THE MOTH'S FLAME

Diane Simmons

authorHOUSE®

AuthorHouse™
1663 Liberty Drive
Bloomington, IN 47403
www.authorhouse.com
Phone: 1-800-839-8640

Published by AuthorHouse 12/23/2011

ISBN: 978-1-4685-0520-7 (e)
ISBN: 978-1-4685-0521-4 (hc)
ISBN: 978-1-4685-0522-1 (sc)

Library of Congress Control Number: 2011962516

In the year of 2015, my husband over dosed on drugs; heroine specifically. The coroners office is saying that he had more in his body than the averaged over dosed victim usually have present. Therefore he was helped and as usual, the first suspects happens to me; his wife.

Before the drugs, Kwame was the type of man every woman dreamed of having. Tall, dark, handsome with a personality that sent shivers up your spine just by conversation. I always knew Kwame was *the one* and **only** man for me. What I never saw in our future was being accused of murder.

The night I found Kwame lying on our bathroom floor was the worst of my life. I had just awoken out of a bad dream when I noticed he wasn't lying in bed with me. After five minutes of waiting I decided to go fetch him. Everything on the second floor where our bedrooms were located looked normal. Just as I attempted to walk down the stairs I smelled an odor that provided a flashback.

"Kwame, Kwame" I spoke in search for his voice.

There was no answer. There wasn't even a sign that he even existed in our dark house. It was storming out, and within each flash of lighting I was able to see a particular part of the room. Walking down the hallway towards our daughters', Kenise, room I saw a figure sitting on our bathroom floor.

"KWAME, KWAME," I yelled. "Got damn it where are you? It's dark and I'm scared," I mumbled creeping towards the form.

Reaching the bathroom I just stood there. Once again, Kwame was caught shooting heroine. He was laid up against the wall with the needle hanging out of his arm. The belt he used to wrap around his limb was still tightly in place. Blood had dripped down his extremity and was now frozen in position.

"Oh...my...gosh," I snapped out of my recollection. "Kwame is doing that shit again," I said running towards the bathroom.

The door was closed. *That's a first* I thought to myself. Trying to be calm I tried knocking. No answer. I knocked even harder and still received no answer. The doorknob was jammed in place indicating that it was locked. Running down the steps as fast as I could my gut anticipating something was wrong. Through the living room and into the kitchen, throwing objects of all sorts around me I found a butter knife. Retrieving what I was looking for I dashed back to the locked door and plucked it open. Kwame was lying on the floor with his eyes open. It was almost as if he knew this was *it* for him. AS if GOD spoke to him his self and said you have a choice to make. You can choose to be healed one day at a time from this substance or you can inject it into yourself one…*last*…time.

I guess Kwame chose death because he's not here.

I've been incarcerated for over a year now. No one can seem to decide my fate. At some point, I began to think I don't have one. The very first time I reached the gates of hell, as I call it, was two days after his death. Our daughter Kenise was with my parents while I took some emotional time to heal. Unfortunately that didn't go so well.

> Lying in our bed with blood shot eyes, our front door was kicked in. Someone yelled "MRS. WOODS WE HAVE A WARRANT FOR YOUR ARREST! PLEASE COME OUT WITH YOUR HANDS BEHIND YOUR HEAD!"

I didn't know what to do. At first I thought it was all a dream, till I heard them climbing my stairs. They threw tear gas cans into the bedroom. Truthfully, when Kwame died, I wanted to die to. As the gas filled the room I didn't even cough. Didn't budge and didn't say a word. I laid there caressing the pillow that he once laid his head upon. Wishing he would come back to me but realizing it's too late for begging and pleading now.

The sheriff snatched me out of bed while placing my hands behind my back.

"Mrs. Woods," he said as he placed the hand cuffs on me while amending me my rights.

I stood lifeless. Tears rolled down my face as I mesmerized our last intimate encounter on our bed.

Sitting on top of Kwame's lap...his tongue deep into my mouth. Pushing his essence inside ever so slowly. Making love...feeling what it's like to be loved by someone so special. Moaning, lip biting and hair pulling. Tip toeing my hands across his shoulders and arms while he stroked me more and more. Feeling that last spike of excitement before orgasm. Seeing the last drip of sweat fall from his locked hair. The last image I'll ever see...of...my....Kwame.

Bryant
Point of View

"I was Kwame's Brother. I loved him dearly; we loved him dearly," I corrected looking at my mom.

"Kwame was always the good child. The one to get the greatest woman, the best of grades, to charm mom so that he wouldn't get into trouble. He was truly a good breed," I laughed recalling the times I had with my brother.

"He loved Karma from the day he laid eyes on her. After getting to know Kwame it was obvious she loved him too.

We met Karma at a job we had working for The Citizens Committee of Youth. She was lost and looking absolutely gorgeous. My brother and I argued and argued *and argued* about whom should be the one to date her. He really wasn't the one to disagree when it came to dating a girl; he'd usually let me have them but when it came to her he really put up a fight. That's how I knew she was the one. The one ordained to him from GOD, if you will.

My brother had never even had sex for gosh sake. Never kissed another woman or even hunched one. You know...the game seven eleven; seven kisses and eleven humps. Well we tried to get him to play that and he ran in the house like a coward," I laughed again.

"He even waited until he was eighteen…I believe, to loose his virginity to Karma and she lost hers to him. When he told me about it I was shocked! I remember telling him he was lying and wouldn't get any until they were married. Karma wasn't that type of a girl. She had plenty of respect for her self; she walked with her head held high in confidence that she could have any boy she wanted. That she was THE shit. Her attitude showed it and she commanded respect. Karma truly was a work of art. After the first time she kneed me, I knew than she wasn't the ordinary girl.

It happened the first day we met her as well. Funny huh? I barely knew her and she kicked me right in the growing. Looking her in her eyes was mesmerizing as it was hard not to want to kiss her. They were so precious and her lips were sweet with a smile of warmth. Just a kiss, one kiss was all I wanted.

Anyway, Kwame came between us comforting her and that was the end of what could have been. He won; I moved on to other girls more willing and less aggressive.

On the second day of seeing her she fainted and guess who happened to be there? You guessed it; Kwame and I.

Getting on the bus and speaking to the driver, "Good morning. How you doing?" Karma spoke.

The driver responded with a warm smile, "Good young lady. Do you need a transfer?"

She returned with a smile saying, "No thank you sir. But thanks for asking."

The moment she turned to her left to take a seat she noticed Kwame and I…pausing as if she'd seen a ghost. Suddenly she didn't look so good. Her head motioned in circles very slowly before collapsing.

The driver asked, "Are you ok young lady?"

Kwame and I ran to her. I sat in the seat near them and watched because he was more experienced first aid wise.

"Young lady, are you ok?"

She tried to stand but lost her balance and fell into Kwame's arms.

He picked her up, than spoke to the bus driver saying, "I will take her to that seat over there by the open window. She needs some fresh air. I know who she is. She's going to work. We work together," he waived his hand over us in a circle. "I can care for her from here."

Nervously and unaware of what to do the driver asked, "Are you sure? I can call an ambulance. She looks as if she needs emergency care."

Sitting her in the seat where the window was open he responded, "Yes. I'm pretty sure." Looking at the crowd on the bus he inquired, "Does anyone have a fresh bottle of water that's unopened?" Looking at me, he suggested, "Some fresh air and nice cold water would probably make her feel better."

A lady passenger said, "I do. I have two of them. She is more than welcome to have one."

Taking the bottle of water from the nice lady, Kwame replied, "Thank you ma'am. You will be blessed for what you just done."

Watching as he poured water into her mouth she countered, "No son. *You* will be blessed for what you are doing for this young lady."

Kwame turned a friendly smile as the other passengers watched in au. The driver continued his route but showed concern by watching in the mirror as often as he could. After about five minutes of coming to her senses, she opened her eyes. The cool breeze blowing through the window must have felt extremely good because she faced more towards the window than she did Kwame.

He put his hand on hers while asking, "How are you feeling?"

She slapped him than crossed her arms and responded "Why is it every time I look up I see your face? Yours and his that is."

"Hey, I'm just watching. I never touched you," I responded.

Holding his face, he replied, "First you kneed my brother and now you slap me. That's a way to tell me thanks for what I just did? At least he did deserve it. I did nothing to."

Giggling and turning towards him to slap him again; she motioned, "I'm sorry. Does it hurt? Where here's another one!"

"Ouch! Now look missy, you are getting way out of line. I just helped bring you back to life and this is how you repay me?"

"I was never dead STUPID! I think I fainted. And I wouldn't have if I hadn't seen you two."

Mocking her in a mumble, "I think I fainted." Rolling his eyes, "Yeah; ya think?"

"Oh shut up."

Kwame said while protecting his face, "No, you shut up."

"You shut up."

"No you shut up."

Over hearing the argument the driver interrupted, "Why don't both of you shut up? And young lady, can't you see the young fellow has a thing for you?"

They looked at each other than just stared. He gazed into her eyes as if he could see every star there ever was in the sky. As if he could see every beat within the rthym of her heart. As if he was watching all of her younger memories flash before him.

Together they looked at the driver and said, "NAH! IT'S NOT LIKE THAT!" Surprised they faced one another and motioned, "QUIT REPEATING ME! YOU QUIT REPEATING ME! WOULD YOU STOP! UUUGGGHHH!"

Crossing their arms over their chest their hands met.

"WOULD YOU STOP! YOU'RE DOING IT AGAIN! NO YOU'RE DOING IT AGAIN!"

"Can you please go back to your seat? I appreciate you *nursing* me back to health; but I'm better now. Is it necessary for you to **still** be sitting next to me?" She spoke calmly through gritted teeth.

Kwame said while standing up and holding his hand out, "I can take a hint. Besides, this is our stop. May I?"

She turned up her nose and refused while looking away. Through the window she watched Kwame as he stood in position. He was serious believe it or not. I was praying that she allowed him to do just that.

Interrupting her thoughts, the bus driver said, "Young lady, we don't have all day. Are you going to take the gentleman's hand or what? I have to get this bus going."

Turning her frustration towards the driver, she stood up and Kwame made the decision for her. Surprisingly, they were holding hands and didn't let go. I felt like they were playing follow the leader and he was it. Like a king, he walked down the steps then turned around to guide his queen protectantly. Afterwards they went for a walk and the whole time I was in au. It was really cool to see my brother happy. With a girl at that. My brother just wasn't the type of guy to deal with girls at that time. He had girlfriends but it was just so people wouldn't assume the usual.

By day three, Kwame said he was in love. He laid in bed thinking about her knowing that her birthday was tomorrow and wanted to make it a special one.

Kwame whispered to me while I was asleep in the bed across from him. Half asleep that is because I couldn't help but to feel his thoughts of love floating in the air.

"Bryant. Pssst. Bryant." And when I didn't acknowledge he threw a pillow at me then yelled, "BRYANT!"

Jumping out of bed, "What? What do you want? And this better be good man?" I said.

Kwame looked at me seriously and said, "I need your help."

Unable to think clearly I paced the floor back and forth, "You need my help. He needs my help," I remember saying sarcastically to myself. Yelling, "YOU WOKE ME UP OUT OF MY SLEEP BECAUSE YOU NEEDED HELP!" Trying to calm myself, "What do you need help with bra that it couldn't wait fifteen more minutes when it was time for me to awake?" I looked at the clock.

"Remember that girl we met Monday?"

"Yeah, Kisses, Kiesha, Kimberly or something. What about her?"

"Her name is Karma and tomorrow's her birthday. What should I get her?"

I sat down on my bed to try to think things out more clearly.

"Why are you getting her something when you don't even know her? You just met her, what…two days ago? You're not obligated to give her any gifts," I said noticing I had ten minutes left to get some sleep.

"You don't know how I feel about her," Kwame said as he laid faced up in bed.

"FEEL ABOUT HER BRO? Feel about her? You barely know the girl bro. Wake up and smell the coffee because the red roses are dead."

"I think…I think…I think I'm falling in love with her."

"I think I'm falling in love with her," I repeated. "Tell me this bro. How do you fall in love with a girl you don't know?"

"I don't know. Just know that I am. She has the most amazing eyes. I feel like my soul is being sucked right out of me every time I look at them. And her smile will break every heart that pass. Her personality is wonderful and she's *feisty*. A real hot tamale. And I love the way she carry herself with respect."

I walked over to him and pinched his cheek while talking like a baby,

"Aww. My brother's falling in love. Aww, and with a girl he don't even know."

Than I bitch slapped him like Karma did yesterday and grabbed him by his shirt.

"Kwame, if you ever wake me up again, *it will be your last!*"

The look in his eyes caused me to let him go and take what he was saying more seriously. He was really in love with this girl.

Kwame reassured while sitting up in bed, "I feel like I've known her forever. Yesterday was amazing."

"What happened yesterday?" Mentally thinking about what the answer would be, I put up my hand and said, "You know what; never mind. Just act like I didn't ask that. Look Kwame, the way to a girls heart is to think like a girl. What do you think she'll want *more than anything,*" I slurred in my girly voice. "Being that it's her birthday?"

"Gifts jerk."

"Aww it seems my little brother has some balls after all."

"Are you going to help me or not?"

"Fine Kwame I will help. What exactly do you need me to do?"

Anxiously, Kwame said, "What should I get her for a birthday gift?"

Sarcastically I replied, "A ring." Than I made fish faces that looked as if I was blowing kisses, "So you can live happily ever after."

Becoming agitated, Kwame said, "Knock it off! I'm serious." Kwame got out of bed and began getting dressed.

"Alright! Alright! Get her a teddy bear, a box of chocolates and a card. You can't go wrong with that."

"Thanks bro, You're a great help. But…I wonder who's going to help you get to work on time? Got to go. Catch ya later. Bro," Kwame said as he closed the door behind him.

I started to yell his names as I heard him slide down the banister laughing. He chuckled so loud that I heard him as he left the house. Checking the clock that now said 7:15 I realized the timing didn't match up with the morning skies. The watch that my brother left behind purposely confirmed that the time shown was in correct. It was actually 5:15am. This meant I still had at least an hr and a half to get some rest. Which also meant it was on me to get him back for this prank.

The day I chose to get him back turned out to be the worst day ever. Not only for myself who could really careless for Karma; THEN, that is, but because of the trauma behind the accident that happened that day.

Kwame and I were on the bus. The two of them had made plans yesterday I suppose, so we all caught an earlier bus. Not that I was a part of their plans. I just happened to be at the right place and at the right time.

Karma must have been running at least five minutes behind because the bus past her by. The light up ahead was red. Karma had just made it to the front door when the light turned green; but by the time the driver made a decision to allow her on the bus the stoplight turned yellow causing her to have to wait for the next green light. Before we knew it she darted across the street to the next bus stop that wasn't too far away. It seems as if the traffic light waited exactly until she got there before turning green. As the bus approached she was gasping for air so hard that she became dizzy and collapsed.

The bus driver immediately pulled over and called 911. Kwame and I witnessed everything. He told the driver it was her fault and that she had asthma. He also told her thanks a lot for putting her in the hospital on the day of her birthday. The driver was speechless and began to cry. At this time I too was speechless. The girl my brother said he was falling in love with just yesterday is lying cold on the concrete.

Kwame showed no remorse; which was unlike my brother. He was always the sweetest guy around. Immediately sitting by her side while looking in her back pack in search of an inhaler he became frustrated because he wasn't able to find it.

"Here let me look," I told him. "Maybe you're over looking it."

"I didn't over look it!" he snapped. "I wouldn't do that to her. Not to my sweet Karma."

I wanted to puke because I still believed he was moving too fast but I kept my cool. He thought to look in her jacket and there it was. Tilting her head back to allow oxygen to flow into her body correctly he administered two puffs while pinching her nose. Nothing. She was unresponsive. Kwame checked her pulse and started to notice change within the color of her lips.

"LOOK WHAT YOU DID TO HER!" Kwame cried. "Do you see this? Do you?" He screeched while holding the inhaler in his hands. "This is her fucking inhaler! I am so going to see that you lose your fucking JOB!"

I stood in surprise as I have never once heard my brother curse. Kwame was so distraught that he spit in the drivers face. Another passenger saw the commotion and tried to calm him down.

"I understand you're trying to help my brother but I think I can handle it from here," I stepped between the two of them placing my hand on the passenger chest in defense.

"Look son, I understand what you're trying to do here but he has certainly lost it. You could use my help."

"Look at her," Kwame cried. "Look…at…her. It's her birthday for gosh sake. This wasn't supposed to happen!"

The ambulance and fire trucks were in the distance as we could hear the sirens. Kwame looked at her pale blue face and attempted to run out into the street towards a driving car. All the while I still had my hands placed on the other passengers' chest trying to keep him away from my brother. So much were going on that we all seemed to just stay frozen.

Someone yelled "NOOOO!" I couldn't make out who it was but I'm thinking it could have been the bus driver.

Looking at how distraught my brother was I released my hand from the passengers' torso.

Placing his hands on Kwame's cheeks with pressure he said, "Look son, you're out of control! Now I'm sure when that little lady awakes she is going to want to see your face. You have got to calm down before the police see you as being unruly and haul you off to jail. And how do you think you're going to be doing in there? Not knowing how she's doing and such? Now if it makes you feel any better I was a witness too and saw the drivers' action that caused this poor girl to collapse. Not to mention you have your brother as well; we will help you son. But first, you have got to calm down."

Kwame listened as tears continued to run down his face. Two police officers arrived at the scene and immediately ran to Karma's side. One officer decided to assist by doing CPR while the other asked questions to any witnesses.

"Ok, who saw what happened?" The officer asked.

"We all did," another passenger said as she stepped off of the bus. "The driver looked at her than looked at the light that had just turned green. I don't know why she didn't open the door for her, she just didn't.

The young lady stood on the side walk and kind of went in a daze as the bus passed her up. The light back there," she pointed. "Was red and so the driver had to stop naturally. The lady than attempted to run for the bus and she made it. When she got there she bent over and looked like she was trying to catch her breath, except seconds later she just… collapsed."

"Maam, I'm going to need you to call the bus station. We are going to have to take you down to the police station," the officer said to the bus driver that was sitting close enough to hear what the female passenger had said.

The driver didn't say anything. She continued to cry, plead and wish that she had made a better decision. All of the passengers continued to look at her in disgust. Even though the ambulance was heard it seemed as if it had taken an hour before it reached us.

"She's still not breathing," The officer said as she continued to do CPR. "I don't even feel a pulse," she said as her watched my chest while pressing down on the vein in her neck with her two fingers. "If you ask me, she's…gone."

The passenger that was keeping Kwame calm looked at him than looked at the officer.

"What did she just say?" Kwame looked at me and asked.

The passenger and I didn't speak.

"What did she just say? You tell me now!" he threatened the passenger who was helping me to calm him.
"Son, it's going to be ok. Everything will be fine. Just stay calm, it's almost over."
"No! You tell me what she just said! You tell me now!"

One of the officers heard the commotion and began to walk towards us. As he began to walk the EMT team pulled into the scene and immediately ran to her side.

"What happened here?" one of the members of the EMT Unit asked the police officer while checking for vital signs.

"I'm not sure but my partner should know. He's over there," the officer pointed.

The officer stopped as he looked at the commotion within our group. He decided that right now that wasn't important, and though we were disorderly, he could get to that later. The officer turned around and walked towards his partner who was thanked by EMT, than asked to step back.

"How long did you do rescue breathing?" One of the members from the EMT Unit asked the officer.

"About five minutes."

"Did her color change any while you did the mouth to mouth resuscitation?"

"A little but not much."

"Ok guys, I'm going to get the defibrillator so we can see what's going on with her body," the woman said from the EMT Unit.

While she did that, the officers asked Kwame some personal information about her.

"I take it you know the victim?" The male officer asked Kwame.

"Yes. Well…not really. We were just getting to know each other. She started work with me two days ago and…I…fell in love with her. We had plans for today. It's her birthday. Her birthday."

"I'm sorry son. Do you happen to know her name? Where she lives? Who we can talk to about the incident that happened today?"

"NO! I just said I met her two days ago. That's not enough time to get to know anyone. But it was plenty of time for me to realize I was in love with her."

"O…K. Thank you son," the officer said as he walked away.

"It's going to be okay. She's a fighter. Don't tell me you forgot what she did to me for trying to kiss her?" I reminded him.

His chuckle caused spit to come out of his mouth as he could clearly recall that incident. It wasn't one I was happy of but at least for the moment he was calm and had laughed.

"OK I NEED EVERYONE TO STAND BACK! I CAN'T TAKE A CHANCE ON HAVING TO HELP SOMEONE ELSE DUE TO CARELESSNESS. UNDERSTAND?" the woman from the EMT Unit suggested.

In the midst of her talking to the crowd of folks surrounded, the rest of the team began to encircle Karma as they provided privacy while placing the pads into its proper places. The AED diagnosed her heart rhythm and said to deliver shock.

"ARE YOU CLEAR?" The woman who just had joined back with her team asked one of her members.

"CLEAR," a member from the EMT Team responded.

"YOU'RE CLEAR?"

"CLEAR," shouted another member.

"IS EVERYBODY CLEAR?"

"EVERYONE'S CLEAR!" They shouted together.

"Preparing for shock," she said as she pressed the button.

"NO," Kwame began to charge towards them.

The passenger and I must have been thinking the same thing as we both grabbed an arm and held him down.

The bunch watched anxiously not knowing what the end result would be. It was so quiet that we were able to hear the shock being delivered. Once, it stunned her, some became uneasy while others were panicking, Kwame had lost all hopes and became numb as others attempted to attack the driver that sat inside of the police car.

After the first shock was delivered the defibullator said to shock again.

"IS EVERYONE CLEAR?"
"WE'RE ALL CLEAR!"
"Preparing for shock."

This stun caused her to cough, gasp for air and her heart began to pick up rhythm. The EMT Team signaled for the helicopter unit ahead to fly her to the hospital. They said that she would get there much faster and needed to be under full evaluation. Kwame ran to her as the crowd cheered the EMT team for their patience and hard work. He held Karma's hand and said he would stay day and night until she got better. And that's just what he did.

Mr. Gentry

Point of View

Karma is my daughter; my only daughter. She has experienced a few rough things out of her life but murdering her husband isn't one of them. She loved him as much as he loved her. I remember when she started her first job and was to be fourteen in three days. You'd thought an Angel died and gone to heaven.

My wife and I were on our way home when we saw Karma waiting to cross the street. Immediately my wife pulled over to pick her up. Karma got into the car and was extremely happy. Apparently she had got the nerve to tell her mother; whom is my wife and I about a young fellow from work; a young man she was beginning to catch feelings for.

"Hey mom, hey dad," she said while placing a kiss on our cheeks.

My wife was totally astonished. She couldn't drive off without looking at her through the rear view mirror.

"What's gotten into you," My wife asked.

"Well….since you asked and we're all here, I'm going to tell you," Karma said while sitting up close with her arms on both the passengers and driver's seat. "I met a boy," she said excitingly.

Her mother had just begun driving before I heard our tires screech to a complete stop. For the longest my wife and I just looked at each other. We were truly astonished.

The rest of the ride home no one said anything. What could one have said during a time like this? We just found out that our little girl was growing up; faster than we expected. I can't vouch for what her mother was thinking but I wanted to get to know this boy and fast! The quicker I got to know him would be a prompt response of getting rid of him, if you know what I mean. Yall wouldn't have to convict my daughter because you'll be convicting me.

We believed we were strict parents and though her mother and I had problems we didn't let that stop us from loving Karma.

After a five minute drive we were home. My wife jumped out of the car while it was still in drive telling me to handle her. I was infuriated by her actions and put the car in park just before it crashed into our home. Chasing after my wife and slamming the front door behind us we begin to argue. I knew Karma could hear us from the car but this was a time I needed to correct my wife and tell her a few things she needed to know about herself. She *stinked*…bad! And have been for quite some time during that period of our life. Moments later I went back to the car and told her to get into the front seat and buckle up that we were leaving for a while. Just she and I. She must have sensed the frustration in my voice because she didn't ask any questions.

We toured the road for hours. I began circling a particular street. One my parents; her grandparents raised me on and reminiscing about the day her mom and I met. Just trying to figure out where we went wrong in our relationship and now with our daughter.

Karma spoke "Dad, this seems to be a nice street."

"Yeah, I know," I said with a scratch in my throat.

"We've road around this same block for at least the past fifteen minutes and you keep looking at a particular house," she said as we were beginning to approach it again. "That house right there," she pointed. "What's up with that house? Why do you keep looking at it?"

"Don't worry about it honey. It's nothing. Really. Just a bunch of old memories is all," I sighed; finally driving away.

We drove five minutes down the road before pulling into a park. Switching gears I ordered her to get out. It must have spooked her because she looked rebellious.

"Why?" she asked nervously.

"BECAUSE I SAID SO," I shouted! "I am sick and tired of you and your mother going at each other's throats daily for my love and attention. She is my queen you are my princess. The two of you will never become any more or any less. So....STOP IT."

She became completely speechless as I saw a tear drop fall from her eye. I never raised my voice at her or her mother for that matter until today. I was at a breaking point and seriously tired of all the bull shit; excuse my French, the two of them was putting me through. When I disciplined Karma it was emotionally or mentally but never with me raising my voice at her. As a man, it just wasn't something I did.

"Honey I love you. And I love your mom. This park is where your mom and I used to play during our childhood. The street we passed over and over again is the street we grew up on. I guess I didn't realize that one day my little girl would grow up as well," I said with a teary eye. "Your mother and I only want what's best for you. You're not even fourteen yet. Haven't had a job for more than a couple of days but you've already met a boy that you really like," I announced while looking out of the window. "Do you know how hard it is to except something like that?"

She continued to listen with her arms crossed as if she felt disgusted by the conversation. And maybe she should have felt uneasy. We were making a big deal all because she said she met a boy. She didn't say she kissed a boy, was going out on her first date or was intimate with a boy.

Just that she simply met one. Looking back on things today it didn't make sense to take things as far as we did but it happened.

After our *long* father daughter talk I drove her back home. While turning the ignition off I ordered Karma to go to her room for the night.

She immediately got out of the car in a rampage like a normal teenager would. But when she walked into our house it was full of smoke and candles that were lit from what I could see. As I followed behind her she began to make her way up the stairs before noticing her mother sitting on the couch smoking a cigarette.

Running down the stairs she screeched, "Mom, what are you doing?"

"Smoking. What does it look like?" My wife responded with arrogance.

"You're smoking?" she asked as if a lot of questions were going through her mind.

"You're smoking?" My wife repeated. "Sister it's a lot you don't know about your dear mommy."

At that point I stepped in and took the cigarette out of her hand. She was so stuck on our daughter that she hadn't realized I walked into the house. My wife turned to face me as if she'd seen a ghost.

Walking away, "I know, I know. Go to your room," Karma said to herself as I looked at her with my disciplining eyes.

We continued to watch each other anxiously. I could tell she was curious about what the results for her mother would be. She always thought of me as being a coward. What she didn't realize was as a man there are some things that we just have to take and put up with. I loved my wife and I knew a long time ago that something was wrong but no one could ever come between what her mother and I felt for each other. So this became a hard period that Karma suffered behind a mistake that her mother made. This particular evening became one of the turning points in our lives as I wore the pants for once. The saying is *happy wife happy life*. But after seeing the way she behaved my wife didn't turn out to being happy that night.

The following morning she and I spoke to Karma as she sat down for breakfast. We understand you're getting older and boys are going to be a part of your life. You have to go to school with them, sit in the same class with them, walk pass them, work with them, play with them; it's impossible for you to avoid a whole race of teenage boys. At some point in your life we are going to have to let you grow up. We also understand this is your social life. This is what you want and probably will do regardless of what your mother and I say. The only thing we ask is for you to remember that you are our only child and sometimes we may be harder on you than we expect to be.

Finishing her breakfast "Ok," and walked out of the house to catch her bus.

During this time her mother and I wasn't sure if we had gotten through to her or not but we sure hoped so.

"So what happened that made you start to change your mind as far as Kwame?" Mrs. Williams asked.

"Oh gosh. That's an even longer story than the one I just told."

"Remember Mr. Gentry, you're here to help prove your daughter innocence."

"Well I have no problem doing that. The problem is do you all have the time to listen to the next story I am about to tell you?"

"Let me put it like this sir. If we don't have time, we'll make time tomorrow."

"Ok. Well fine," I told her while straightening myself and trying to get comfortable on the witness stand. "Do you think I can have a cup of water? I'm going to need it after this."

Mrs. Williams fixed me a glass of water than handed it to me.

"Is it good and cold sir?"
Taking a gulp "It sure is," I swallowed.
"Good, because the court room and I are anxious to hear the next story you have to tell."

My daughter had an accident three days after she started her first job AND met Kwame. Her mother and I didn't find out about it until 3pm that afternoon and were furious. We couldn't believe she had been in the hospital for nearly twelve hours and no one has called.

My wife and I had just gotten home. I love to turn on Channel 12 News the moment we walk into the house. All sorts of crazy things are always happening. I was in the kitchen fixing a cup of orange juice while she was attempting to take a shower. She must have taken her last piece of garment off when she heard me scream gruesomely because she was standing in front of me looking gorgeous I must say," I winked at my wife who was sitting behind Karma.

"Baby what's wrong? What happened? Are you okay?" she asked concerned, a voice I hadn't heard in a very long time.

Unable to speak I pointed at the television. By the time she looked a commercial had come on. Continuing to look in shock I said nothing; just stood there.

"Darling what did you see?" she asked alarmed.
"I…I…I thought…Karma," I said uncertain.
"What about her?"

"Television," I pointed.

"Did she do something to it?"

"I SAW HER ON THE TV," I screamed at her due to frustration.

"Well what was she doing there?"

"On the damn news," I became more agitated.

"Karma? There's no way. Look at what time it is," she pointed to the clock. "It's nearly 3:15pm. She should be home from work by now."

"Well did you check on her while you were up there?"

"No I didn't. Our baby girl has always been pretty mature *and grown*," she tried to mumble. "I didn't see the need to."

"I know what I saw. That was our daughter who got hurt earlier today."

"Got hurt?" she questioned. "How?"

"Would you just go check on her please? Something's not right. I can feel it in my bones."

"Fine. I will go upstairs and look into her room. I'm almost positive she is napping like she always does when she gets home," she said optimistically.

I don't remember much of what happened during our moment in the house. What I do recollect is my wife running from room to room, and flying down the steps like a mad woman saying I was probably right.

We stormed into the hospital demanding some answers. My wife and I were so distraught that we couldn't think of what our daughter's name was as we were standing at the information desk. A nurse over heard the conversation and pulled us to the side. She said to calm down that she had worked with Karma personally and can assist us with any problems or concerns we may have. We begin speaking together confusing her. My wife was complaining of the timing of the incident while I was pissed for not receiving a call. The nurse was very understanding to our distress. She also said if we had a cellular or even emergency numbers placed within our daughters coat; being that she's asthmatic, that someone could have been reached a lot sooner.

The room became quiet. I assume my wife and I were thinking and jotting mental notes of some things we need to do once we got home; if it wasn't too late. Finally the nurse uttered that no one was to blame while guiding us into an empty conference room so we could talk more privately. For us to thank GOD that someone was around to get to her as soon as they did else she wouldn't have made it.

"I'm not going to sugar coat anything," the nurse discussed while looking both of us into our eyes.

We begin to feel tense while listening attentively to what was about to be said.

"This isn't easy to say but your daughter has Pneumothorax."
"What? What is that? What does that mean?" I asked while standing up.
"Calm down sir. I need for you to stay calm and be strong for your daughter."

My composure began to change as I sat back down. Mentally I began to repeat to myself, *stay strong for Karma. I…need to…stay strong for Karma. My baby girl.*

"Pneumothorax is a fancy term for collapsed lung."
"Oh my gosh, is she okay?" My wife asked tearful.
"Yes ma'am, she is fine. A bit scared and unable to talk due to the shortness of her breath, but she is fine."
"What do you mean shortness of breath?" My wife asked.
"Because she is asthmatic and her lungs did actually collapse on her she is currently on oxygen. There is a mask placed over her face and nose to give her adequate amounts of oxygen. Although this is helping her, Karma may be tired from her accident and may need to rest before she's going to want to do any talking."

"Good, cause that little helfa has a mouth on her," my wife; *her mother*, retaliated as she straightened up and crossed her legs.

In the midst of trying to stay strong I rolled my eyes at her and didn't respond. In the back of my mind I imagined myself strangling her until she respected me more and did a better job of being a mother, *for once*.

"Pneumothorax is an accumulation or increase of air in the space between the lung and the chest wall also known as the pleural space. As the amount of air in this space rises or expands, the pressure against the lung causes it to collapse. This prevents your lung from expanding properly when you try to breathe in, causing shortness of breath and chest pain. You see, when you're breathing, your lung shrinks inward while your chest expands outward. When the oxygen flow is inadequate, it causes shortness of breath which in this case caused the lungs to collapse."

"So she is going to be okay right?" I asked heart broken.

"Yes sir she will be. We have taken a chest x-ray and drew some blood. The x-ray confirmed that Karma did have Pneumothorax. Blood was drawn to see the amount of oxygen that was flowing in her body. Our results showed that she was at twenty nine percent without the oxygen mask. With the oxygen mask, her oxygen flow immediately rose to ninety three percent."

"When can we go see her? Or are we allowed to?" I asked.

"I can take you to her if you will follow me. Oh by the way, she is needed for observation so make plans to stay tonight."

"Is it mandatory for us to stay?" my wife; *again her mother*, asked.

Being sure to word her self correctly and keeping her personal opinions aside, the nurse answered "No ma'am; It isn't. Just make sure the front desk is aware that you will be leaving so that someone from the hospital, such as myself can keep an eye on her and make her stay here at Jackson's Hospital, a pleasant one.

My wife didn't respond and I couldn't help but to think of how snobbish she was acting. Her mother was acting like a woman with no morals or values. She had no respect for herself, daughter or me; her husband. Not only did she embarrass herself but was also embarrassing me. Being the calm gentle man that I was I chose to put my focus on our daughter.

Once we got to her room, the nurse knocked twice and peeked in before entering.

"She's asleep," she whispered to me respectfully. "You may stay in here with her as long as you are quiet. If you disturb the patient in any way I will have to ask you to leave," she said as politely as possible to my wife. "One other thing, being that she is *my* patient, if for whatever reason she requests for you to not be in her room, I will have to remove you because the patients' health, needs and concerns comes first. Although you are her parent, she has the first and last say so here at Jackson's Hospital."

"Well you won't have to worry about that because I won't be here with her no way," my wife; her mother retaliated.

I looked at my wife and rolled my eyes again than placed my hands over my face in complete humiliation before taking a long, deep breath.

"What is your name again Miss," I asked taking the nurse by her hand.

"Patricia. My name is Patricia."

My wife became extremely jealous and pissed at this. Her mouth dropped as if I disregarded her presence. Some nerves huh? I simply wanted to tell Patricia thank you for all she's done.

"Thank you…so much…for taking care of my baby girl. She's the only child I have. My *only* child," I persisted hugging the nurse than inhaling and exhaling one last time before seeing my baby girl.

Patricia, became teary eyed as if she felt my pain. She whispered for me to go see my daughter. That once I saw how good the hospital was taking care of her I'd feel a lot better. The nurse gave me a Kleenex that was nearby for me to clean my face. All the while my wife; *her mother*, cleaned her nails and could care less that I was in pain. She always was a selfish cunt during this time. After I built up my strength, I walked over to my baby girl, took one look and began to feel a sharp pain in my chest. At first it had a feeling of heart burn but then the pain continued to become greater and I dropped to the floor.

Patricia ran to my side as I continued to clinch at my chest. She ran out into the hallway screaming WE NEED A DOCTOR IN HERE. THERE'S A MAN HAVING AN ACUTE MYOCARDIAL INFARCTION! All the while, my wife sat there with her mouth wide open. I assumed she didn't know what to do and was in complete disbelief. After two doctors ran into our daughters' room and checked my pulse I blacked out.

"Honey," I whispered unconsciously as the room was a blur. "Honey," I continued as the area began to become clear. "Honey...HONEY, HONEY..."

"I'm here," my wife said calmly. "How do you feel?"

"What do you mean how do I feel? And why am I hooked up to these machines; hell, what am I doing in a hospital bed?" I pronounced trying to sit up. "Ouch, and why is my chest so soar," I whimpered lying back down. "Where's our daughter? Where's Karma?"

My wife kept quiet. I assume she didn't know what to say or do at this point since Kwame was sitting directly in between Karma and I.

"Hush darling. Everything will be okay. That is until I tell you how daddies little girl has grown up in unspeakable ways," she mumbled.

"What do you mean everything will be ok? I want to see my daughter!"

I sat up in bed, ignoring the unbearable pain and unhooked myself from the machines. They beeped to alert the nurse up front that I needed immediate assistance. Attempting to stand up I couldn't help but to notice a young fellow sitting nearby. He had to be about 5'9" and maybe 180ibs. I remember thinking, my gosh this is a big boy. Than the thought of who he was crossed my mind. The child must have seen the expression in my face change because he stood than stepped towards me. I didn't know rather to hit him or embrace him in my arms. A bit confused and GODLY I might say, I allowed him to make the first move.

"How are you Mr. Gentry? My name is Kwame..." he stated with his hand out before being interrupted.

"Kwame are you in the right room? This room is for Karma Gentry and I have never heard of or seen you."

"Well sir, no disrespect, but your daughter and I work together," he answered before being interrupted again.

"Oooooh. You're him. The kid my baby girl was telling us about last night."

"I'm not sure about what you're speaking of but I'm pretty sure that I am…the kid you're referring to."

"You told the doctor that you and our daughter had plans of hooking up this morning," My wife invaded in on the conversation just as I was beginning to like the kid.

"Well Mrs. Gentry, you are correct. We did have plans on seeing each other this morning, but we also work together. I apologize; I may have left that part out."

"*I apologize; I may have left that part out,*" my wife repeated before speaking to my father. "So tell me something, *darling*. Still think daddies little girl is so innocent?"

I must admit; at this point and time I was speechless. I honestly didn't know what to think or believe anymore; even though my heart told me otherwise. My baby girl never gave me a reason to not trust her. She has always been honest. Even after meeting this young fellow she felt comfortable enough to tell both my wife and I. Not to mention the two of them hadn't gotten along in years.

I looked at Kwame one last time than laid back in bed. It was all too much for me to deal with than. Not to mention I had just dealt with my wife and daughter just the night before. At the time I had mixed feelings but couldn't help but think she was right. My wife was right. *She was right she was right she was right,* I mentally wrestled. *Where did I go wrong? Lord tell me where I went wrong? My wife and I haven't gotten along in nearly ten years and now I don't know my daughter. My sweet baby girl. My princess. Lord please tell me what I am doing wrong?* As I contemplated with my eyes closed Patricia walked into the room.

"Mr. Gentry I came as fast as I could, are you okay?"

"I don't know," I wailed.

"Is there anything I can do to make you feel any better?"

"I have one. Why don't you stay the hell out of his face. I see your little fast ass," my wife verbalized. "You must be a hoar because everyone knows only type of women become nurses so they can separate happy homes.

I snorted and nearly choked on saliva when she said the word happy. We haven't been happy in years; she can't honestly think that the two of us are happy with our marriage. She looked at me disgusted and I pretended to cough as if I was choking instead of grunting.

"Mrs. Gentry I am only doing my job. I apologize if I have offended you in any way."

"Mrs. Gentry I am only doing my job. I apologize if I have offended you in any way. Yeah I'm sure you are *just* doing your job. Just know…your job *isn't* going to be my husband," she snapped before leaving the room.

She closed the door behind and I could tell she was lying against it because I saw her shadow underneath. I assumed she felt embarrassed for the way she was acting; jealous. And I must say, it was sexy being that I never saw her this way.

By the time my wife came back, Kwame and I were actually getting to know each other. He really was a sweet kid and I could tell by the conversation just how mature he really was.

"What's going on in here?" her mother asked shockingly.

"Well I figured since Kwame was here we at least got to know who our daughter is involved with."

"We're not together," Karma crackled.

"Yes Mrs. and Mr. Gentry, we are not." Kwame added on before noticing who voice he just heard. Panicking, "How are you feeling? You gave me quite a scare. Oh, and by the way, happy birthday. I missed you while you were a asleep."

"My chest and ribs hurt. What happened?" she asked while trying to sit up.

"No no, Karma. You have to stay rested in bed. And your body is soar because you collapsed earlier today."

"What... do you... mean I...collapsed?" she puffed between words.

"Well, you were running for the bus and you crumbled."

"Well did the bus driver at least attempt to wait for her?" my wife asked, as if she was concerned.

"In the beginning Karma wasn't at the bus stop when the bus passed her by. She stopped at a red light not too far away from the bus stop and attempted to try to catch the bus there. When she got in front of the doors the driver looked at her than at the light that had just turned green. She paused a second and looked back at Karma liping *I'm sorry*, before trying to go through the light. Only thing is, by the time she decided to go through the light, it had turned yellow and she stopped instead. Karma saw that she stopped and ran through the light to the following bus stop. I guess in her mind she knew that naturally the bus would have to stop for her. Karma made it but bent over and collapsed. I'm assuming because she was waiting for the bus that that's the only reason why the driver stopped for her. I think given the drivers reactions today, had it been anyone else on that ground, the driver would not have stopped."

"Ok, so what happened next?" I asked.

"Well naturally the police was called and the fire department except in this case, the ambulance was contacted and told to show at the scene."

"Ok, than what happened?" my wife asked.

"Well the woman was taken downtown and Karma was flown to the hospital. Oh, and they had to place a defibrillator on her and send shocks to her body three times I believe."

"And she made it?" my wife, *her mothered* mumbled.

I rose from my bed like a lion preparing for his first roar after awakening. Standing tall, but calm, because that's just the type of person I was, I looked into my wife's gorgeous eyes. It reminded me of my beautiful baby girl and always made me feel weak in my knees. Just crippled like I couldn't take another step if I chose to. I always told her looking into them would make the tides come in hours early.

I took my hands and pulled the pony tail out of her hair so it would fall down her shoulders. She looked even more attractive especially when her hair blew in her face. Combing my hands through her curls until it was the way I loved to see it I began to caress her face. I could tell as she closed her eyes and began to drift away that she has yearned for this touch. Unfortunately it wasn't my fought she wasn't getting the affection she needed. She refused to let me be anything but good to her.

Guiding her lips to mines I kissed her ever so passionately. The type of a kiss that will make the dead rise. The door to the side of us had opened as I contacted Miss Patricia to come to my aid what seemed a long time ago.

"Patricia, now that I'm a patient and I have rights too of who can and can't be in our room; can you escort my wife off of the premises please?"

"WHAT!" My wife yelled at me as if she was honestly hurt. "How could you? HOW COULD YOU? She continued on. "She's my daughter too."

"Your daughter? You don't give a damn about your daughter. So do us both a big favor," I said caressing my hands through her hair once more, "Go home, shower or bath and think about how much your daughter and I mean to you. I told you before you will not continue to disrespect our daughter. I also told you that either you started acting like her mother or sign away your rights, *which*, in doing so I will be asking for a divorce."

"But..."

"Shhh...shh...shhh," I kissed her lips again. "I'm serious. Go take some time to think about what's more important," I stressed sternly to her. "Sorry to take some of your time Patricia, but my wife, is ready to leave now."

"No disrespect sir, but I'm glad you told her," Patricia whispered in my ear.

"So am I Patricia. Believe me...So am I."

My wife grabbed her purse than stopped and starred at Patricia. She wanted to say something cruel but knew if she had spoken; it would only make things worst for our relationship. Patricia looked at her in disgust as she escorted her out. Karma seemed relieved as she closed her eyes and allowed a tear drop to fall. I can't say how she felt about what happened but I can say she fell asleep almost immediately.

After my wife left Kwame and I had a very interesting conversation. He told me how much he loved my daughter and I could tell this was true else he wouldn't have been there with her. I'm sure his parents were worried sick as he was so concerned with my baby girl that he never once called home. At least not to my knowledge or that I saw with my own eyes.

"So why my baby girl? Why Karma?" I asked him.
"Why not Karma?" he replied.

I couldn't help but to smirk to his response. But it did make sense and I admit it was a silly question. Why not my baby girl? Hell she was the most stunning, well respected, young lady walking. Her mother and I taught her well.

"What are your intentions with my daughter young man?" Sitting straight up and looking him square in his eyes.
"Sir, to be honest, I really don't have any. I just want to be her friend. If we could just be friends I'd be happy with that. Karma isn't your everyday girl," he answered folding his hands.
"And what type of girl is an everyday girl?"
"Well I don't know personally. Some of my friends tell me things and I always chose to be different."
"The oddball huh?" I continued to look at him in an uncomfortable way.
"That's exactly it sir."
"And how is it that you and my Karma met again?"
"We work…" he started before being interrupted.
"I know yall work together. I'm saying to tell me the story behind how the two of you started talking," I pressured.
"Oh," Kwame laughed. "Well it was her first day at work. She was standing in front of us lost. My brother spoke to her first because I just couldn't gather the words to speak. It was like seeing an angel sir. I'm

sure you know how beautiful your daughter is so I don't think I need to remind you."

"Unhuh," I warned.

"The way she walked and carried herself. The way she was dressed; not that I was looking at her in that way sir, I'm just saying she was a sight for eyes. I mean, she looked gorgeous."

"And," I continued to bully for information.

"Well she asked for directions to get to the office and my brother told her how to get there. She walked by and I stood there with my mouth still open pretty much."

"And."

"And we ended up meeting after work, not by chance though sir and she asked for our names. Well, before than, we asked her for her name so in return she asked for ours."

"Unhuh," I crossed my arms flexing my strength.

"Well, after we got acquainted we ended up catching the same bus home together."

"Oh so you…and your brother just so happen to live nearby?"

"Well, I don't exactly know where you live at sir. I was never invited to your home."

"Oh, so you've never came over huh?"

"Well…no sir. I hadn't had any plans on coming over anytime soon."

"Unhuh. Tell me more about you and my daughter."

"Well sir there really isn't much to tell. Oh, the second day I tried to treat her out for breakfast but it was packed so we only drunk a cup of orange juice. Than she said she liked to swing so we walked to the park and I pushed her."

"You pushed my baby girl?"

"No sir, not pushed like shoved her down. But I gently moved her swing back and fourth while she kicked her feet."

"Oh so you were moving my daughter huh?"

"Ok sir, this isn't going so well."

"Oh it's going fine. And your only intentions are to be her friend.

No sex, no video tapes or nothing else crazy that you young teenagers are doing these days?"

"Sex," he throttled. "With Karma? Heck no. She's not that type of girl."

"Yea so I've been told. Well come here son and shake my hand. You passed with flying colors."

"My gosh sir, I thought you were going to kill me."

"I never said that I wasn't," I chuckled. "Now if you excuse me I'm going to get some sleep. The old man is tired," I said lying back in bed slowly.

"Sure sir," he said while placing the blanket over me.

After seeing him do this I knew he was the man for my Karma. He was very respectful, polite, honest and seemed to have real man qualities. I would have been crazy to tell him to stay away from my little girl when her prince was right in front of her. Don't too many young ladies find their prince and definitely not at a young age.

"How did you feel about the two of them getting married?" Mrs. Williams asked.

"Well I couldn't have been happier for my daughter. I admit I cried a little bit but that's because my little girl was going to become a woman now. Well, she already had become one when she had my grand daughter Kenise. But this was the real thing of my baby girl transforming to a woman. She had already started a family." I paused. "I couldn't have been more grateful for the two.

"Did you attend the wedding?"

"Of course I did. I said she was my only child. Why would I miss something like that?"

"I didn't mean to offend you sir. It was just a question. Why don't you tell us about the wedding."

"Well to make a long story short, I walked her down the aisle because I couldn't see her before the wedding due to the superstition of bad luck. But the moment it was time for me to walk her down that aisle and I saw how beautiful she looked I couldn't help but cry. I whimpered like a big baby. She saw my tears and immediately sobbed too. Walking her to her husband is one of the most treasured memories any father could ever have. Especially if the husband was a good man like Kwame."

"Were there any times that you were concerned for their relationship?

"If you are asking me if Karma told me about his drug addiction, than the answer is yes. At first she tried to keep it a secret but I knew better. Her hair began to fall out. They went from visiting every weekend to not showing up for months at a time. Then when she did show it was always without Kwame. So one day as we had Sunday dinner; her, my wife and Kenise that is I spoke to her.

"Karma…baby," I began and could see the uneasiness of her as she placed her fork down on her plate.

"Yes daddy," she replied.

Daddy was a term she hadn't used in many years and was like a clue that something was wrong. It was as if she wanted me to ask her questions so she could finally tell the truth.

"Is everything ok…" I began trying to choose my words wisely. "Between you and Kwame that is?"

Her mother watched waiting for a response. Karma looked at Kenise who in return was giving her a look of reassurance. She looked at her mother than looked at me before speaking.

"Kwame's on drugs," she murmured.

"What do you mean he's on drugs honey?" her mother asked alarmed.

"Mom…it's true," she pleading. "He's on drugs. I caught him more than a few times."

"Well what type of drugs?" my wife asked. "Prescription pills, Marijuana, Nyquil type of drugs."

"I wish mom but much worst."

The whole time I couldn't believe what I was hearing. This man whom I vouched for was the best she could ever find has given his life away for drugs. For fucking drugs? Becoming agitated I immediately stood up with my chair falling backwards with force.

"What type of drugs is he on Karma," I threatened.

"Heroine," she cried.

"And you are for sure?"

"Yes daddy! I caught him in our bathroom with the needle sitting next to him while he sat unconscious in the tub."

"Where is he?" I roared.

"Home I guess."

Kicking the chair out of my way I grabbed my car keys and went for the door.

"What are you going to do?" My wife asked stopping me in my tracks.

"What do you think I'm going to do?" I glared at her.

"Baby, NO!" she shrieked placing her hand on my chest.

"Woman if you don't get out of my way," I pressured.

"NO," she stood secured.

"Woman," I growled. "Move...now!"

"What good is it going to do?"

"I'm just going to talk to him?" I tried to reassure.

"Now honey we both know that's a lie. We've been married for nearly thirty years. Did you really think I would believe that?" she said crossing her arms with no doubt in her mind I was going through this door.

That's what I loved about her and why I never gave up during the hard trials of our marriage. She was feisty when needed to be and the woman could fight. Deep in her heart she knew I'd never harm a hair on her head. That's why she was able to stand assured in front of the door.

"Grandpa don't hurt my daddy," my grand daughter hugged me. "He's not used to not working and taking care of home. Tell him mommy...tell him," she said talking to Karma.

"It's true dad. He lost his job a year or so ago and haven't been the same since," she reassured me.

"Has he hit you?" I asked her through gritted teeth.

"What?" she looked impractical.

"Has...he...hit you?" I asked again startling her.

"No daddy. He hasn't," she said.

Again she used the word daddy which meant they have had some kind of battle. Before it got any worst I was going to correct him. My wife looked at me as if I had turned into the Incredible Hauk. Her hands came down to her sides very slowly as rage filled my eyes. I looked at her one time and she immediately knew I was out of control. My wife moved out of my way as I opened the door and walked out.

"I'm letting you know I'll be sending an officer over," she threatened.

"Good," I continued to walk. "Cause I'm gone need one."

When I got there, I kicked the door in, in search for Kwame. He was no where to be found at first sight but I smelled an odor. One that I knew dealt with drugs.

"KWAME!" I bellowed trying to listen for any noise that would lead me towards his direction.

A noise was heard upstairs and I immediately ran skipping three steps at a time. I stood at the top and looked both ways but couldn't see him. The smell became stronger and so I followed it. Walking down the hall I kicked each room in. To the left the door was locked. The little bitch must have known why I was here. Anger as well as adrenaline filled my feet as I kicked the door literally in half. It went slamming into his face as it caved in.

Picking him up with one hand I shook him in the air saying "You put your hands on my daughter?" I snarled.

Kwame didn't say anything. He continued to dangle in my arms. Shoving him out of the bathroom door while hitting his head on the top of the entrance I carried him out into the hallway. Drooping him over the banister he was so high from the drug that he didn't realize what was going on. I became so pissed and hurt that I threw him down a flight. He landed on the living room floor and just said "Umph." Seeing him like this began to make me feel sorry for him. I sat on the staircase nearby and cried as I watched him attempt to stand and couldn't. Moments later the police came in.

"Mr. Gentry I presume," the officer said with his gun facing my direction.

"Yea. Are you here to arrest me?" I asked.

"Well...it depends sir?"

"Depends on what?"

"Depends on what Mr. Woods can tell us about what happened here, if anything happened," he acknowledged looking at Kwame continue to trynand to stand.

"Good luck with that," I mumbled.

"Sir why don't you go home to your family," he said placing his hand on my shoulder. "We'll take it from here."

"Ok. But what are you going to do with him?"

"Well he is going downtown until he detox his self. From there he will receive a court date where he'll probably be forced to go to rehab."

I went home and cuddled with my wife; telling her how much I loved her. Karma and Kenise slept in her old bedroom while hoping for the best.

"So did it get better?" Mrs. Williams asked.

"No it did not but I'm sure Karma could do a better job discussing her life then I could."

"I agree," she said. "No further questions."

Mrs. Gentry

Point of View

I am Karma's mother. The one Mr. Gentry spoke so highly of during her childhood and some of her teenage years. Yes, I wasn't the best parent but that's because I had some skeletons in my closet that was keeping me from enjoying my daughter, husband; family, like I should have been doing.

While Karma was in the hospital, it was true. I was nothing but a disaster. A tornado blowing through the wind. A lioness ready to pounce on its next pray. I was worried sick my husband was going to leave me if he found out about a one night stand I had prior to Karma being conceived. If it wasn't for GOD speaking through to their doctor I don't think my husband and I would be together right now. And I'm almost positive Karma could care less about anything that would have happened following the news that was sure to get out.

My husband hugged the nurse than inhaled and exhaled one last time before we saw our daughter in her hospital bed. Patricia, became teary eyed as if she felt his pain. As he laid on Patricia's shoulder I couldn't help but to feel that should have been me. He should have been confiding in me. Patricia whispered for him to go see his daughter.

That once he saw how good the hospital was taking care of her he'd feel a lot better. She gave him a Kleenex that was nearby for him to clean his face. All the while I cleaned my nails and pretended to care less that my husband was becoming attracted to this woman that I could have stabbed by now. After my husband built up his strength, he walked over to our daughter, took one look and began to grab his chest. Patricia ran to his side. He began to rock as he continued to clinch at his torso. She ran out into the hallway screaming WE NEED A DOCTOR IN HERE. THERE'S A MAN HAVING AN ACUTE MYOCARDIAL INFARCTION!

All the while, I sat there with my mouth wide open while being in complete disbelief. Two doctors ran into the room and began to check his pulse.

"Patricia what happened," one of the doctors asked as they assisted my husband.

"Well he is the father of our patient Karma, here, and he was already nervous about her being in the hospital. The moment he saw his daughter he began to clinch at his chest and naturally fell to the floor.

"Does he have any allergies to any food or medication?" he asked Patricia.

"Mrs. Gentry, is your husband allergic to any food or medicine?" she directed the question to me.

"Uumm...uummm...no. No he isn't."

"Ok Patricia, because it's minutes within his acute myocardial infarction and he doesn't have any allergies I am going to give him tenectaplase. In the process, I need for Mrs. Gentry, sometime within the next hour to get her husband signed in so we can keep an eye on him as well. Due to this estranged situation and Mrs. Gentry can't be in two places at one time, I am going to have a bed placed in this room so that Mr. Gentrry can be next to his daughter and Mrs. Gentry be available to take care of the two of them.

"Uum. I can't do that. I have to work," I announced.

"Mrs. Gentry, I apologize for life's mishaps but your family comes first. Someone other than Mr. Gentry is going to need to be here to care for the two."

The transportation team entered our room with the extra bed and equipment needed to assist my husband. In the midst of them preparing our room, I was still trying to plead my case with the doctor *until* a teenage boy entered our room that I was unaware of.

It didn't take long before I became disgusted. He truly was the last person on Earth I wanted and probably needed to see at that moment.

"Kwame Mr. Gentry has just had a heart attack. I need for you to step to aside so that you're not in the way," Dr. Collins said.

"You know him?" I asked devastated.

"Of course I know him. Well, not know him literally but as far as his stay here so far with your daughter ma'am."

"And you allowed him to stay without our permission?"

"Well, your daughter needed someone by her side when she awoke. Kwame didn't seem like the type of child to take no for an answer. Am I right Kwame?" he directed the conversation to him.

"Yes sir and thank you," Kwame responded with courage.

"Just a personal note ma'am, you should be thankful that Kwame was available to see what happened to your daughter as well as stay here with her. My gosh, no one was able to get in contact with yourself or your husband for nearly twelve hours. The numbers we tried were outdated; there weren't any emergency contacts that we strongly recommend for all of our patients. He was the best choice for the patient at this time."

What the doctor said had nothing to do with the way I felt about Kwame. The problem was the skeletons I had in my very own closet. How could I have accepted this child who was willing to do so much for Karma when I didn't even except her myself? Didn't have any respect or dignity for myself? Didn't love myself and couldn't tell you what love was since I had denied it for so long.

"Mrs. Gentry I hope it isn't too much to ask for but I would really like to stay here with your daughter. I…lo…I need to be here," Kwame suggested.

I knew what he wanted to say but I assume he felt this wasn't the right time or place. He was a very respectful child.

"I came in with Karma by helicopter earlier today," he continued. "I witnessed everything that happened. She was supposed to meet me this morning."

"That will be quite enough. You can stay…AS LONG, as you stay out my way."

"Stay out your way; sure. I can do that. Doing that," he sat down. "Right now. Nothing else, not a word," he zipped his lips. Unzipping his lips, "That is unless Karma wake up," he zipped them back.

The look I gave him was clear into what I was feeling.

"Mrs. Gentry is there anything I can do to make your stay here any better?" Dr. Collins asked.

"Wow doctor I really don't know?" I spoke sarcastically. "My daughters' *apparent* boyfriend that I and her father just heard of is here in the hospital…with my daughter. By the way who can't talk and looks like she's in A FUCKING COMA BUT YOU WANT ME TO BELIEVE SHE'S ASLEEP."

"Mrs. Gentry, here in this hospital we have rules. We will do whatever it takes to make sure our patients are protected at all costs. From parents as well. This is not your house. Your rules and the guidelines you follow are for your house only. Here at Jackson's Hospital, we show respect to our families and expect respect in return. I apologize for the situation with your daughter. I truly do. But be thankful this young man was there to assist when she collapsed, else she *wouldn't* have made it. Now if you'll excuse me," he said as he began to talk to Patricia. "Patricia, will you be able to work extra tonight? I would really like to keep this families business private and not up for discussion among the other nurses. Can you handle the extra hours?"

"Uum…sure doctor. As long as there are some demands met on my behalf which I will talk to you about *away* from the patients."

"I'm sure they will be quite interesting and approvable," he said as he walked out of our room.

I stood in front of Kwame with my hands crossed as he sat back in his chair. Funny thing is; he never became uncomfortable. He stared at me just as well as I was doing him. I remember thinking this big headed little boy has the audacity to engage in a staring contest; possibly studying me as I was him.

Eventually our event ended and I sat down as well but faced him. So many thoughts over flowed in my mind. My husband and daughter are both in the hospital. Her boyfriend is here with her; which I should be thankful for but wasn't. And she was planning on going to see him this morning.

Is she still a virgin? If not, how long have she been having sex and with how many people? Is she even working or was that a scam to get out of the house to meet up with Juice or whatever his name is. What is really going on with my daughter and why did I feel like I don't know who she is anymore.

A mental thought slapped me saying "That's because you haven't been a mother to her. You've been too busy making her suffer for the mistake you made when it wasn't her fault."

"Shut up!" I yelled aloud.

Kwame didn't say anything. He tried not to look at me after my outburst that wasn't directed to him. Kwame placed a kiss on Karma's hand than cut the television on. As he flipped through the channels, my husband opened his eyes. It was as if he saw what had just happened.

"Honey," he whispered. "Honey," he continued. "Honey…HONEY, HONEY…"

"I'm here," I said calmly. "How do you feel?"

"What do you mean how do I feel? And why am I hooked up to these machines/ Hell, what am I doing in a hospital bed?" He pronounced as he tried to sit up. "Ouch, and why is my chest so soar," he stated as he laid back down. "Where's our daughter? Where's Karma?"

I just kept quiet while he spoke. I didn't know what to say or do at this point. How to tell him that daddies little girl has grown up in unspeakable ways.

"Hush darling. Everything will be okay."

"What do you mean everything will be ok? I want to see my daughter!"

He sat up in bed, ignoring the unbearable pain, than unhooked himself from the machines. They beeped to alert the nurse up front that he needed immediate assistance in his room. My husband than stood up and began to step towards me. As he was about two feet away, he saw Kwame. Respectfully, Kwame stood up and held out his hand.

"How are you Mr. Gentry? My name is Kwame…" he stated before being interrupted.

"Kwame are you in the right room? This room is for Karma Gentry and I have never heard of or seen you."

"Well sir, no disrespect, but your daughter and I work together," he answered before being interrupted again.

"Oooooh. You're him. The kid my baby girl was telling us about last night.

"I'm not sure about what you're speaking of but I'm pretty sure that I am…the kid you're referring to."

"You told the doctor that you and our daughter had plans of hooking up this morning," I articulated.

"Well Mrs. Gentry, you are correct. We did have plans on seeing each other this morning, but we also work together. I apologize, I may have left that part out."

"*I apologize, I may have left that part out,*" I repeated before speaking to her father. "So tell me something, *darling*. Still think daddies little girl is so innocent?"

My husband became speechless. At this time he didn't know what to think or believe anymore. As he closed his eyes nurse Patricia walked into the room.

"Mr. Gentry are you okay?"

"I don't know," he wailed.

"Is there anything I can do to make you feel any better?"

"I have one. Why don't you stay the hell out of his face. I see your little fast ass," I verbalized.

"Mrs. Gentry I am only doing my job. I apologize if I have offended you in any way."

"*Mrs. Gentry I am only doing my job. I apologize if I have offended you in any way.* Yeah I'm sure you are *just* doing your job. Just know…your job *isn't* going to be my husband," I snapped before leaving the room.

I honestly believed she was trying to come on to my husband. In all actuality, she was just doing her job and I was in the way. After noticing how silly I behaved I decided to go for some fresh air. As I leaned up against the door, Doctor Collins came from around the bend with some papers in is hands.

"Mrs. Gentry, are you okay?"

"Of course I am. I was just…um…on my way to get coffee. Yea, that's it, a coffee," I said walking away hoping he was persuaded.

"Uum, Mrs. Gentry, our coffee machine is the opposite way in which you are going," he smiled sensing that something wasn't quite right.

"Um…that way…right. I…knew that."

"Mrs. Gentry, why don't you step into my office. I don't know why, but I feel that there is something else on your mind that you may want to talk about. You just don't know how to," he assured now walking with me.

"Not really, but thanks anyway," I spoke while trying to walk ahead.

"Mrs. Gentry before I became a doctor I was a psychologist. One for many years."

"Oh so now you think I need to talk to a shrink?"

"No I'm not saying that at all," he laughed. "I am simply saying that maybe if you told someone of this secret you are holding so deep inside, it might just help improve your attitude. You see…Mrs. Gentry, I read my families like I listen to the heart beat of my patients and I can tell something isn't right with you. But…if you insist that there's nothing wrong…than maybe there isn't," he insisted. "Well, I guess I'll be going. Oh by the way, the coffee machines are two doors down from where we're standing."

"Oh…ok, thanks."

"Oh, one last thing Mrs. Gentry."

"Yes."

"Do you remember the way back to your room?"

"No, not really but I think I'll be ok."

He took a few steps before turning around again.

"Oh, one last thing Mrs. Gentry. My name is Doctor Collins."

"Oh…ok. Thanks."

We departed ways and I was left with the stress of a secret pounding at my heart stronger than ever. The thought of the cup of coffee helping to ease what I was feeling at this current moment didn't and wouldn't help regardless of how I tried to convince myself otherwise. By the time I got back to our room Karma was awake and my husband; her father and Kwame were talking. Actually getting to know each other. I was devastated. *Wow, I've only been gone for fifteen minutes and I've missed a lot.* My husband was engaging in conversation with the last person on earth I wanted him chatting to. I'd rather him talk to Patricia than to be making friends with our daughters boyfriend.

"What's going on in here?" I asked.

"Well I figured since Kwame was here we at least got to know who our daughter is involved with."

"We're not together," Karma crackled overhearing the conversation as she awoke.

"Yes Mrs. and Mr. Gentry, we are not." Kwame added on. "How are you feeling? You gave me quite a scare. Oh, and by the way, happy birthday."

"My chest hurt. What happened?" she asked while trying to sit up.

"No no, Karma. You have to stay rested in bed. And your chest hurt because you collapsed earlier today."

"What do you mean I collapsed?"

"Well, you were running for the bus and you crumpled."

"Well did the bus driver at least attempt to wait for her?" I asked trying to sound concerned.

"In the beginning Karma wasn't at the bus stop when the bus passed her by. She stopped at a red light not too far away from the bus stop she was at and Karma attempted to still try to catch the bus. When she got in front of the doors of the bus, the driver looked at her, than at the light that had just turned green. She paused a second and looked back at Karma while before trying to go through the light. Only thing is, by the time she decided to go through the light, it had turned yellow and she stopped instead. Karma saw that she stopped and ran through the light to the following bus stop. I guess in her mind she knew that naturally the bus would have to stop for her. That's when she bent over and collapsed. I'm assuming because she was waiting for the bus that that's the only reason why the driver stopped for her. I think given the drivers reactions today, had it been anyone else on that ground, the driver would not have stopped."

"Ok, so what happened next?" my husband asked.

"Well naturally the police was called and the fire department except in this case, the ambulance was contacted and told to show at the scene."

"Ok, than what happened after that?" I asked.

"Well the woman was taken downtown and Karma was flown to the hospital. Oh, and they had to place a defibrillator on her and sends shock to her body three times I believe."

"And she made it?" I mumbled.

My husband rose from his bed looking mighty strong. He gazed into my eyes for what seemed like an eternity. Taking his hands to pull the pony tail out of my hair so that it would fall down my shoulders I fell into a spell. Combing his hands through my hair until it was the way he loved to see it, he began to caress my face. I closed my eyes and began to drift away with every touch. He guided his lips to mine and ever so passionately kissed me. The sound of the door forced open my eyes as I snapped out of it.

"Patricia, can you escort my wife off of the premises please?" my husband said very stern.

"WHAT!" I yelled. "How could you? HOW COULD YOU?" I continued. "She's my daughter too."

"Your daughter? You don't give a damn about your daughter. So do us both a big favor," he said while caressing his hands through my hair, "Go home, shower or bath and think about how much your daughter and I mean to you. I told you before you will not continue to disrespect our daughter. I also told you that either you started acting like her mother or sign away your rights, *which*, in doing so I will be asking for a divorce."

"But…"

"Shhh…shh…shhh," he said kissing my lips once more. "I'm serious. Go take some time to think about what's more important," he stressed. "Sorry to take some of your time Patricia, but my wife, is ready to leave now."

"No disrespect sir, but I'm glad you told her," I overheard Patricia whisper to my husband.

"So am I Patricia. Believe me…So am I," he agreed.

I grabbed my purse than stopped and starred at Patricia. I wanted to say something cruel but knew if I had spoken; it would only make things worst as my husband was watching. She looked at me in disgust as she escorted me through the door. On the way down the hall we saw Dr. Collins.

"Hi Patricia, can I assist you in any way?"

"No sir. I am escorting Mrs. Gentry off of the premises."

"Off the premises. Sounds serious. What happened?"

"Well Dr. Collins, Mr. and Mrs. Gentry had an altercation. Because Mr. Gentry is now a patient and I was asked to escort Mrs. Gentry off of the premises, I have to do just that."

"I totally agree Patricia. You have done nothing wrong. Here, why don't you let me help you with Mrs. Gentry and you go check on Mr. Gentry."

She walked away leaving just the two us. He didn't give me a choice of rather or not I wanted to talk. He walked and I just knew to follow. When we approached his office, he pointed to a lounge chair and said to lye down, try to relax. To take deep breaths and try to focus on what was causing problems within our marriage.

"What do you mean what's causing problems within my marriage?"

"Well obviously something has happened that has you so distorted that you can't enjoy the regular life of being a happy mother…wife and etc."

I couldn't help but look dumbfound. *Was I that easily read?* And if Dr. Collins noticed it in as little as twenty four hours, did my husband know? I began to cry huge water fall tears. Dr. Collins didn't dare approach me. He stood a distance allowing me to continue to allow what ever was causing so much pain out.

"I'm so sorry," I continued. "I'm…so…sorry. My husband…I need to talk to my husband. I cheated on him and made a terrible mistake. It's a possibility Karma might not even be his. Oh GOD, we named her Karma because she was the most beautiful thing he'd ever seen. She's our only child. We don't have any more kids. What if she's not his? I can't live without him. I love him so much. Oh GOD…I am so sorry. Please make this pain go away. I can't take it anymore. I need your help, lord. I need for you to make things right."

"Mrs. Gentry, God is giving you a second chance right now to come clean to your husband. The time is now, while he's already in the hospital," Dr. Collins joked. "Not to mention, the two of you will be safe and I won't allow anything to happen. I have already talked to Patricia earlier about staying over time so that she can continue to be your nurse until you guys leave and I also will be staying over to assist with your medical needs. I don't want your business to be lurking the halls and although we have a strict confidentiality rule here at Jackson's Hospital, we've had altercations of our patients business running the halls. In which, the situation became much worst because of this. Anyway, you and Mr. Gentry seem like a loving couple. I actually haven't seen a couple like the two of ya's in a very long time. I can't say how long cuz than you'll have an idea on how old I've become. One thing's for sure, you two will get through this."

"Do you think he'll ever forgive me?"

"I'm sure he will. The way he looks at you shows just how much he's in love with you. As I've said before, it's a look I haven't seen in many years. And to make things better. I am going to do something for you but it has to stay between us."

"Ok," I sniffled.

"Since we already have your husband and daughter as patients and the two of them both had blood drawn, I will get a paternity test done during their stay here. We'll make it first priority and have it ready by tomorrow morning."

"In other words you want me to go home, get some rest and come to court in the morning?" I smiled in a thanking way.

"I wouldn't necessarily call it court. Just going on a good hunch. At least, when you come back tomorrow morning, you will have thought of what to say to your husband. The results will be in and we can provide them to him, free of cost AND hope that things will die down right there and than. Your husbands a strong man. He'll forgive you but you have to trust me. And when you go home, make sure you pray and tell God thanks for all that he has done," he said while showing me to the door.

The following day Kwame was there next to Karma as he had been. He was feeding her breakfast and I must admit it was very sweet. Reminded me of my husband; her father. After she finished her breakfast he fluffed her pillows for her and engaged in conversation.

"How are you feeling?" Kwame asked.

"A little better, I think," Karma responded.

"I'm sorry I had to meet your parents so soon and in this way. I know you probably weren't ready for that but I just couldn't leave you. I had to make sure you were okay."

"That's okay Kwame, really. I had just told my parents about you yesterday; which didn't go so well," she mumbled. "But everything happens for a reason. Maybe this happened so that my parents would become closer as well as get to know you."

"Maybe," he paused before smirking.

"What?" she caught on quickly.

"Nothing," he said sitting back in his seat.

"I know you; well not literally. But I think I can vouch for that smirk of yours?"

"Unhuh. So…you really want to know what this smirk is about huh?"

"Yes, I do. Now tell me."

"I'm just curious on what made you tell your parents about me?"

Karma became quiet. Her father and I tried to look away as if we weren't listening for a response.

"We'll talk about that later," she suggested while sending him signals that she knew we were listening.

"I want to…" my husband started before I tapped him to shut up.

"What," he tried whispering.

"That's the reason why she won't talk now. You have to learn how to listen without actually listening."

"What?"

"We'll discuss our little situation later too" I said while signaling we too had an audience.

After prying in on our conversation Karma tried to lift up in bed.

"No, no, no. You have to stay lying down and rested. Here," he said messing with the up and down buttons on the bed. "One of these should position you in a way that is more comfortable."

The bed frame moved in all directions. Finally he found the correct button to position her cadaver in a way that was most comfortable.

"There," he spoke in confidence. "How does that feel?"
"Much better."
"Do you have to go to the restroom or anything?"
"If she does I will be the one to take her," my husband intervened.
"No disrespect sir, but I wasn't going to watch her use the restroom. I was just going to walk her there."
"And I appreciate your help but I will feel comfortable taking her myself," He said looking at Karma from his bed. "And daddy won't look," he spoke sarcastically.
"Honey, why don't you let Kwame take her if she needs to go? You can barely move yourself," I suggested.
"What...what got into you this morning? I can't believe you of all people actually feel comfortable with letting a boy we barely know take Karma to the restroom. Now I may be sick but I'm not dumb," my husband said.
"He started to sound like me," I thought. "Baby we both will be right here in eye vision of the two of them," I pointed. "You need your rest as well. The way I see it is allow Kwame to care for Karma while I care for you. Besides the point we really need to talk."

Kwame turned the television on and kept Karma entertained as I assume he knew something was about to go down.

"Talk about what?"

"About my behavior for the past ten or so years."

My husband looked me in my eyes in search for the worst. I could see the tears forming as he tried to hold them back.

Trying to sit his self up "So tell me."

"No, no darling," I said while fixing his bed for him just as Kwame did for Karma. "There…that should help. How does that feel?"

"It would feel much better once you get to whatever you have to tell me."

"Ok," I inhaled. "Remember…No, no," I continued to try to reword my thoughts. "Ok…ok. I'm just going to come out and say it. Before Karma was born I had a one night stand."

"WITH WHO?" he roared as he already anticipated this day to come.

"Well right now that isn't important. There's more to say."

"How could you?" he asked with hurt and pain in his eyes. "How… could you? All these years. All of this," he waved his hand. "Everything I've gone through for nearly ten years or more is because of a mistake you made?"

"I'm sorry."

"Yea, you are. Real sorry."

"Well since I got your attention it's only right for me to tell you the rest," I hesitated. "Karma might not be yours."

"WHAT?" Karma implied. "There is no way he is not my father. I won't accept any other man to be a father to me."

"Kiddo, I will always be your father. No skeletons in the closet will ever scare me away."

"And…being that the both of you have gotten blood taken, Dr. Collins was willing to do a free paternal test…that is…if you want to know?"

"No, no,no," he disregarded.

"But daddy, even though you will always be my father, I would like to know."

"Karma are you sure you can handle all of this pressure right now? My gosh your lungs just collapsed," Kwame asked concerned.

"Kwame I will be ok. But now that the truth has been told...I really need to know."

He took her by the hand and kissed it. I couldn't help but notice the love he had for her. The way he looked at Karma was full of it. Like she was his personal seraph.

"Ok but if it's alright, Mr. and Mrs. Gentry I would like to stay to support her through this?"

"Sure honey. I think Karma would like that," I said.

Dr. Collins and Patricia walked through the entrance.

"Hello everyone," Dr. Collins said. "I'm sure Mrs. Gentry has discussed the news with you all because it's written all over your face," he began to sing. "You don't have to say a word," he continued. "Tell me yall don't know about that song," he tried to be cheerful. "Ok...guess not. Well let's get to it. In the case of Mr. Gentry and Karma Gentry, you are..." he looked around before continuing.

Kwame squeezed Karma's hand. I tried to hold my husbands hand but he wouldn't allow it. His eyes closed as he waited for the rest of Dr. Collins sentence to be disclosed.

"THE FATHER," he yelled excited. "Now fix this mess you made Mrs. Gentry. And remember, it starts with GOD," he said as he and Patricia walked out of the room.

"Yes it does. And I know deep in my heart that my husband will forgive me. Now I can become a better mother as well as wife," I mentioned while looking at my husband than Karma. "And Karma baby, I know I missed nearly all of your life since birth because I accused you of my infidelity, but we will get through this and I will make it up to you."

"Fourteen years mom! Fourteen years I've been nothing but a shadow in the corner and now you want to try to be my mother," she begin to cough.

"Honey are you okay?" I asked her as she continued to cough.

"Karma," Kwame said looking at the machine.

Her oxygen level begin to decrease drastically almost as if her lungs had collapsed again.

"Karma...Karma...GET THE DOCTOR...NOW!" Kwame Yelled.

I ran towards the entrance as if I was going to tackle down the door.

"WE NEED A DOCTOR! SOMEONE GET US A DOCTOR."

"MRS. GENTRY WE ARE AWARE OF KARMA'S SITUATION. THAT'S WHY WE HAVE CAME TO THE DEFENSE SO FAST," Dr. Collins said running by me.

He checked the machine and saw that Karma had about fifteen percent of oxygen left in her body.

"We are going to have to put her mask back on her face and increase her air flow."

"That's fine," I said. "Whatever you have to do."

"We are also going to give her a steroid to help keep her lungs open."

"Ok."

"What's happening with my baby girl?" My husband demanded.

"Oh no you don't," I looked him in his eyes. ? "Not you too. You just stay calm and strong for our little girl. She's going to pull through.

I prayed for this and I believe GOD will keep his word because I have faith."

My husband began to cry. I held him as tight as possible in my arms. Shortly after, Karma lungs were at one hundred percent but she was asleep. Dr. Collins said her blood pressure was normal and she was breathing fine. That she will need to continue resting and to keep her oxygen mask in place. When she awoke, they would take more x-rays of her chest and to expect to be here for a few more days.

Following Karma's accident as well as the incident at the hospital I became a changed a woman. I knew I had to make up to both my husband and Karma and it would be best if I started right away. I began to prepare breakfast for my husband and daughter before work every morning. My husband was invited for neighborhood walks so we could spend more time together and also to invite him on getting to know the real me that had been buried decades ago. Karma also was taken to and from work, *when she was ready*. Not that she didn't have a curfew because she did, but as a token to give her a little freedom and privacy.

The day before she was due to return to work Kwame called the house. I was sitting in the bed in my pajama with my husband. We had just got finished reading the bible when my husband turned on the television.

"Hi Mrs. Gentry how are you?"

"I'm fine Kwame and you?"

"I will be better when I hear my Karma's voice," he said seriously.

Chuckling, "Hold on honey let me get her for you."

"Mrs. Gentry, before you do that; I understand this may be a bit to ask for, but when it comes to her I'm willing to do anything it takes to please and make her happy."

"Well…what is it Kwame?" I asked concerned.

"I Know tomorrow's her first day back to work since her incident and I would really like it if I could take her out to breakfast.

"Well Kwame," I cleared my throat. "I understand completely what you want to do but I don't think I comprehend to why you're telling me."

"Well, she told me that you will be taking her to work for now on.

"O…k."

"I'm asking if you can drop her off at Bagel Brothers instead of taking her to work. Say…about 6:45am?"

"Before I answer you I need to ask Karma first to see how she feels about that."

"I'm almost positive she will love the *surprise*," he hinted.

"Ohhh, surprise. O…k. Well," I looked at my husband who was looking at me as if he already knew what was going on. The remote was in his hand still pointed at the television that had suddenly stopped changing channels. "Sure, I will take her."

My husband looked away and continued to view channels as if he was no longer needed.

"Thank you so much Mrs. Gentry. You truly are the best."
"You're very welcome Kwame," I said almost hanging up on him.
"Uuum; Mrs. Gentry."
"Yes Kwame."
"May I speak to Karma now?"
"My gosh I nearly forgot just that quick. Yes Kwame give me a moment to get her."
"Thank you."
"You're very welcome hun."

The following day I did just as I promised. Karma seemed to be in good spirit today as if she already knew what was happening. She kissed my forehead before stepping out of the car confused.

"Mom, this isn't where I work."
"I know honey. Why don't you go inside? There's a special young man waiting for a special young lady," I smiled encouraging.
"Really?"
"Yes, and I have you hear exactly on time so don't be late. Go, go," I motioned her with my hands
"Thank you so much mom," she said teary eyed.
"Don't cry baby doll. That's just going to make me cry."
"I can't help it mom. I haven't felt this close to you in years and now all of a sudden," she stopped wiping a tear from her eye.
"I know baby I know. This is a change I'm getting used to myself but we can put our old memories behind us and move forward," I said blowing her a kiss. "Love you."

"Love you too mom."

"Now go."

Kwame must have seen the commotion outside because when Karma turned to walk to the door he walked out of it embracing her in his arms. At that very moment I fell in love with Kwame and he became my son. Soon to be in law.

"Mrs. Gentry, wasn't there a time that you had to have a mother daughter talk with your daughter because she up and...left Kwame?" Mr. Ohio asked.

"Well at the time she believed she had reason to."

"And why is that?"

"She said they had a disagreement and he stayed out all night."

"Didn't he leave their home due to Karma not wanting their child she was carrying?" Mr. Ohio stood firm and asked.

"I suppose."

"No no no Mrs. Gentry. That's a yes or no question. He told you why he left when he called you right?"

"Yes," I sighed looking at Karma.

Mr. Ohio saw this and walked towards me. He stood in front of me in a position that I wouldn't be able to look at Karma.

"What did he say...specifically?"

"I can't remember specifically?"

"If you can't remember specifically then there's no need for you to be counted as a viable witness because you have a," He put up quotation marks, "Jogged memory. Correct Mrs. Gentry?"

"He said she didn't want their child and he was hurt. He left to take some time to his self as well as give her space to think about what she was going to do."

"And this was her first child correct?"

"Yes," I sighed again.

Mr. Ohio took his seat and Mrs. Williams walked towards me.

"Mrs. Gentry, do you have any other children?" she asked.

"No ma'am I don't."

"And how did you feel when you found out you were pregnant with Karma?"

"I was devastated. I felt exactly the same way she did. What was I going to do with a baby when I wasn't ready to become a mother?"

"Thank you Mrs. Gentry. Now when Karma contacted you, what did she happen between the two of them?"

"That she had called his phone and someone else picked up the line. Another woman to be exact. Karma said the woman placed the phone down and she was able to hear their conversation. That he had just gotten out of the shower and asked for help from the woman. I believe her name was Thickness."

"And?"

" Let me start from the beginning," I waved her.

"Hey dad," Karma answered assuming it was her father returning the call.

"This isn't your father honey, its mom."

"Oh. Hey mom. What's up?"

"I don't know. You tell me."

"Nothing much. Just met up with Denise earlier and am spending time with her."

"Oh really?" I asked trying to lead her on that I had talked to Kwame who told me otherwise. "How has she been?"

"She's fine now that we found each other again," she said playing in the back ground.

"Well I'm glad to hear that, but the person I'm referring to is Kwame."

"Oh," she stopped in her tracks.

For a moment I didn't think she was on the phone.

"What about him?"

"What do you mean what about him? He's been calling here worried sick about you. And….he told us."

"Told you what?" she said troubled.

"About the baby?"

"What baby?"

"The one you're carrying and neglected to tell your father and I about?"

"Wow, I can't believe he would do that."

"I can't believe you would keep your pregnancy a secret from us."

"I wasn't keeping it a secret mom. I just wasn't ready to tell anyone. This isn't easy for me."

"I understand darling. That's why you're father and I are here. Anytime you need someone to talk to, come to us. Or Denise," I joked. "But most importantly; to us. Never feel like you can't talk to us. Even if it's the smallest thing or concern. Ok?"

"Yes ma'am."

"Ok. Now where are you?"

"I'm over Denise house. I'm going to stay here for awhile."

"What do you mean you're going to stay there for awhile?"

"Mom, I don't know how else to shed more news on you but Kwame cheated on me last night and I won't be returning home to him. I was actually on my way back home to you guys till Denise and I bumped into each other."

"Karma there is no way that Kwame would cheat on you."

"Mom, I heard the woman's voice with my own ears. He even called her Thickness. That's what he calls me mom!"

"I'm sorry darling but we're talking about Kwame here. I just can't believe he would do something like that. It isn't in him to do so."

"I used to think the same thing till I heard the lies myself."

"Well darling, I'm going to tell you something your grandfather used to tell me. *In life, things aren't always what we perceive them to be.*"

"In life, things aren't always what we perceive them to be," she softly repeated trying to mentally gasp onto what I was saying.

"Well darling, I'll leave you to Denise. Tell her I said take good care of my baby. I love you and call me anytime of day or night. You're always welcome."

"Thanks mom but you and daddy never answer your phones. No matter what time I call," she laughed.

"Yes that is true darling. But…we always return the call…eventually," she joked. "Love you baby."

"Love you too mom. Bye."

Dr. Collins
Point of View

I was the doctor of Mr. Gentry and Karma Gentry during their stay at Jackson Hospital. Kwame was also in attendance during this stay. He was a very kind gentleman. Well spoken and very polite; nothing you would have saw during those times.

After we took Karma to her room I went into the waiting room to see if anyone was waiting for her. I had heard of the young fellow waiting there but I hadn't had the chance to meet him yet.

"Party of the Gentry's," I said while looking through my paper work.

"I am here for the Gentry's," he said hesitantly.

"You're a bit young aren't you? Where are your parents?"

"Well…sir," he said scratching his head. "I'm not a part of her family. Her family isn't here. I don't think they know what happened."

"Well do you know their number? We can give them a call. You have to be at least eighteen in order to be alone with her."

"Karma and I just started working together Monday. I don't have a phone number or even a house number to call her on, let alone get in touch with her parents."

"Well given the circumstance," I started before being interrupted.

"Please sir. Please. I need to be with her. I don't want her to be alone when she awakes. You understand, don't you?"

I looked around the room than told the child to walk with me.

"What is your name son?"

"Kwame."

"Kwame huh? Kwame and Karma. What are the odds of that?" I joked. "Because her parents aren't here and we have no number listed for them I am going to allow you to stay. I don't think I need to tell you the rules here because you don't tip me off as being that type of teen," I mentioned pointing him to make a right.

Kwame just listened. I don't think there was anything else I could have said to him that wasn't already said. He really was a sweet kid. I showed him her room and told him to take good care of her till I got back. I also told him I would be back every hour to check on her; her vitals, oxygen level and such. He just walked to her nearly in tears. I could tell the kid was heart broken. And seeing the mask on her face as well as other things that were hooked to her I'm sure didn't make it any better.

"What else can you tell us about Kwame and Karma?" Mrs. Williams said trying to jog my memory.

Well he never left her side. I don't even recall seeing the kid eat. There was so much commotion going on it was almost impossible to keep an eye on everyone but my patients.

"Well that couldn't be true because Mrs. Gentry testified that you had time to do a personal favor?" Mr. Ohio the prosecutor interrupted.

"Yes I did sir, BUT out of good faith. All I had to do was send in the order for the paternity test. No work was personally done at my hands. Therefore I couldn't have personally sat in and listened to the majorities of conversations discussed between Karma and Kwame."

"Were you finished?" Mrs. Williams asked Mr. Ohio.

"Sure," he said uneasy.

"Please continue with what you remember about the couple."

Well by the time Mr. and Mrs. Gentry approached the hospital and were guided to their daughter's room Kwame wasn't there.

"How do you know he wasn't there?" Mrs. Williams asked.

"Because he was with me. He was nervous about what her parents would think about him and needed some advice."

"And what did you tell him?"

"I told him to be his self. That he looked like a pretty good kid, well respected and polite. Her parents would appreciate him being there with Karma."

"No further questions."

Patricia

Point of View

I was Karma's and Mr. Gentry's nurse. I will never forget the couple because Karma's mother was a real bitch; excuse my language. She was so nasty and I just couldn't believe this good man had dealt with her for as long as he had. The word shocked couldn't explain the way this woman was towards her daughter. In my opinion, she literally couldn't stand her. Mrs. Gentry had no respect for herself or husband let alone the family period. Because of some of her statement's I actually wrote a mental note to check in more than usual so that the child would be safe. When Mr. Gentry asked me to escort her off of the premises, I couldn't have been happier to do my job.

"Patricia what happened," Dr. Collins asked assisting Mr. Gentry.

"Mr. Gentry is the father of our patient Karma, here, and he was already nervous about her being in the hospital. The moment he saw his daughter he began to clinch at his chest and naturally fell to the floor.

"Does he have any allergies to any food or medication?" he asked.

"Mrs. Gentry, is your husband allergic to any food or medicine?" I directed to Mrs. Gentry.

"Uumm…uummm…no. No he isn't."

"Ok Patricia, because it's minutes within his acute myocardial infarction and he doesn't have any allergies I am going to give him tenectaplase. In the process, I need for Mrs. Gentry, sometime within the next hour to get her husband signed in so we can keep an eye on him as well. Due to this estranged situation and Mrs. Gentry can't be in two places at one time, I am going to have a bed placed in this room so that Mr. Gentrry can be next to his daughter and Mrs. Gentry be available to take care of the two of them.

"Uum. I can't do that. I have to work," she announced.

"Mrs. Gentry, I apologize for life's mishaps but your family comes first. Someone other than Mr. Gentry is going to need to be here with little Gentry."

The transportation team entered their room with the extra bed and equipment needed to assist the father.

"So much has already been said that I don't really know if there's anything left to mention," I motioned uncomfortably.

"How about you tell us the type of person Kwame was? What do you recall?" Mrs. Williams asked.

"Well like Dr. Collins said, he was a very sweet boy. He didn't leave Karma side at all."

"Well that can't be true because Dr. Collins said he came to talk to her during a time that neither Mr. or Mrs. Gentry was available," Mr. Ohio mentioned.

"Yes, yes. That's very true; but,"

"But what Miss Patricia? Did I mention you are on trial and can be sentenced for perjury?"

"Well sir I'm aware of that but I think you may have misunderstood. I can only account for one time that Kwame wasn't in view in the room. It wasn't until I heard Dr. Collins on the stand that I heard just exactly where he was. I thought the child was in the restroom. Like I said, he wouldn't leave her side."

"He wouldn't; but did."

"Well I guess so according to Dr. Collins."

"No further questions."

"Mrs. Williams will you like to cross counter the witness?" Judge Lanai Brown Brown asked.

"No maam. Not at all. Miss Patricia has said plenty," she smiled.

"Patricia, you may step down."

Tamela

Point of View

Kwame was my son. Though it hurts me dearly to take this stand... there's just no way Karma would hurt him. They were truly in love with one another.

I remember the first time I heard about Karma, well the first time Kwame and I actually sat down to talk about her anyway. She had an accident of some sort and he was crazy out of his mind for her. It wouldn't have made since to split the two love birds apart or punish him in any way because he was love sick. He was really devoted to her.

I was lying in bed in the after hours when he came knocking on my door.

"Mom...can I talk to you?" he asked.
"Sure baby come in."
He said "Mom...I can't sleep."
So I says, "Why?"
"I keep thinking about her?"
"Thinking about who?"
"Karma."

Her named ranged like music to my ears because I knew at this point in time, my son was in love; a situation he'd never experienced before. You see, he didn't know that I knew the little girls he was calling his girlfriend was just to please everyone else. But I knew better. Kwame barely called them, allowed them to come over and I never once heard him say "Mom I'm going to the movies with such and such." But when he spoke Karma's name…I knew…she was the one.

Sitting up in bed, "Ok tell me about Karma."

"She's wonderful mom. She has the most beautiful eyes and the smile to match. Every time I see her smile my body melts beneath me."

"Ok."

"Well, the problem is…I can't sleep. I keep thinking about her. It's better when I'm next to her. The feeling of being comfortable and where I belong has never felt better."

"It sounds to me son that you are love sick."

"Love sick?" he repeated. "What's that?"

"That's when your soul finds the one you are destined to be with and it aches every moment you are away from him…or her in your case. What you have to do is BE PATIENT. Get to know her and allow her to know you. Don't too many people find their soul mate as young as you have."

He looked dazed as if he was dreaming about future plans. Like it was being written right in front of him.

"Let me ask you a question. How are you so sure that she is the one?"

That's when he broke down for me the type of day they'd had. He told me about the bus ordeal and how Bryant, my other son, went one way and he and she went another. That she had fainted into his arms and became feisty once she awoke.

The sun rose the sky was a mixture of orange, blue and yellow. Kwame really didn't know how to feel at this moment. It was a feeling he's never felt. Emotions of butterflies and loss of breaths as his eyes snuck peaks at hers.

Kwame pointed down the street and convincingly said, "There's a Bagel Brothers there and they have some delicious food. We can stop in if you like? It will be my treat?"

"Umm. I'm not sure that's a good idea," Karma hesitated.

"Well you weren't sure taking a walk would be a good idea either but you came along anyway. One bite to eat isn't going to harm anything. It's not like I'm going to poison you. *And*, we can still *pretend* to not like each other the moment we get back to work. Deal?"

"Um, Ok. Sure. But, this is not a date!"

"Fine. Not a date. Gotcha."

Nothing else was said until they got to the restaurant. There was a long line of customers waiting to be served. The aroma of the food smelled delightful. The sight of a clean atmosphere made him feel extremely comfortable.

Kwame turned to her than asked, "Would you like to sit down and eat? We will get served a lot faster?"

"Sure. Why not? I don't have to clock in till 8am. Its only 7:15am."

He chose a table by the window. My son loved to watch the clouds move through the sky.

She spoke with a smile as he pulled her chair out from under her, "And here it is I thought you were trying to show me off. Good choice."

Kwame giggled, "I couldn't have said it better."

The waiter walked over and asked "What can I get you two?"

Looking at Kwame she motioned, "I will take an orange juice please."

The waiter than asked, "What to eat?"

"I don't want anything to eat. Thanks anyway."

Kwame interrupted saying, "Are you sure? The food here is excellent and always help me to start my work day."

"That's understandable but by the looks of the line and those folks that are standing over there looking at their watch repeatedly; I don't think we will be eating anytime soon."

The waiter whispered, "I'd take her advice. She's a smart gal. I'd keep her if I was you."

Amazed at her attentiveness Kwame said, "Ok, well I will have an orange juice too." Pulling the waitress in closer to him, he whispered, "She's not my girlfriend. Not yet anyway."

The waitress looked at her than looked at him and said, "Whatever floats your boat," as she walked away.

"What was that all about," Karma asked.

"Before I tell you should I expect to get slapped," Kwame asked.

She placed her hand on her chin, leaned in closer and said, "Hum, well that depends on the answer you give me."

"In that case, I'd rather not tell you."

"Don't tell me you're scared of being hit by a…by a…girl," she joked.

Kwame mumbled, "You sure don't hit like one."

"What was that," she overheard.

"Oh I was just saying, how you're quite a girl. A girl indeed."

"Now I don't believe that's true. I'm…going…to have to hit you," she scared him.

He covered his face to protect it and she just laughed and laughed. Kwame peeked through his fingers to see if she was serious or playing another joke. It took minutes before he uncovered his face. Kwame watched me as she continued to laugh. He was in shock. There wasn't any way to believe as mean as she had been to him that she actually had a sweet, charming side. Kwame also flashed back to their entrance just a little while ago into Bagel Brothers and how in less than five minutes she was able to tell how things were going in a restaurant she'd never been to. He was truly amazed. All these qualities she possessed made him like her that much more.

Eventually she stopped laughing and noticed just how comfortable he had gotten. His staring at her started to make him feel nervous as he began to feel butterflies again. He'd felt them at first sight of her and now he was feeling them again. Immediately gaining composure she began to look out of the window. Through the reflection she was able to see Kwame, who was still gazing at her. He said she was so beautiful that gaping just became a habit. She noticed he was making her feel awkward and like she was backed into a corner that she couldn't get out of.

Turning to Kwame," Can you stop?"

Looking innocently, Kwame replied, "Stop what?"

"Staring."

"What's wrong with me staring?"

"It's rude," she snapped.

"What's rude about me starring at you?"

"It makes me feel weird?

"Weird like how?"

Becoming irritated with the whole ordeal she responded, "Why is it every time I ask you a question you ask me one back?"

"Well…truth of the matter is…you make me nervous too."

Glancing pass him, towards the waitress that was coming their way, she said, "I bet you say that to all the girls?"

"Nope. Just you," he quickly replied as the waitress got between the two.

Placing their drinks down she said, "Here is your orange juice," as she served Karma's drink first. "And here is your orange juice and bill," she said placing it in Kwame's hand.

Kwame laughed saying, "You females sure do stick together."

Smiling at Kwame, she agreed, "Yes we do."

She gulped her juice and noticed the time; 7:22 I believe Kwame mentioned.

Kwame than looked at his watch and implied, "Wow. Pretty soon it will be time to clock in. What do you say we go for another walk when we're done here?"

"Sure. Why not?"

Just as they finished their orange juice the waitress had returned.

"Is everything ok? Do you need anything else?"

"Everything is fine. Thanks," Kwame said as he pulled out his wallet. "Do I give you the money for our bill, or take it to the cashier?"

"I can take it for you; but you know that requires a tip," the waitress giggled.

"Good, cause I had planned on giving you a tip anyway. I love your personality by the way."

"Thanks. I get that a lot. That's one of the glories of me being me."

"Yes it is," Kwame said as he stood up after pulling out a ten dollar bill.

"I'll be back with your change."

"No need to. Keep it," Kwame replied as he pulled Karma's chair from under the table and guided her to a standing position.

Leaning over towards Karma the waitress said, "Girl you better keep him. Don't too many men offer to take on the responsibilities of paying a bill, let alone, give a tip. He's a good man. But I'm sure you know that already."

"Jennifer, I need your help," someone yelled.

"Welp, that's me. I really enjoyed being of service to you two and won't forget you. Yall have a good day as you have truly made mine."

They shook her hands than shared a smile. He said it was as if Cupid had shot a love arrow at him during that moment. He was so nervous that he looked away. Reaching out for her hand he led the way. Looking at his watch, there was thirty minutes left before their shift started. He opened the door for her to go through; than followed. The two strolled down the street, hand in hand, swinging them back in fourth, sneaking smiles at each other intermittently. After hiking for five minutes, she spotted a park in the distance.

"Hey, there's a park ahead. Do you know if it has swings?" she asked Kwame.

"I'm pretty sure it is. Would you like to go take a look?"

"Would I? I love to swing. It's something about being so high up in the air," she said dragging him in the direction of the playground.

Sitting down on the swing and looking at Kwame, she motioned "Aren't you going to sit down?"

Looking uncomfortable, Kwame answered, "Nah. I think I'm just going to enjoy pushing you."

"Ok," she retorted beginning to move her legs back and forth.

There was silence. The whole time he couldn't help but think *please don't let me mistakenly touch her butt as she will think I'm a total creep.*

Higher and higher she went till she was able to lay her head back and see Kwame behind. This always made me feel so dizzy. Kwame checked his watch saying they had about ten minute so he was going to stop her swing. The speed of the swing dragged him so many feet backwards before finally coming to a complete halt. When it ended, Kwame was holding her in his arms, or at least it felt that way. His body was next to Karma and they intertwined. He could feel his heart as it began to beat fast. Could smell her sweet perfume and even the soap used. What than felt like a daydream brought him to reality because she jumped out of the swing as if seeing a ghost.

"What's wrong," Kwame asked as he walked towards her.

"Nothing. I just got dizzy, that's all. I'm ready to go to work now. To go file some papers and…um…" she said refusing his hand as he held it out.

When they arrived at work, Kwame gave her a hug and told her to have a great day. He also said how much fun that he had and he would love to do it again if she could. She never answered and he never lost hope.

"So the very first time they spent together went well…as if it was heaven sent?" Mrs. Williams asked.

"Sure. That's how it sounded to me when he told me the exact same story."

"How are you so sure to recall every memory by correct date and time being that it happened nearly ten years ago?" Mr. Ohio asked as Mrs. Williams finished.

"Why wouldn't I be able to remember? The times we spent together are all the memories I'll have to keep for the rest of my life."

"No further questions."

"Tamela, you mentioned this not being the first time that he'd told you about Karma correct?"

"Well…yes."

"How many other times have he told you about her?"

"Several times I guess?"

"Do you mind sharing one other event with us?"

"Sure. Let me think.

There was a pause.

After the accident that left Karma hospitalized for about a week Kwame decided to make it up to her; especially being that he missed her birthday. He adored Bagel Brother's and felt that it would be the best place to make up for their lost of a meal the last time they visited. Particularly since it was a place she was already familiar with. Of course this time he was sure that she would have more than an orange juice. Especially after everything that has happened; it was the least he could do.

Kwame seated her just as he did before and when the waiter arrived he did all of the talking. He ordered a ham, egg and cheese on sourdough bread for himself and an egg and cheese on sourdough bread for Karma; six chocolate chip cookies, warm, and two glasses of orange juice. Mentally the thought of the egg and cheese on sourdough sandwich teased her stomach because he overheard it growl in excitement.

"So you and your mom appear to be getting along," Kwame said sparking conversation.

"I know. It actually feels weird. I'm not used to this at all. Well, maybe up until a few years ago."

"What happened a few years ago?"

"Well I don't know actually. Everything was fine. The only thing I really remember is she gone to my dad's job than she came back all distorted. I asked her what was wrong but she yelled at me. I was so upset that I ran to my room and slammed my door than laid in bed. I looked to my posters to calm me down, that's when…"

"I'm sorry to interrupt you guys but here's your orange juice and cookies. Can I get you anything else?" The waiter asked.

"Well ma'am, no and yes. We don't need anything else as of now besides our plates when they are ready; and I have a question. More less a concern. I asked for our cookies to be warm. They are warm right now at the moment, but when we are ready to eat them, which I'm sure will be after we've had breakfast, I'm not so sure they will be hot still," Kwame replied.

"Ok," responded the waiter as if she didn't understand anything he had just said.

"Um, my question is, can you take these cookies back and we signal you when we're ready to have our desert?"

"Oh, yes. Certainly. I'm sorry, I've had a long night. I have a baby at home."

"A baby?" Karma intruded.

"Yes," she reacted embarrassed.

"How old are you?"

"I'll be sixteen next month."

"SIXTEEN! You're sixteen? With a kid? Already? What happened?"

"My mother was on drugs and while she was high on crack, my stepfather was in my room molesting me night after night. So it's not my fault. She called me a hoar and kicked me out. Pregnant and all. I've been on my own for the past two years. Feeding myself and my baby, working and trying to finish school."

"Wow. You're so young. I thought God blessed everyone. Looked out for all his children. Why did he let that happen to you? Why didn't he stop it?"

"You know I used to ask myself that all the time. Looking into the positive aspects of life I am very blessed to have my son. Without him I wouldn't have the motivation needed to get me through life's mishaps."

"Can I hug you?"

"Sure."

He said Karma later told him that hugging the waitress made her except the foughts of her mother even more. At least she didn't do drugs, she didn't smoke until that very last moment, but even than Karma haven't seen it sense. She don't drink, she works. And lately she has been trying her best to make up for the years lost.

"Can you believe that? Sixteen? With a baby? Wow," she said shockingly to Kwame.

"Yea, that's pretty sad. And she said her step father did it right? Or did I mishear things?"

"No you're right. I just don't understand why her mother would kick her out when she did nothing wrong. She was molested for who knows how long just to end up pregnant by the guy and no one still seemed to care. Not even the hospital I'm assuming because the baby is in existence." There was a moment of silence. "How can she even want to raise a child she bore with her step father? I just don't understand."

"That's because that's her life. It isn't meant for you to understand. God has chosen a life for you and has also chosen a life for her. Her life is for her to make sense of, not you," Kwame replied.

"Since when have you become an expert at life?"

"I haven't. It just seemed like the right thing to say. Since when did you become so sensitive? Aren't you supposed to be tough like a boxer or something?"

"Now see that would have got you hit but the waiters' coming."

"How do you know?"

"Eehum," Karma said clearing her throat.

"Sorry to interrupt you two again. Here are your ham, egg and cheese on sourdough bread," she said to Kwame. "And here is your egg and cheese on sourdough bread," she said while speaking to Karm. "I didn't forget about your six chocolate chip cookies, warm," she smiled. "As soon as the two of you are ready for them just wave me down and I will be right over. Can I get you two another glass of orange juice?"

"Sure," They spoke together.

"Alrighty, I'll be right back."

The two began their meal. He said Karma looked very thankful for taken his offer to eat breakfast this time; not realizing how hungry she was. The food was excellent, just like he promised it would be. By the time the waitress came back with round two of their drinks, she was finished with her sandwich.

"Wow, you *were* hungry," Kwame acknowledged.

"I guess I was," she smiled.

"Would you like another sandwich?" The waitress asked.

"Yes she will," Kwame spoke up.

"I think she would too," the waitress added. "I have never seen someone eat a sandwich so fast in my life," she chuckled.

Speechless and possibly embarrassed, Karma kept quiet. The waitress walked away and was back within five minutes with a newly prepared sandwich. The sight of it caused her stomach to roar all over again. The cookies were even better. They had become so full that neither could move.

My sweet boy said he enjoyed his self so much that on their walk to work, he asked her out for lunch afterwards. My heart crammed with joy when she told him she would love to as long as he promise to have her home an hour before she was due to check in. He was so filled with joy that he couldn't keep from laughing.

"What's funny?" she asked.

"Nothing. That's my happy laugh. When I'm around you I just feel like laughing and shouting for joy at the same time," he assured.

"Oh. Ok. Well continue on. I guess."

As they approached the front doors to their work place, Kwame looked at his clock, saying to his self, *ok we have seven minutes*, than turned her to face him. At this point I held my breath as I knew he was going to say he'd kiss her but I should have known better. Kwame was always very respectful of the ladies. Even of ones whom had no respect for themselves.

He looked into her eyes and suddenly she must have felt like she did when his brother, Bryant, tried to kiss her.

Placing her arms to his chest "Un un Kwame. No. Not again."

"Just go with the flow," he directed.

"I don't know how to. I've never been,"

Before she was able to say anything else Kwame lips were a space away. Closing her eyes she had to envision her happy place because she began to sing unconsciously.

"I said no worries, about a thing. Cuz every little thing, is gonna be alright. Said no worries,"

"Karma,"

"About a thing."

"Karma,"

"Cuz every little thing."

"Karma,"

"Is gonna be alright."

"KARMA!"

"Huh? What?"

"Um, we're going to be late for work."

"Really? Wow. What happened?"

"Well, I assume you thought I was going to kiss you and it made you nervous."

"I wasn't nervous."

"Really?"

"Yes really," She said while crossing her arms.

"Than why did you begin to sing?"

"I wasn't singing!"

"Oh really?"

"Yes really."

"Hum. Ok, well I guess it's time for us to get to work," he said as he took her by the hand. "Oh and by the way, I was only going to kiss your cheek," he mentioned guiding her up the steps. "Cuz every little thing, is gonna be alright," he chuckled while looking at her.

"Shut up!" she shoved. "Jerk."

"I said no worries," he continued while opening the door. "About a thing."

"Ooh you are so going to get it at lunch."

"You know, maybe you should be a singer. I think you'll do a good job," he continued jokingly. "See you later."

"Yea you too."

"No worries," he continued singing; echoing in the hallway. "About a thing."

That afternoon he watched her through the glass doors as she punched her time card. She had no clue that he was awaiting the queens' arrival just down the steps as if he knew she was getting off early.

Upon greeting he kissed her cheek and gave her a single Lillie. I remember saying awwww after he mentioned this. My son had become prince charming in just a few weeks.

After seeing her blush, he pulled a box of chocolates full of cherry cordials from behind his back. He said she gave him the biggest hug.

Guiding her by the hand he opened the door. At the street there was a cab waiting. Kwame opened the door and directed her to get in.

"This is for us?" she asked.

"Yes. I told you I was going to get you home before your parents expected you."

"Yes you did," she said while entering the car.

"Golden Corrall on Montgomery Road, right young man?"

"Yes sir," Kwame replied.

"Alright, I just need everyone to buckle up and than we can be on our way."

Kwame buckled her seat belt making her feel exceptional. High class or elegant if you will. Like she was queen of the world and nothing else mattered. The cab driver watched in au. It must have reminded him of his younger days.

Their cab pulled in front of the restaurant and Kwame got out opening the door.

"Aren't you going to pay?" she asked.

"Why pay when I already have?" Kwame responded.

"Honey you are one lucky lady. You hold on to him for the rest of your life," The cab driver spoke while giving Kwame a wink.

"So I keep hearing," she responded. "Thanks for the ride."

"Don't thank me young lady. Thank your date. He paid. I just did my job."

Turning towards Kwame, "Thank you. I really appreciate all you have done for me."

"And I appreciate you allowing me to do all that I am willing to do and so much more."

"My father always said that nothing is for free. So what do you want in return?"

"How about a good time?" Kwame asked while they were walking hand in hand.

"A GOOD TIME!" she stopped releasing his hands.

"Sure. Why not? Everybody's doing it."

"TAXI!" she yelled.

"Hold on, hold on, hold on. Calm down. I was only joking."

"Well this is what I think about your joke," she said offended, forcing her knees into his penis.

"Oof!" he bellowed. "I expected…you…to…slap…me not knee me. Aw it hurts. Really bad," he held his hands between his legs with his legs bent inward as if he was knot kneed. "Are you going to sit there and just watch?"

"Yes," she replied crossing my arms.

"But I was just kidding."

"So was I."

"But your kidding hurts. Really, really bad."

"Does it? Karma asked sarcastically.

"Yes. It really does."

"Aww. Poor baby. Let me help."

"NO! NO!"

"No."

"Yes. *No*! You're just going to knee me again."

"Wow, you learn fast," she said while slightly slapping his face twice. "Now lets' go eat."

Limping the rest of the way making sure to keep a distance between the two, he allowed her to lead as he followed. As they reached the entrance, he opened it, than turned his back shielding his jewels away from Karma avoiding any possible injuries she may have envisioned.

"Will it be just the two of you?" The cashier asked.

"Yes please," Kwame coughed still trying to gain his composure.

"Will the two of you be having just our buffet for lunch or would you like to place an order for a fine meal and have it ready on your way?"

"That won't be necessary. We're just planning on having the buffet. But thanks for asking," he said while reaching into his pockets.

"Alright, for the buffet it's $8.99 per person and does not include a drink. Would you like something to drink with your meals?"

"Yes please. I will take a Dr. Pepper and she," he stated before being interrupted.

"I will have a Red Cream of Soda."

"Good choice. That's my favorite soda," the cashier explained.

"Mine too. The first time I taste it I dranked a whole two liter non-stop. I dranked so much that it broke my face completely broke out and when I went to school, I was sent home early because the nurse didn't know what was wrong," Karma chuckled.

I recall seeing Kwame blush during this part just as he told me. He really was infatuated with Karma.

"Wow, that's some story," the cashier laughed back. "Sir, the drinks are $1.99 per person and there's only one size."

"Ok," Kwame acknowledged as Karma continued talking.

"Your price is $25.36," she said as Kwame handed her two twenty dollar bills. "Ok, out of forty. Here's your change, you can seat yourself wherever you like. Have a great day. And ma'am, try not to drink too much Red Cream of Soda," she chortled.

Kwame took her by the hand and guided Karma to a seat near the window. He said he chose that restaurant because it had multiple choices of food to eat.

Karma was so eager that she walked from the top of the buffet to the bottom making mental notes of what she planned to eat. He was too busy watching her to really think of anything to consume. As long as they were together she would be his food.

The whole time Kwame looked at his watch making sure he kept up with the time; just like he promised. At one point of time he excused his self but didn't say why; but it was later told it was so he could call her a cab home. My boy was quite the gentleman.

Once the cab arrived he walked out and talked to the driver. Kwame than walked inside and gave her a kiss on the cheek, telling her there's a cab outside prepared to take her home; as he promised and that he had already paid for it.

"How did it make you feel to do something so charming for her," I asked.

My baby told me "These are the things a real man is supposed to do and that he anticipated doing so much more."

Again he made sure she was secure as he strapped her in. After looking into her eyes he just stared. He said he wanted to kiss her but knew it was too soon for something like that. Not to mention taking a chance of getting kneed again. Instead he blew a kiss and closed the door. Kwame was so nervous that he shut the door not giving Karma the chance to respond.

As the cab pulled off he waved her goodbye and through the rear window could see her doing the same. At this point in time, Kwame was more than confident, he was in love.

Denise
Point of View

Karma and I have been best friends since ninth grade. The moment I seen her I knew we were meant to be pals so I grabbed her by the arm and made it official.

That day I was standing on the side of the steps outside of school when I saw them.

"When you say *them* you're referring to Kwame and Karma?" Mrs. Williams asked from her seat in front of Denise.

"Yes."

"Thank you," she said writing on her yellow table. "Please continue."

From what I saw the two haven't seen each other in a period of time. Karma was looking down at her paper and ran right into him. She had began apologizing while lifting her head and he was saying that's ok. He said she had a voice like a young lady he had met over the summer, but was too frightened to look up because he knew there was no way possible she could be her. After hearing his voice, she too became nervous and fearful of looking up because she said she didn't want to be upset if he wasn't who she wanted him to be. After a short pause he said they would count to three than both look up at the same time. One, two, before he got to three he had already lifted his head. When they locked eyes they both froze not knowing what to do. I assumed they were thinking of hugging or kissing just as teenagers would during those times.

Kwame took the initiative to pick her up and spin her around. He was so happy. They both seemed very pleased. He continued swinging faster and faster until they fell down laughing. And of course everyone was staring at them. Kwame was the hottest boy in school; fooling around with the new girl. No one knew exactly what was going on but I could tell, Kwame was truly in love with Karma; as I'd never seen him pay this much attention to any girl. It just wasn't in him to do so. Kwame's concern as far as I could tell was his school work, his brother Bryant and every now and again a female acquaintance but not in that form. Sexually I'm saying. He didn't have that type of reputation to hit it than quit it. If you asked me, I don't think he was sexually active at all during those times.

When Karma started our school it was like she was a Godsend. She was perfect in every way. Sweet, beautiful, skinny but thick in the right places with the most gorgeous eyes. It was hard for any guy back then to keep their eyes off of her. But she too only had eyes for Kwame. I followed them inside trying not to gain too much attention as I listened more into their conversation. I wanted to know who this girl was and what was her secret?

"What are you doing here?" Kwame asked her surprisingly.
"I go to school here. This is my first year," Karma responded.

"Wow that means you're a freshmen. You will get teased a lot by us sophomores and we will get teased by the juniors and seniors. But it's nothing to be scared of. Everyone goes through it."

"Oh ok. So how are you?"

Walking together side by side Kwame said, "I'm better now that I get to see you again and for the next three years. I am a sophomore you know. I don't mind helping out fresh meat every now and again," he chuckled while taking her backpack off of her shoulders. "Well can I at least take you to class?"

"Sure, since you didn't give me the chance to say no."

"I missed seeing you. I hated that our summer job had ended so soon. I never thought I'd see you again."

Karma didn't respond. He took her by the hand and led them inside of school. She seemed to look as if she was loving the attention. How he was carrying her backpack in front of everyone; being a gentleman. It was like he wasn't ashamed to be seen with her. *And should he have been?*

As I was walking to class I continued to watch the two of them. I actually had to walk pass them into the classroom because they stopped in front of the door. Taking my seat with my eyes on Kwame with his sweet lips and Karma with her dazzling smile I couldn't help but to yearn for more on this love connection. He looked at the wall that showed our room number and teacher. Lip reading, his response was Mrs. Turner.

Looking at the wall as well Karma replied "What about her?"

"That name sounds familiar," he said reaching into his backpack.

"Familiar good or familiar bad?"

"Wait...a...second," he spoke while reading over his schedule than hers. "Oh my. Ohhh Myyyy."

"What is it?" she asked trying to see what he saw.

"WE HAVE CLASS TOGETHER!" he shouted so loud the whole class heard him and stopped to look at the commotion.

Except for me because I was already looking.

"Look," he showed her while pointing. "This one and this one."
"Which one?"
"This one silly. Our first class together is Spanish than before school gets out we have gym."
"No way!"
"Yes way. Let's go before we're late," he said.

The bell ranged and the two of them walked in class holding hands. He helped her to a seat than sat beside her. Luckily for me I sat directly behind Karma because I was able to lip read as well as over hear any conversation the two decide to have during class. *If* they chose to.

As he sat attentively I couldn't help but sigh and smile. For so long I wished I was Karma but after that day I decided to give all feelings away for Kwame. Karma and I became friends and I immediately understood while he fell in love with her.

Kwame whispered, "Uuum. We worked together and now we attend the same school. Isn't that weird?"

After hearing Kwame say this I quietly said ah, while once again wishing that I was the one he was speaking those words to.

"Yea it is. I never even heard of this school. Believe it or not this was my mothers' idea."

"Smart woman."

Spanish seemed to be one of her favorite subjects as she spoke it very fluently.

"Good morning class. *Clase de Buenos Dias*. My name is Miss Turner. *Mi nombre es Miss Turner,* "she continued in English and Spanish as she wrote on the white board.

Karma looked extremely excited. After class I found out she took Spanish in Junior High and thus became very familiar with the translations. Miss Turner turned around and asked for the class to say their name in Spanish. She asked who wanted to be first.

"Me llama Karma. *My name is Karma,*" she stood up and said.

"Excelente Karma," Miss Turner responded. "Se le habla en Española?"

"Muy Fluido," she said while noticing she was at the center of attention.

"Estoy impresionado,"

"Glacias,"

"For those of us that didn't understand the conversation; I asked Karma if she was fluent in Spanish? And she said that she is very fluent. I than told her that I was impressed and she said *thank you.*"

She turned to face the white board, held the marker up than turned back to the class.

"By the way, *excellente*, means excellent. Is there anyone else that is *muy fluido,*" she said while smiling at me "very fluent, in Española?" She looked around the room and paused a minute. "Nadie, *anyone?*"

She continued to search but no one answered. It was obvious no one knew Spanish but she and Karma. This girl is good I thought as I watched Kwame give her a brownie point.

"Ok. No need to get nervous. By the time your term ends with me;

everyone, *todo el mundo*, will be muy fluido in Española. Let's start by taking attendance. When I touch your shoulder, I want you to stand up and tell me your English name. After you are finish, I will tell you you're Spanish, Española name, in which you will repeat," Miss Turner said while getting her attendance book. "Ok. You are?" she said while starting at the seat next to Karma.

"Kwame," he said while sitting in his seat.

"Your Española name is easy. It's the same as your English name," she said while marking him down in her book. "Remember to follow directions and stand next time; it's a part of your grade," Miss Turner said while moving on to her next student.

I decided to pay attention instead of watching the couple but couldn't help myself. It was hard to not want what Karma had. Kwame was the definition of drop dead gorgeous. The man was so fine I began to daydream about him and smiled as I did so. Of course the bell interrupted those thoughts just as I saw myself taking Karma's place but that's fine. I now see that he was her's all alone.

I smiled at Karma who returned a smile back. I could tell she wasn't embaressed by the things I just said. She already knew of my feelings for Kwame during those times. She also knew that if he would have allowed me to I would have fucked him too but again Kwame wasn't that type of man.

Approaching Karma from the side and locking my arm onto hers, "Hi Karma. I'm *Denisee*," I said rolling my tongue. "Also known as Denise."

"Hi Denisee," she responded nervously.

I take it she didn't have many friends I jotted mentally.

"Ok, it says I am to go to History.... in room....147," Karma read from her schedule.

"Cool, that's my next class too. Hey, let me look at your schedule," I said taking it out of her hand. "We have all the same classes. Yeeaaa! We can say that we are sisters. When is your birthday?"

"June 17," she implied while being guided down the hall.

"Aww. You're a Gemini. Cry now laugh later."

"Sometimes," she chuckled. "But I'm nothing to be scared of."

"Really? Wow. Hey, for fresh meat, you're pretty cool."

"Wait, aren't you..."she started but left the thought alone while continuing to walk.

I assume I confused her being that I was also fresh meat. What she didn't know is I actually had to repeat the ninth grade due to some issues with my mother passing away.

"Yessss. I'm fresh meat too," I laughed to make her feel more comfortable." I just wanted to be the first to pick on you since we are *best friends.*"

Karma began to turn red in the face. I thought I may have offended her but I guess as time went on it was meant for us to be the best of friends.

"Oh, ok."

"Most of our classes are down here in the basement; so it's best that we pick a locker down here, that's close to class," I said as I picked her out a locker. "You can have this one and I will take that one next to you."

"Ok. Looks pretty clean," She said while placing her Spanish book inside.

"Did your mom buy you a lock? You're going to need one."

"Yes, I have one. But she didn't buy it. I bought it myself."

"How did you do that?"

"I worked for the money needed to purchase a lock, my school clothes, shoes and supplies."

"You got to work this summer?" I stated excitingly.

"Yesssss," she responded as if she was shock that I didn't get to.

"I didn't get to; but I would have loved to."

"Why not?"

"My father would rather get me what I need than to allow me to work for it."

"Wow. That must be nice sometimes. My mom signed me up like a month before the program started."

"Sometimes it can be. I wish my dad was like that."

(Ding.Ding.Ding.)

"Class is just right here. We aren't late at all," I said while escorting her to class.

"Alright class, I am Mr. Meyers, and when that bell rings you have exactly thirty seconds to be inside this class before I close my door. Not only will my door be closed but it will also be locked. That means, if you get to class and the door is closed...and locked, you will need to go to the office, that is just around the corner there and get a late slip. Do I make myself clear?"

"Yes Mr. Meyers" everyone said.

"All right. I know it's the first day of school so we are going to talk about some rules other than the ones we just discussed.

- Rule # 1 is Always being to class on time.
- Rule # 2 is Come to school ready to learn.
- Rule # 3 is Expect a challenge.
- Rule # 4 is Be respectful
- Rule # 5 Stay in your seat.

Any questions?"

No one said anything. He had our full undivided attention. I sat beside Karma. She always stayed so focus. When class was over I took her by the arm and led us to our lockers.

"He seems like he is going to be very strict?" I spoke.

"I don't think so. I believe he is just putting his foot down now so that no one tries to test him. You know how adults are? Especially with us being teenagers."

"Yeah, I guess you're right. He's actually new here. Our teacher last year couldn't handle the behavior of some of the students here so she resigned."

"How do you know about last year?"

"Because I'm repeating ninth grade."

"You? No way."

"I wish it wasn't true but it is. My mother died last year and I couldn't handle it. I became very depressed and wouldn't have imagined that I would be here today."

"Wow. I'm sorry for asking you a personal question. I wasn't trying to pry into your personal life."

"That's ok. I'm over it now. It was yesterday's news. Now I look forward to tomorrow."

"Well I guess we better be getting to our next class; Math. Yippee."

"I love math too. Hey we have something in common."

"Yes we do."

"We are going to have something else in common if we don't hurry along to class."

We laughed while locking arms again and skipping down the hallways just as best friends would do. We made it to class right on time before the bell ranged again.

Math class wasn't so bad. Karma and I tickled and pinched each other the whole time. Our schedules said that it was time for lunch. We packed our belongings in our lockers and skipped again to the lunch room. While we bounced it felt as if all eyes were on us. And what can I say...I loved being the center of attention. *Especially after all of the attention Kwame had given her earlier.* I had Karma next to me so I wasn't alone. I liked having a friend. A female friend. It felt good to have someone to share my thoughts with. Someone to laugh with and enjoy their company as much as they enjoyed mines. She was like the sister I never had. Funny, smart, sweet, cute. And I don't mean that in a bi-sexual way but just saying she was nice looking.

When we got to the lunch room, there was a long line of hungry teenagers waiting to get their trays of food. On the wall, it showed we were having pizza; which there was a choice of pepperoni or cheese; with a side item of french fries, frozen fruit Jell-O, and white or chocolate milk. The alternative was salad which was lettuce, shredded cheese, sliced carrots and crackers.

"So what are you eating for lunch?" I asked.

"I am going to have *pizza*," she said while sliding her hands back and forth as if trying to keep them warm. "I love pizza. I can eat pizza every day. What is your favorite dish?"

"I like pizza too. My favorite is pepperoni and pineapple."

"Yuck! But I won't tell anyone. It will be our little secret, fresh meat,"

I laughed as we were far enough in line to pick up our tray.

I chose a slice of cheese pizza, french fries and a chocolate milk for lunch while she chose a slice of pepperoni pizza, french fries, fruit Jell-O and a chocolate milk. We chose to sit by the vending machines that sat on the far left side of the lunchroom. We were able to see in the lunchroom that sat across from ours through the opening in the middle of the room. While I ate and joked with Karma, someone walked behind her putting their cold hands on her face. I froze, not knowing what to do or say.

"No shit," I spoke beyond jealous. I thought they wouldn't catch up till later on for gym but here he was.

"Well Denise, tell me who it is?" she snapped.

"Oh no! I'm staying out of this one," I giggled with a sexy voice hoping he noticed. "Honey, you are on your own," I stood than walked to the next table in front of the couple.

"Ok. So who are you?" she asked crossing her arms.

"It is only I *little red riding hood*," he said in disguise.

"Ummm, that isn't a good enough hint," she said struggling to remove his hands.

"Don't remove my hands or I will huff and I will puff,"

"Those fairy tales doesn't match. Try again."

"Ok, ok. It's me," he said. "Turn around and look."

She turned around slowly to see her mystery person was Kwame.

"Kwame," she squeaked in total shock. *She really had no clue.* "Are you supposed to be here right now?"

"Sure I am silly. But I usually don't sit over here with *fresh meat*. I sit across the hall with my friends."

"Really? Then, *why* are you here?"

"Because I saw a girl that I am really, really interested in and thought I'd say hi."

"Oh Really? And who might that be?"

"I don't know. I couldn't catch her in time," he said while walking away.

"Jerk."

"Do you know who that is?" I ran to her as fast as I could.

"Yeah. Kwame. A guy I used to work with and now I attend the same school with."

"No, honey. He is much more than that. "

"Well what do I care," Karma said with attitude.

"Girl, he is the cutest guy in school. Every girl wants him. Do you know how hard it is just to engage in conversation with him?"

"Really?" she asked eating a spoonful of Jell-O.

"YES!" I sat down. "So did you do it?"

"Do what?"

"Do it? Do *it?* It…"

"*It?*" she said while chewing into her pizza.

"It," I continued while looking in her eyes for the answer.

"It….it…heck no," she choked, nearly unable to catch her breath. "I can't believe you asked me that. That's nasty. I'm only fourteen. Why would I want to do *it*, with a guy I barely know. Gross," she said while cleaning her tray.

"Why not? I started having sex at eleven."

(Ding.Ding.Ding.)

"Eleven? Eleven? When I was eleven I was too busy reading books and playing soccer. Wow, she snatched her backpack in pure disgust.

"So you've never done it?"

"It? NO!" she said seriously with a rosey red face.

"Ever?"

"Never…Ever."

"Oh my…You're a …you're a …virgin. Wow. That is so good."

"So you're not mad?" she stopped than turned to me.

"Of course not. You're a virgin…and…I'm not," I locked arms with her leading into skipping down the hall. "Hey, my friend is a virgin," I said to someone standing around as we skipped.

"Why would you do that?" she asked embarrassed.

"What's wrong with it? It's a good thing to be a virgin. Isn't it?"

She looked at me than together we laughed. I knew I hurt her feelings because her beautiful eyes had strokes of water rising but she held them back. Throughout my years of knowing her she was always strong. Strict parents are what taught her to respect herself as a lady.

I can remember her saying "My body is a rare gem that was meant for only one man to have." And she kept to her word as Kwame was her first and only.

Before school ended Karma and I exchanged numbers. She said she'd be expecting my call.

"I can't call you if you're too busy with Kwame," I teased.
"Is it that obvious?" She asked.
"Duh; and girlfriend let me tell you. If you ever and I mean EVER, don't want to take up this fine and rare opportunity with Kwame, do you think you can scold him a word or two for me so I can become Mrs. Woods?
"Girl you are silly. You can have him now; but oh that's right. He has his eyes on me," she said getting the last laugh.

I walked her to our last class which was gym. Of course I knew Kwame would be there that's why I took the pleasure in taking her. I had to see him just one last time before I started tomorrow with eyes for a new prize. He sat at the bottom of the stairs nervously. I assumed he was waiting for her and possibly thinking of something to ask or talk about because I over heard him speaking of a date or something. When we approached him he became extremely nervous. It was in a way I've never seen. I hugged Karma and left the two, as I knew she and Kwame had plenty to talk about, than blew a secret kiss at Kwame. He turned around just to see the kiss coming towards him; I suspected, than frowned.

"What's up with your friend?" He asked Karma as I walked passed them into the gym room.
"I'm still learning her myself," she smiled at me.

Waving one last time as I approached the bathroom stalls I couldn't help but to think of how lucky Karma was. Oh gosh and she got to work with him. Whew, I would have loved it. But…he's taken so on to the next.

Gym was a drag. The two love birds giggled as they jogged side by side, and snuck peeks as they exercised. One gym session Kwame got too close to Karma and she slapped him. I can still see his reactions I laughed. It cost her a Saturday; one that wouldn't have been right if Kwame wasn't there as well. To get on the list, he wrote on the boys bathroom stall, "I'm in love." Our gym teacher Mrs. Applegate was not happy. I laughed and laughed at how pathetic he was; wanting to be next to Karma. She had him wrapped around her finger. Of course being that I was the third crowd and couldn't help but to watch the love connection blossoming from the two of them I had to find away to get on that list as well. I walked over to Kwame and decided to give him a slap. He wasn't happy and it damn sure didn't make Karma happy but when I explained to her they both laughed.

"Kwame you mean to tell me you got on the list just to be in the same room with me?" She asked him.

Snorting, "A-Duh! The boy is madly in love with you Karma. Damn can't you see that," I cupped my mouth at the end of my sentence. That wasn't supposed to be said out loud.

Kwame blushed embarrassed and looked down at the floor.

"I'm so sorry Kwame. I…I didn't mean to," I spoke to him.

"And you haven't made things any better missy," Karma snapped.

"You two could be doing better things with your time but instead chose to give up…three hours… of your time for Saturday school; just to be with me. Thank you guys," she hugged us teary eyed.

Mrs. Applegate said we had exactly ten minutes to get ready to go home. Kwame walked us towards the girls' locker room than stopped Karma.

"Can I walk you to the bus stop…since you don't know where the bus will be picking you up at?" he asked leaving the part out of him riding the same bus.

He took a moment to dread the fact that he missed catching the bus this morning because they could have held conversation than.

"Sure I guess. If I don't let you Denise is just going to do the job for you," she laughed.

"No sister. I can't do that. My bus is the first bus to leave and I can't afford to miss it," I joked while hugging her. "With that said I'm going to go get dressed. I'll call you later girly.

Two weeks into school and Karma has become the most popular girl, which caused a lot of girls to be jealous because they wanted what she had. To be treated like royalty, while still holding on to their virginities. His ex-girlfriend even tried to stir up problems but he fixed her right away. She went around school saying they were back together. When word got around to him during our Spanish Class, he got a restroom pass and went to the office while the secretary was doing the morning announcements and started shouting *I'm in love with Karma! She's the only girl for me!* Of course normally one would probably get suspended but because he was a good teen, he was given In School Suspension.

Naturally this pissed his ex off but not Karma. She seemed to like the other girls wanting what she had. It didn't affect her one bit. And when he announced how he felt for her through the intercom she blushed. Embarrassed and covering her face I stood up and shouted *WHEWWW! KARMA. That's your man on the intercom.* The class began to clap. Miss Turner did nothing but smiled as she seemed to understand puppy love.

Kwame never made it back to class. Karma had taken his things with her. She said he knew her code to her lock as she also knew the code to his. The only problem was she didn't know where his locker was at and wasn't sure if he knew where hers would be. Not wanting to be late for class I talked her into putting it in her cubbyhole.

"Trust me Kwame can get any information needed…that easy," I snapped my fingers.

"Really?"

"Of course. We're talking about Kwame. The Kwame that was around and about before you were even heard of. Trust me Karma, he will get the information needed to where your locker is. It wouldn't surprise me if he didn't already know," I teased.

"Yeah, you're right. Let's get to class before the bell rings."

We didn't find out what happened to Kwame until our three way conversation that night. The phone rung and I was nervous to the point sweat was breaking loose. Praying for Mr. Gentry to answer the phone my heart paced more and more. By the second ring I told myself one more ring and I would hang up.

"Hello," Mrs. Gentry answered.

Too late, thought gone. "Hello Mrs. Gentry," I tried to address myself as polite as possible.

"We're not interested."

"I'm sorry; I'm actually calling for Karma."

"Oh. Well who's calling for Karma?"

"I'm Denise, her best friend from school."

"Denise, her best friend from school huh?"

"Yes maam," I responded while over thinking why is she mocking me.

"Karma, I have Denise, who wants to speak with you."

The phone went quiet for a moment before she took the line.

"Hey Denise, how are you?"

"I'm fine girly. What's up with your mom? She scares me."

"She's cool actually. She scares me too sometimes. I forgot to tell her that I gave our number away at school."

"Oh so you and Kwame haven't talked yet I assumed?"

"No we've talked. But he always call the moment I get home from school and my parents don't be home yet."

"So what do you guys talk about?"

"You are one nosey chick."

"I'm sorry I'm sorry. Have you talked to him today about his punishment?"

"Yup!"

"What did he get?"

"In School Suspension."

"He is so lucky. Anyone else would have gotten suspended without a chance."

"Yea I guess so."

We began to talk about Math homework until she got a beep on the other end. I waited patiently for her to click back to me but she never did.

Returning the call, I asked "Chick what happened?"

"Oh I am so sorry. Can you believe we spoke him up?"

"Spoke who up?"

"Kwame!"

"Really," I tried to sound happy for her.

"Yes; so girl I am going to have to call you back."

"Ditch the best friend for a boy. Sure."

"Aw. Don't say it like that."

"Well why not it's true; but for you to talk to Kwame...it's worth it."

"Really?"

"Yes girly. I'd give anything; before today that is, to talk to Kwame over the phone. But I meant what I said. You better keep him or give him up to someone that will."

"Girl you are too silly but I will keep that in mind. See you tomorrow."

"I'll be there, hovering over you and Kwame in Spanish class."

"Ok girly."

"Bye."

"Denise, while Karma was in custody she mentioned that the two of you had lost several years together," Mrs. Williams asked.

"Yes, we did."

"How did she take that?"

"Well I can't say how she took it because we lost contact. There wasn't any communication after my father took me away."

"Ok…let me rephrase the question. How did she cope *before*…you left?"

"She coped well. Of course she was heart broken; hell we both were.

Karma and I were very close. We became closer as the school year went by. In our last month of school, right before school ended for that school year my father got a job offering in Canada. Can you believe he took it and took my best friend away from me? My only best friend. There wasn't anyone else.

She was funny, honest, smart and knew how to have a good time. Karma knew things that I didn't know and I learned a lot from her. My father said I was too young to stay in the states alone. Her parents even actually offered to care for me; they knew how much we loved each other. Especially being that we were their only children, so it was like having the sister we didn't and wouldn't ever have. But my father declined that too. Said *he couldn't imagine leaving his little girl on someone else to care for. I was all he had since my mother died.* I always spoke of him being so over protective but never saw this coming in a million years. The day that something like this would happen could only happen in my dreams.

I couldn't even tell her goodbye because it meant I'd be gone forever and didn't plan to be. She was promised that one day, upon my return we would have each other back. A slit was going to be cut into my hand by a knife I bought from a hunting store. Never hunted but I knew where to get the perfect knife for the ritual I had prepared. I told Karma she had to cut her hand too. Of course she said no, that I was crazy for even doing that to myself. Reassuring her she could trust me, she gave the privilege for me to do it. To…cut her hand.

Afterwards we had to put our hands together and say *best friends forever.* This is what I explained to her and she thought I'd gone mad. But years later as you will hear, it worked. It actually did work.

I spent the night at her place for the weekend. It was the last time we'd ever spin together since I was leaving in two days. Anxious to encounter my discovery, I steered her outside in the backyard. Looking at me fanatical she caused me to become so nervous that my hand began to tremble.

"Stop shaking or I'm going to cut you wrong and it won't work," I threatened.

"Are you sure this is necessary? Why do you have to cut me too? Can't you just cut yourself and be done with it? You already seemed well prepared anyway. Obviously you're experienced in these types of things." She motioned.

"Yes silly. This is very necessary. And I wouldn't consider myself experienced. I saw it on TV and thought of it being a good idea. That's when the *experience* part came in. You know; the part that you play in. Kind of like my guinea pig."

"I don't think this is a good idea. Especially since I'm your guinea pig!"

"Look Karma…we're best friends. *Best…friends*. We've been the best of friends since the day we met. Have I ever lied to you? Better yet, will I lie to you? Your best friend, Denise. Think about it. Come on. Say it to yourself. *Have my **best friend Denise** ever lied to me about **anything**?* Go on."

I've *never* lied to her and could have lied about being a virgin, wanting to sleep with Kwame *and* her father but didn't. To be so honest about something as hurtful as that meant she could trust me because I was going to speak the truth, and at all times.

"N…no," she stuttered.

"Have I ever lied to you?"

"No."

"Do you trust me?"

"Yes."

"DO YOU TRUST ME?" I asked with excitement.

"YES!" she yelled followed by an "OUCH!"

"All finished."

"That hurt!"

"Sorry. Now we have to finish by placing our hands one in to the other, kind of like high fiving."

"Yea…like I want to high five you for cutting me," Karma crossed her arms.

"I had to. Don't you understand I will die without you?"

Karma looked at me with speculating eyes before finally given in.

"I am truly going to miss you," she looked at me.

"And I am truly going to depressingly miss you too," I returned with a sigh. "Let's finish our ritual, if you will. Place your hand into mine and,"

"Best friends forever!" We shouted together.

The night seemed as if it was going as fast as the wind. The stars were so exquisite but never stayed still. It seemed as if they bounced across the sky.

"We will always be able to find each other now. I am in your blood and you are in mines," I mentioned. "Let's go inside."

We cried and hugged each other one last time than held hands like she and Kwame always did but not in the same sense or with the same feelings.

"Denise, you mentioned that the ritual work; correct?" Mrs. Williams asked.

"Yes."

"How are you so sure that it worked?"

"Well, because we met up again and it was out of no where. There wasn't a phone call or any post card. We just happened to be in the wrong place at the right time."

"What do you mean by wrong place at the right time?"

"Well, I was on the way home but had to use the restroom and was not going to make it. So I pulled over to the nearest gas station to release the explosion. The whole time I'm trying to tinkle; if you will, my neighbor in the next stall's phone kept ringing repeatedly. Not only did it keep buzzing but she didn't have the audacity to hit ignore or silent so no one else would be disturbed.

"WOULD YOU CUT THAT THING OFF?" I finally yelled at her.

"You know, I was thinking the same thing," she said sarcastically.

"Kar-ma?" I barely whispered.

"Yes. That's my name but I don't recognize who I'm talking to," she responded pulling tissue from its dispenser.

"It's me, Denise."

"No it's not. Quit playing with me," she said beginning to sniffle. "I've had enough shit to deal with today and don't have time for no more games."

"It really is. Open up the door, when you're finish of course and you will see for yourself."

"I am finish. But I'm scared. I don't believe you. Tell me something that only she and I would know."

"How about I show you," I declared sticking my hand underneath the door for her to see the healed cut.

She paused a bit as if memories from that night had flashed.

"Best…friends…"

"Forever," I finished.

"Oh my gosh it is you," she said nearly braking the door down to get out of the restroom stall.

"I told you it was," I placed my arms around her. "Oh my. Look at you. Are you…pregnant?"

Karma shook her head with a smile in agreement.

"No way. Not you. Not little Miss Virgin," I giggled. "Hey, are you and Kwame still dating? You know he's only had eyes for you."

"Yeah," she sighed. If only that was true."

"Well what do you mean?"

"I just found out today that he cheated on me last night."

"Kwame, no way."

"Yes way."

"How did you find out?" I asked concerned.

"I called his phone and another chick picked up. Is that enough evidence for you?"

"Oh my Karma. I am so sorry. Is this…his?" I asked pointing to the baby that's developing inside of her stomach.

"Of course it is silly. You know how I was."

"Well I have been gone for a few years. You could have changed."

"Me…Denise? Little Miss Virgin lol."

"Aw, mommies being a big, fat meany," I poked my lips as I rubbed on her belly.

"Am not."

"Am too."

"Am not."

"Am too," I articulated while opening the door for us to exit.

"Am not. And I'm not fat. I'm not!"

"I know you're not girly. I'm just teasing. It's been so long. We have so much to discuss and talk about. Why don't you come over to my place?"

"I would love that. Do you mind if I stay a while? Just…till I get myself situated."

"You Karma…never. I could never get tired of seeing you. Stay as long as you like."

"Wow. Who would have ever thought we'd be grown and getting to spend as much time as we like together without the hassles of our parents?"

"I know. This is going to be so much fun. First I'll make us some hot cocoa cause you're pregnant and all so no caffeine. Than we can light some candles and just talk the night away or watch a movie. And do you want to know the best part?"

"What's that?"

"When I bought my three bedroom house, I placed a double bed in my room. I didn't know why at the time, but now everything is so clear. It was placed there for you bestie. We can share a room, unless you'd rather sleep away from your best friend that's been missing you for years now."

"Awww; and never bestie. Long as we don't have to share beds," I giggled.

"Share a bed with you," I snickered. "I wouldn't fit! Look at all this belly," I rubbed.

"Awww."

"Best friends forever," we sighed together.

All of the time and attention I was giving her must have taken her mind off of Kwame because she didn't discuss him or even look teary eyed at times like I thought she would have. Not to mention her phone had been off since we met earlier in the restroom stalls.

"Maybe you should check your phone to see if there are any missed calls?" I encouraged.

"From who? Kwame; the guy who has Thickness to keep him occupied. So engaged he couldn't call his pregnant girlfriend to tell her he wouldn't be home."

"I don't know why girly but in my heart I honestly feel this may be a mistake."

"Well whose side are you on?" she snapped.

"Bestie I'm just being a friend. What do you want me to say?" I crossed my hand and changed my voice. "Why don't you go out and sleep with another guy? Especially while you're carrying his baby; that will really tick him off."

She looked at me than snorted loudly.

"Ha ha," she said grabbing her phone out of her purse. "You're right; I'll at least check my voicemail."

Watching her quietly as she hit the button on her phone I could see the nervousness written all over her face. Butterflies must have filled the pit of her stomach as I and she knew she would have all sorts of text messages, voice messages; paged who knows how many times and whatever else he could have thought of to do to get in contact with her.

"Karma...what are you doing?" I asked after she placed the phone on the table.

"I can't do this," she cried. "How am I supposed to listen to his lie after lie when I heard the truth for myself?"

"Like your mom said, sometimes things aren't what we perceive them to be. You have to remember that. It's a true statement," I embraced her.

She sobbed and sobbed in my arms until she became playful. Karma pinched me on my boob.

We're best friends and I'm sure we're not the only ones who have played the pinching boob game. Only difference now is I have some boobs; than she was just pinching nipples.

That thought caused me to laugh in reminiscence.

"Ooh you sneaky little thing," I said throwing a pillow at her face.

"You are so going to pay for that."

"You'll have to catch me first pregos."

"I bet I can," she chased me around the couch.

I tried throwing a pillow at her but she dodged it. To be pregnant she was good. Guess it really does have its advantages.

"Too slow fat girl," I teased.

"I'm not fat! Not yet anyway," she stopped and begin to cry.

"I am so sorry. I didn't mean to,"

"It's not you. It's Kwame. I'm hurt. He waited all these years to confess his love to me just to cheat on me. All because I had intentions on not keeping our baby."

"Whoa, whoa. You didn't tell me that girly. How did he find out? And what were you thinking?"

"I was scared. Just like any normal first time parent would be. We both had noticed change in my stomach I guess you can say. One day after work I took the test but was so tired that I left it on the bathroom sink and went to sleep. It said I had ten minutes to wait and I was drowsy as well as in denial that I could possibly be pregnant. As if Kwame and I wasn't fucking lol. Thinking about things now it was kind of stupid to assume there was no possible way that I could have been. Anyway, I went to sleep and he came home and saw it on the sink. Woke me up, we argued and that was the last time I saw him."

"Wow Karma. You slut," I teased. "Say fucking again, it sounds cute to hear you curse little miss goody two shoes."

"I was not."

"Name one time that you ever got in trouble?"

"The time that I had to do Saturday school,"

"AND Kwame and I got in trouble on purpose just to be there with you," I interrupted laughing afterwards.

She hooted so loudly that she was crying again.

"Well…if it makes you feel any better…I have a confession. It's not one I'm particularly proud of but it will make me very happy to share this secret with you."

"I'm listening, "she calmed herself between sniffles.

"I don't know if it will make you feel better but it's worth a try. At least it will help me to get over my past."

She stopped and looked at me seriously.

"After my father took me away from you I ventured out."

"What do you mean?"

"You and I were extremely close. You were the sister I never had. I missed you dearly and needed the love and attention. Daddy was at work all the time. You know the situation with my mother. I didn't have any one."

"I'm…so…sorry. I thought things would have gotten better for you."

"Just the opposite. It got worst. I started to give my body away to any and everyone. The only way I felt any type of love was through a man fucking me," I bawled. "And do you want to know what was so ironic about each fuck?"

"I'm not sure I do but I'm listening."

"Each time and no matter who I slept with, I thought…of you."

"You thought of me? Really?"

"Unhuh," I smiled while wiping away the tears.

"Wow, I'm honored… I guess," she said confused.

There was a pause while we both took in the years that we lost being in touch.

"You're not a lesbian or anything are you?" Karma inquired.

"No silly. That lasted every bit of two years and I decided to seek counseling."

"Did it help?"

"I'm here aren't I?"

"Yea, I guess you're right. Wow, who would have known," she said trying to change the subject.

"Yea," I sighed. "Who would have?"

We sat there staring at the blank walls, deep into thought. I've been through hell these past few years and hers just recently began. At least I can help her get through it since I've been down this road already.

As I stood up to go out onto the balcony getting a breath of fresh air her phone rung. The moon beamed down on my back while I watched her body language. She appeared to be calm so I knew it couldn't have been Kwame. Walking into the living room while closing the balcony door behind her I overheard Karma say

"Love you too mom."

"Love you too mom," I disguised my voice and teased.

"Oh shut up."

"So what was that all about?"

"Apparently Kwame has told her EVERYTHING."

"Everything?"

"Everything."

"No he didn't?" I still was unconvinced.

"Yes he did. She knows about the baby and about me accusing him of cheating. "

"So what are you going to do?"

"I don't know. I love my mother and I know a mother knows best but deep in my heart I believe that I need some time to think about what I want to do; without being instructed into what to do. Do you understand?"

"Of course I do. This is your relationship. Only you can make the decision, good or bad, for your relationship and for your baby," I hugged. "Now, I know I'm the Godmother."

"Of course you are bestie. I couldn't imagine a better mom."

"Did you check your voice messages yet?" I asked sneakily.

"No. I chased you around the couch than my mom called. It totally slipped my mind."

Picking up her phone she dialed voicemail.

"Put it on speaker, put it on speaker," I harassed.

She did as was told and placed the phone on the table.

"You have twenty one unheard messages. First message," the recorded voice said.

"Karma please pick up the phone. It's not what you think," Kwame panicked.

She seemed disoriented. I could tell she was feeling down all over again so I started to laugh. Cheering her on to giggle with me and not allow it to get to her I repeated the same phrase *it's not what you think*. If that couldn't get you an award winning Grammy or Oscar I don't know what else would I teased.

"Next unheard message,"

"Karma I love you. I would never do,"

"Anything to hurt you," we interrupted while laughing again because our predictions were right.

"Next unheard message,"

"Please,"

"Call me back," we said while laughing even louder.

What once was supposed to be a sad moment became ComicView. Kwame pleading and begging had turned into a game of Charades. After about the twelfth call Kwame began to confess his love for her just as she said he did on their very first night of intimacy. And after the twentieth call, he was crying. He said he couldn't believe that she wouldn't answer his calls and that he wouldn't call anymore until she called him.

For about an hour he really felt that technique would work. And maybe it would have; who knows. But unfortunately for his luck, her phone was off which caused him to call one last time. His last call was the most heart braking. I actually felt sorry for him, more than I ever could have given this type of situation. I could barely make out anything he was saying. Everything was a mumble due to his crying.

As much as I would have wanted to make things better at this moment for the two of them my heart suggested Karma just wasn't ready to. The look in Karma's eyes was indescribable as she rubbed their baby. It had to be hard on her to deal with the emotions of this. And what could I say at this point but Kwame messed up. He seriously got his self in a disaster.

"Aww girl I'm so sorry. Maybe it wasn't a good idea for you to hear his messages. BUT…I will say this. You two love each other. Regardless of what happened last night that is your man and you don't let no one take him from you. Not even me cause girl you know he fine. And if you don't want him..well we share blood so it's only fair for me to have him right?" I teased hoping it helped her to feel better.

She gave me a *bitch I'd kill you* look and I got the message real fast.

"I was just trying to make you laugh. Everyone who knows everyone who knows everyone else knows that Kwame ONLY has eyes for his Karma. There is NO other woman *or man* who can come between that."

"Oh girl stop," she smiled. "Kwame aint gay now."

"Well I thought if I had you imagine a man in place of another woman you might have felt better."

"Not necessarily. I think I'd rather it be a woman."

"Come here and give me the biggest hug pregos. You're going to get through this. And you two will still be madly in love. Now it's getting late and I don't think I'm going to make it any longer. And NO, you can not sleep in my bed," I said guiding her towards the bedroom.

Another hug followed by how much we missed each other ended the evening as we both departed into our beds. Beds that were just inches apart, nothing like how things were in our childhood.

That night I awoke to see Karma in a sweat. It was obvious she was having a nightmare. I yelled her name trying to awake her and it must have worked because she rolled over instead and was sound asleep again.

The next day I fixed her breakfast; only because she's *the bestest* friend in the world as well as pregnant and really didn't eat much the night before. She must have smelled the aroma because she zombie walked into the kitchen with saliva hanging from her lips. Not literally but it made me think about a zombie movie.

"You're awake?" I asked.

"Uh-duh! How can I resist the smell of bacon and I'm pregnant? I feel like this baby intentionally woke me up just to eat," she chuckled.

"Girl you is a mess," I laughed in return. "How did you sleep pregos?"

"I slept fine...I guess."

"Un...huh. I saw you last night," I mentioned scrambling eggs over the stove.

"Saw me what?"

"Having a nightmare."

"I was not!"

"You were too."

"Was not," she continued uneasy.

"Than who?" I asked switching the subject to an old song I recalled.

"You," she laughed.

"Who stole the cookie from the cookie jar? Not me, than who? You," we sung together.

"You still remember?"

"Of course. How could I forget? Mr. Meyers used to give detentions for those who blurted that song out across the room.

Breakfast had just been placed on the table. Four pancakes, four blueberry and strawberry waffles, four French toast sticks, six pieces of bacon, two sausage links, scrambled cheese eggs with onions, four slices of wheat toast with a pinch of butter and strawberry jam, hash browns, diced potatoes, a pitcher of milk; orange juice and water with a lemon added with two glass cups..

"I didn't know what exactly you'd like being pregnant and all so I fixed you everything. I wanted to make sure I covered your sweet tooth as well as your thirst. Beside the point, I stay in this huge home alone so I'm not use to fixing anything for anyone else except myself."

Karma was speechless as she helped herself to as much food as she's liked. It must have been tasty because she kept one eye on her plate and the other on me. With every bite full I could hear her "Mmmm," as she licked the fork clean. After so many mouthfuls her phone rung. She looked at it than at her plate as if she wasn't sure if she wanted to take one more nibble before answering it. The thought must have been over whelming because she decided to take it with her.

"Hello...Hello," she reacted hoping not to have missed the caller.

There was a pause of silent. The look in her eye confirmed who the caller was; Kwame.

"Um, hi," she retorted placing a spoonful of eggs into her mouth. "Who is this?" she played dumb.
"No. I'm eating and can care less who this is."
"When you say me, I hope you're not referring to Kwame?"

There was a pause.

"Oh, so this is you huh?" she smiled devilishly while placing her plate onto the coffee table.

After seeing this I knew Karma was about to snap.

"Let me tell you something...first of all I don't appreciate you staying out all night and I damn sure don't appreciate calling your phone to hear another woman's voice. And you called her Thickness. What the fuck is wrong with you?"
"If I come home you'd better have every fork and knife in the kitchen hidden from me, cause it's not going to be pretty.
"Every heel?" she continued.
"Boots too?"
"Shin guards, cause you know I can kick a homerun down there?"

She began to laugh and at that moment I actually thoughts things between them was back to normal.

"Yea. I guess it's just as good to be able to…without crying.

"Uum…yeah"

"Promise?" her lips quivered.

"Awww. Well if you love me so much, I need you to prove it!"

"That woman's voice that I heard and will NEVER forget…I need to see and talk to her. I need to hear her say that you did not cheat on me. That you stood awake all night crying and wailing of how in love with me you are. Then I'll be satisfied."

"Really?"

"Yes, you are absolutely right. I do need to meet Miss Thang. Miss *Thickness*," she teased.

"Give me two hours."

"Because Denise fixed me breakfast and I was in the middle of eating."

"Yes, Denise. Oh. You don't know she's back."

"I just did."

"I just found out myself."

"Tell her yourself, she's coming with me."

I shook my head "no" while waving to get her attention. Karma glared her eyes at me insisting that I come. Looking away while mentally pouting I got the point.

"Than I will."

"We won't be," she said before hanging up the phone with a wide smirk.

"You owe me big time," I mentioned.

"I know. I know," she said finishing breakfast. "This is good!"

"Quit trying to suck up."

"Am not."

"Am too."

There was a pause.

"Well I guess I'll go get ready to see your baby daddy," I said unpleasantly.

"Ok," she said while drinking her orange juice.

"Ok. Aren't you going to get dress too?"

"No. I'm wearing this."

"Honey, you are not going with me looking like that. I don't care if you are pregnant."

"What's wrong with what I have on?"

"Go look in the mirror and you tell me."

"But I'm still eating."

"And. Put...the plate...down."

"But I don't need to look in the mirror. I know what I'm wearing."

"Well fine. Than you also know that we're going shopping to get you something better."

"No. I didn't know that. But as long as I get to finish my breakfast now or on the way it's fine with me."

We didn't get to Kwame till about six thirtyish. By that time he claimed to been worried sick.

"Where have you been I've been calling you all day?" Kwame asked.

"I didn't know I had to answer your calls?" she responded.

"Hi Kwame," I interrupted, overhearing the two as I walked through the front door.

"Hi Denise; how are you?" Kwame responded.

"The question is how are you?" I retaliated while standing directly in front of him with my arms crossed. "And how are you going to be when she's done with you? You know you don't mess with a pregnant woman and her hormornes. Come on now Kwame, tell me you at least knew that much?"

"It's not what it looks like."

"I know," I stepped forward. "Just know that you dug yourself into a deep hole. Good luck getting yourself out mister," I whispered to Kwame walking pass to sit down.

"Well why would you think that?" Kwame said cutting back into the conversation with me.

"Maybe because your girlfriend thinks you cheated on her."

"I didn't cheat. The only thing I'm guilty of is not coming home or having enough decency to call and let her know that I was ok."

"So if you didn't cheat who was the woman that picked up the phone?" Karma intervened.

"Are you talking about Thickness?"

"Did you hear that Denise?" she said turning to talk to me. "She has a name," she mentioned turning around to sock Kwame in between his nose and eyes.

"You know I'm going to start calling the police on you when you hit me," he motioned while holding his nose

"Call em. They'll agree that you needed it. And every time that I hit you as well."

"But you hit me for no reason!"

"I hit you," she said kneeing him in his jewels. "Because…YOU CHEATEEEEED!!!!!"

She screamed so loud that the house shook.

"Ok. It's getting a little wild around here. Pregos is going crazy and I don't want to be a conspiracy to murder," I said walking out of the front door.

"Denise, WAIT! YOU CAN'T LET HER DO THIS TO ME! YOU SAID YOU KNEW I WAS INNOCENT!" Kwame shouted.

"Ok. Ok. He's right bestie. Wait till I actually leave out of the door, get into my car and drive off to kill him. Oh, and try not to get dirty. You're looking good girl!" I mentioned as I closed the door behind me.

I called to check on her about an hour later and the couple was fine. I was able to hear Kwame and he sounded alive and well. Karma was laughing and had rays of love shining though the phone. She said that the two of them had spoke and he was telling the truth. That he was able to prove he didn't cheat. Yet and still consequences were distributed as she couldn't have him start something she wasn't willing to put up with.

"You mentioned she was pregnant during this time, correct?" Mrs. Williams asked.

"Correct," I answered.

"And you were the Godmother, correct?"

"Am, yes."

"Were you there when she delivered the child?"

"A girl, Kenise, yes."

"How did that go?"

"Her labor? I asked with attitude.

"Yes. Let me rephrase that. Was Kwame there when Karma delivered the baby?"

"Of course he was. He wouldn't have had it any other way."

"So being that he was there means that conversations were held?"

"Naturally."

"Tell us about them."

"Well what exactly would you like me to tell you?"

"Why don't you start from the beginning?"

It's 8:45 pm Thursday evening, May 19. She must have been in labor for almost twelve hours and was in a lot of pain. The contractions are coming every fifteen minutes and were very strong. Doctor Montauk had just broken her water four hours prior and still no baby. She was due May 7th but because this was her first child Doctor Montauk didn't want to induce the labor.

"Breath Karma. Huh Huh whew. Huh huh whew," Doctor Montauk coached.

"I am fucking breathing damn it! Huh huh whew. Huh huh whew," she breathed.

Kwame and I breathed with them to show support. She was having a very hard time delivering my Goddaughter.

He took a rag and wiped the sweat away from her forehead than grabbed her hand, "Huh huh whew. Huh huh whew. Keep breathing honey. You're doing a good job."

"Shut…up!" she yelled.

I gave him a look to let him know that was normal as he continued to breathe while the doctor watched the machine. It showed her blood pressure rising, a temperature of 101.2 and due to her heart rate increasing slowness of breath.

Doctor Montauk asked while standing next to her taking her other hand, "Karma how are you feeling?"

"How the hell do you think I'm feeling? I'm in pain. *A lot*…of pain."

Seconds later she quieted down. Gasping for air she laid in bed frozen. The doctor placed a face mask over her mouth and nose. Karma closed her eyes and drifted away, fell asleep is what I'm saying. I don't know how during the mist of the pain she was feeling but she was asleep.

"Doctor, what just happened," I asked.

"I increased the medicine in her Epidural which took a lot of the pain away as you can see."

"And the face mask?"

"That's so her and the baby can both get the amount of air needed to support their lungs. If mommy can't breathe, baby can't either. That's why it was best to increase the medicine. Also, as you can see, pain gone, so is the boost of blood pressure."

I looked at the machine than at Karma. It was obvious she was feeling a lot better. Her contractions were still strong which suggested the baby was ok as well. Kwame didn't understand what was going on. I think he just rested his faith in the doctors' hands and stood clear out of the way. If anything was wrong, he would be able to tell right away; probably a lot quicker than I since he knew Karma longer than I did.

Karma continued to rest and everything seemed to be well until about an hour later. The doctors and nurses came rushing in and said they had to give her an emergency cesarean. That the baby was showing distress which possibly could mean has stopped panting.

"I thought you said she was ok? That everything would be fine?" I said shocked.

"And everything should have been. And it will be. You can count on that," Dr. Montauk reassured. "I need the two of you to hurry up and put this clothing on," she shoved in our arms. "You have to hurry! We don't have much time."

Kwame and I did as was told. The whole time I was amazed how calm he had stayed. It was as if he knew everything would be fine. He never once panicked, although the look in his eyes suggested that he wanted to.

It didn't take anytime for the deliverance of Kenise after our scare. Some kind of way the baby was playing with the placenta until it got forced contracting through the birth canal as well causing the baby to suffer from lack of air. Not to mention the oxygen mask that Karma was still wearing wasn't given enough supply either. She had lacked oxygen so much that her body was using it all for herself giving her baby about ten percent of what was left over.

Kenise was the most beautiful little girl I had ever seen. She looked exactly like her dad with a pinch of some of her mother's features; such as her lips and hair. The first time Kwame laid eyes on her he fell in love instantly. He literally cried at the beauty and joy overflowing for their daughter. His kisses made Kenise turn her head towards his lips as if she was trying to kiss her daddy back. It was the most precious thing I've ever seen.

"Kwame, I know you are in the bonding stage with your daughter but we have to clean her and get her nice and ready for when you get back to your room. You two will have all of the time needed to bond as I'm sure you wouldn't have it any other way."

He smiled and continued to rock his daughter side by side. When he gave her to the doctor she let out a little weep that was so cute. She turned to look at her father as if she already knew who he was. Tears continued to roll down his face as he watched them take her into the next room to get her clean.

Karma on the other hand was doing a lot better. She was getting stitched on the inside which made me sick to my stomach. I walked over to Kwame to keep him company.

"She's beautiful isn't she?" Kwame asked.

"Yes she is. Looks just like her dad," I assured him. "You know we can still hook up since Karma's asleep," I teased.

"You always were funny Denise. I'm glad Karma has a friend like you," he shoved me gently. "Now that we have a child together and we've always been madly in love I think it's time,"

"Time for what?" I interrupted excitedly.

"You know," he hinted.

"No…no way."

"Yes way. I want her to be my wife."

I screamed so loud that Karma turned her head. For a moment we thought she was awake and so we ran to her.

"Karma baby, did you hear that? I want you to be my wife."

"Karma girl you better wake up and answer this man. He talking about marriage and if you won't answer him you know I will," I teased.

"Karma…Karma…Doctor she's looking kind of blue this end.

Doctor Montauk looked at her face than at the machine.

"GET OUT, NOW!" she yelled!

"What the fuck is going on doctor," Kwame spoke so sternly.

"This is serious. You trusted me before; I need you to trust me again. But you have to leave and let us do our job she tried to speak calmly."

I took Kwame by the hand as we were led to the waiting room.

"Don't worry. Everything will be ok. You know the two of you are made for each other."

He couldn't hold back the tears that were sitting in his eyes. They overflowed like water running from a faucet.

"I can't lose her Denise. I…can't…lose her. I love her."

"I know you do Kwame. You always have. Everyone knows including

GOD; you two are a match made in heaven, there's no way he's going to depart his two angels."

"You know…there was another time similar to this one when I thought I'd nearly died too."

"Really? When and where was I?"

"You two hadn't met yet. This was while we worked together; before she had even started at our school."

"Well what happened?"

"She was trying to catch the metro bus on her birthday and the bus driver wouldn't open it up for her because she was at the light I guess. So the traffic light changed back red and Karma dashed across the street to the next bus stop."

"Where were yall at when this happened?"

"Near where her parents stay."

"Wow."

"Tell me about it," he wiped away tears. "When the bus went through the light, Karma collapsed right on the concrete."

"Really?"

Kwame gave me a look that didn't give off a pleasant feeling.

"Her lungs had collapsed on her. The medical unit had to pump her chest."

"What do you mean pump her chest?"

"They had to send electric shocks to her because along with her lungs collapsing her heart had stopped suddenly too."

"Wow. She never told me this story."

"That's because she didn't remember anything that happened and I never told her."

I was in shock. They had experienced unspeakable things together. That's why the two of them are so close. Shortly after Doctor Montauk walked in and asked us to follow her.

"Well...I did all I could," she started before being interrupted.

"You told me it was going to be ok," Kwame started crying.

"And everything is ok Kwame. I was just going to say she and your little one has been taken to a room. She is still asleep, but your daughter sounds as if she is ready for her first feeding which we typically allow the parents to do."

"Show me the way," he suggested.

She directed us to our room in silence. Doctor Montauk stopped when we got in front of their room.

"I just want to let you know she will be asleep most of the day. She has a lot of medicine in her system not to mention after having a baby some women can become very restless; nothing that's out of the usual. We will continue to keep an eye on her," she finished as we started to hear Kenise cry.

Kwame didn't take any time at all getting to his daughter. He entered the room, immediately washed his hands, prepared a bottle, sat in the rocking chair and fed her while rocking calmly back and fourth. Their eyes connected during the whole feeding. Afterwards he placed a blanket over his shoulder than placed her on top of the blanket as well. Patting her back than rubbing her in circles until she finally gave out a loud burp. His smile was one of the most beautiful ones I've ever seen. He always did have a beautiful smile but this smile was a smile of love, happiness and the joy he had in his heart for his daughter.

Kwame was in the restroom and I was in the bed with Karma asleep when I felt her move. Throughout the night she must have rolled onto her side because she was facing me and I her. She sat up feeling her belly that was sore I assumed as she hissed with each movement.

"WHERE'S MY BABY?" She panicked!

She removed the sheets from the bed and saw that each of her legs was wrapped in a bandage that squeezed them every so many minutes. Than she must have began to feel light headed because she laid back down with force. Before I knew it she was asleep again, uncontrollably. By the time she had awakened the second time there was vomiting everywhere.

As I cleaned her, she had her eyes on a bigger prize; Kwame holding their baby. He was wrapped nice and snug inside of a white blanket that had blue and pink stripes on it. Kwame looked so happy. He held her in the cradle position and smiled and smiled while making silly gestures. The baby seemed to be responding well. She too stared up at her father as if she enjoyed the silly faces her dad was making. As I watched in au, not wanting to spoil the moment; the nurse came in to check on Karma.

The nurse spoke to Kwame saying, "How is mom doing?"

"Well I'm not really sure. This is her first time awaking since delivery."

"Um…" I put up my index finger knowing that what I was about to say was going to upset Kwame. "This is actually the second time she awoke."

"What do you mean the second time?" Kwame asked.

"Well, she woke up about 5am and looked me dead in the eye. Than she rubbed her belly and noticed she was no longer pregnant and panicked. Than she became flustered when she noticed all of the machines that was on her legs and such."

There was a pause.

"It was 5am in the freaking morning. I was tired; what did you expect me to do? Call a nurse when she awoke just to say oh, she went back to sleep? Yeah right. She went back to sleep and so did I?"

I gave them a *I wish you would say something* look. After that long delivery I felt like I had had a baby too.

"No one's judging you Denise. I may have done the same thing had I been the one to see what happened. Watching her de-," he caught his self. "Attempt to deliver a child, just to end up having a cesarean is a bit tire sum."

"Lets not forget her turning blue," Doctor Montauk joined in.

We all laughed at that.

"Yea, how could we forget to mention the main event of the evening?" I asked.

"Well she appears to be well. Everything with her vitals is back to normal."

"Is it safe for her to hold our daughter being that she has that medicine in her system?"

"Well…the medicine can be tricky. Some folks react sooner than others. Why don't we try to allow her to hold your daughter and see how she does?"

"Baby, how do you feel about holding Kenise?"

"You named her?" Karma asked.

"Yes. I know that Denise," he looked at me. "Is your bestest friend in the whole wide world and would like nothing better but for her only Goddaughter to be named after her. So I came up with Kenise. I switched the D for a K; giving her the first letter of both of our names, and the ending will be spelled exactly like Denise's," Kwame said putting Kenise in her arms.

"Kenise," she spoke while looking at her beautiful bundle of joy. "Kenise…hum…I like that."

"You better and she's named after me," I said to her. "Kwame, you're the best," I motioned excitingly.

"I figured you would," Kwame supposed.

"Ohhhh, and I know something you don't know," I walked around like a princess excited to spill the news.

"What do you know that I don't know?" she asked.

"Should I tell her or should you tell her?" I asked.

"You tell her," Kwame surrendered.

"I can't tell her; I was only joking. You tell her."

"Well I can't tell her, you tell her."

"You're her man."

"And you're her best friend."

"Tell her," I gritted my teeth in a threatening way.

"You tell her," he gritted back.

"Ok…ok. Why don't both of you tell me?" she demanded.

"Both of us?" Kwame and I said together. "We can't. I mean he/she can't," we continued. "Hey, stop that. You stop."

"HELLO!" Karma became irritated. "Why don't both of you tell me what the hell," she looked down at Kenise. "Heck is going on before I get up and smack both of you silly."

"We can't," we recited.

"What do you mean you can't? The two of you was just sitting here rambling back and fourth about something I should know and now all of a sudden," she stopped and paused. "Oooohhh. I know what it is. You just couldn't keep your fu-…freaking hands off of my man huh Denise?"

"Huh?" I asked confused.

"You weren't going to be satisfied until you slept with him huh?" she sat up in bed.

Kenise must have felt the tension flowing because she started to cry.

"Here, why don't you give me Kenise while you two talk," I mentioned trying to take the baby from her.

138

"Get your sleezy hands off of my baby."

"Karma, you need to calm down."

"Oh I am calm. You just be blessed that I can't get out of this bed."

"Tell her Kwame. Tell her now!"

"Yeah, Kwame. Tell me how for the second time now your sorry as-, butt broke my heart again."

"KWAME!" I yelled getting inpatient.

Kenise had calmed herself but started to cry again.

"It's ok baby; mommy smells a skank when she sees one."

"Skank? Skank? Girl if you weren't in that bed I'd slap you sensible."

"Oh honey we can get it started," she threatened starting to disconnect the wires that were attached to her.

"Karma you can't do that. You just had a C-section. You probably won't be able to stand."

"Like hell I won't. You fucked my man and bitch I'm about to whoop your ass."

"Kwame," I begged. "Tell her for Pete's sake.

"Tell her for what? The woman I wanted to marry has truly lost her mind," he said taking Kenise, an extra blanket and exiting the room.

I looked at Denise in a sickening way. Things weren't supposed to happen like this. He was supposed to tell her his plans for marriage and show her the ring via his phone he was thinking of getting and she was supposed to say yes. But she just accused this man...this GOOD...man of cheating; with her best friend at that.

When I confided in her I didn't mean for her to turn my past against me.

It happened during her stay at my home. The same day she and Kwame made up after she thought he had cheated than because of "Thickness." She had just got off the phone with Kwame telling him she would be to talk within two hours. Naturally, anywhere I go, I have to look damn good.

I walked into the living room with a purple dress on that went to my knees. My hair was curly; since it was just washed and in it a purple flower that looked perfect with the dress. Black butterfly ear rings with a matching necklace and bracelet came with the package naturally as well as flat, black, sandals and a purple ankle bracelet. I was gorgeous and knew I was the shit. The plan was to help Karma to look like "the shit," too because she was going to be walking around with a Diva.

"Wow! You look nice," Karma gazed.

"You like?" I asked while taunting clockwise.

"Yes. I do, I do. I hope that's how you plan to make me look when you're finished."

"Of course, of course darling. You have to look the best to be considered the best," I spoke in a fancy voice. "Let me grab my black purse and I am ready to go."

Karma walked me to my bedroom closet and stood as I turned on the light. She must have been in au as she viewed the tons of purses all of different colors and styles that were neatly organized.

"Why so many?" she asked.

"A girl has to have more than one with more than one choice," I replied grabbing a shoulder purse. "I'll drive."

"Sure," she motioned allowing me to lead the way.

We walked around to the back of the house and Karma looked as if she was in a chill. Cars of different colors were parked all over the back yard.

"Bestie, why do you have so many cars? Better yet, are they all yours? Like cashed out yours?"

"Yes darling they are…all mine. Cashed out, paid up front and bought," I smiled.

"But how?"

"Good pussy."

"Good pussy? What does that mean?"

"I told you about my past encounters."

"Yea, but you didn't tell me you had nearly a dozen cars that are all paid in full."

"Let's just say they were a gift."

"A gift from who?"

"Do I have to spell everything out bestie. You know for you to be so book smart, you have no street smarts at all."

"I never need them."

"Everybody needs them silly. And to answer your question each car was a gift from a different guy. Told you I got around then," I snapped. "But I'm clean now. A girl can't have too many cars either I guess."

"I guess too."

We drove the purple Toyota Camry. It went perfect with my dress. After we reached our destination I placed my purple shades on my face, got out of the car than locked her arms with mine. A charming young man walked our way and was giving me the eye but I ignored him.

"When I told you of my past, I was grateful when you kept it in my past. I'm not this skank that you accuse me to be. I am actually a true, loyal friend. Not to mention you have a damn good man. If I wanted to fuck him and he wanted to fuck me don't you think it would have happened already? We had plenty of opportunities. With your attitude you're going to run him away. A man can only take so much," I stressed grabbing my purse and departing.

I didn't even think to close the door behind me. With her nasty ass attitude she needed some fresh air to accompany her. Kwame was walking down the hall with his back facing me. As much as I wanted to apologize for her outburst I felt it was best for me to just leave. No good bye kisses to Kenise, no hug from my best friend, just me departing the place where I was no longer welcome.

Karma must have felt bad and embarrassed about her outburst because she called me apologizing over and over again; none in which I answered but did allow her to leave a voice message. She texted me and said Kwame refuse to talk to her until she made things right with us. Of course the moment that I read the message I immediately felt as if she was only making up for Kwame. That she was too good to ever apologize on her own. But then I thought of her personality and this was nothing like her. Karma knew deep down I would never sleep with Kwame; even if she was dead and gone.

"So you forgave her?" Mrs. Williams asked.
"Of course I forgave her, she was my best friend."
"Continue."

I waited until the day she was due to go home to visit her again. Walking through the entrance couldn't have seemed more welcoming. Kenise was in her fathers arms; of course and Karma was resting.

"Is she ok?" I whispered to Kwame.

"Yea, she still had traces of medicine in her system though. She's just been doing a lot of resting probably due to the stresses of her body. They said it could take up to six months for her to get better and some even a year."

"Well I'm sure she'll be fine. She has you to help care for the baby until she gets well."

"Of course she does. She'll have me for the rest of her life if I can help it."

"Speaking of which, why didn't you tell her?"

"I froze up…became scared. Looking into her eyes was just like looking into them the first day I confessed my love for her."

"Kwame you know she's going to say yes," I hindered.

"Say yes to what?" Karma awoke.

"Kwame," I gave a light shove of encouragement.

He reached in his pocket and pulled out a pink box that had a gold ribbon on it. I was shocked that he was able to pull everything off the way that he'd did. I'd only been gone two days and he'd already had a ring. But how?

Placing the box into her hand he said, "Open it."

Tears filled her eyes; mines too. I never imagined their proposal to be in a hospital but I know how much the two loved each other. Kwame could have had her dig through cow manure looking for earthworms and she still would have responded as I expected her to.

"What do you say?" he asked getting down on one knee. "Karma, I've loved you from the moment I've laid eyes on you. No other woman could ever fill my heart the way that you do. You've given me the true meaning of love. Watching you bring our daughter into the world was the most beautiful gift you could have ever given me. All the times of being kneed, slapped and kicked just made me respect you that much more and made me that much stronger. I love you Karma. Please say you'll give me the honors of being my wife?"

There was a pause. Karma fidgeted with the ring placing it on and off of her finger.

"Kwame are you sure we're ready for this?"

"Of course we are baby. How couldn't we be? We've known from the first day we met that we would end up married. Well maybe you didn't but by first glance I knew you would be mine. That's why I was staring at you the whole time speechless. I dreamed of this. Of all of this," he stood up. "I dreamed of you," he held her hands. "This couldn't be truer. We are made for each other."

"Yes we are," she smiled than sniffled. "Yes…Kwame. Yes…I will marry you."

Kwame dashed out of their room for joy and ran up and down the halls shouting "I'M GETTING MARRIED AND TO THE WOMAN I LOVE!!!!"

The doctors and nurses rushed into the room and began to clap in excitement.

"Well Mrs. Gentry, you appear to be doing a lot better and can be released home shortly if you feel you are ready," Dr. Jackson suggested while checking the necessary.

"What do you think?" she turned to Kwame and asked.

"How about," he started placing Kenise in her hands. "We start by you holding your daughter a little longer than you have. I don't think you've gotten to bond much with her. You were heavily drugged due to the cesarean."

She looked at their infant and was speechless. Nine pounds five ounces, twenty one and a half inches long, caramel complexion, her light brown eyes and a head full of silky hair.

"She is so beautiful," Karma begin to cry.

"So you're the one that was causing so much pain, huh?" Karma kissed her.

Kenise continued to look into her eyes as if she understood what was just said.

Kwame looked at them with teary eyes and asked, "How are you feeling?"

"I feel soar. How..what happened? I really don't remember much of our baby being born."

He climbed into bed holding the two of them in his arms and replied, "Well honey, you gave us quite a scare."

"What do you mean?"

"You had to get an emergency Cesarean done."

"Well I know that much cause you've been saying it lately?"

"Oh; sorry. You were having a lot of complications."

"Such as?"

"Honey let's not talk about that. It was very hard on me to see you experience that and knowing I couldn't take it away from you hurt me more."

"I'm sure it was but baby I need to know. This is what I remember," she tried to recollect. "It was about 12am. I was in labor for quite some time. I was seven centimeters dilated. Contractions were coming every eight minutes. Medicine was given to me in my IV to speed my contractions...but it wasn't working. You were holding my hand than wiped the sweat away from my face and I said that I had to poop. Together you and the nurse were attempting to help me out of bed when I began to push uncontrollably. The nurse called the doctor in to the room and told him I was ready to deliver and had already begun pushing. I remember peeing on myself and the nurse cleaned me. Feeling a contraction coming I began to push again. The doctor rushed in to our room, washed his hands and put his gloves on. He told me to feel down there where I was able to touch my baby's hair. He also smiled and said we're about to have a baby. I remember him saying our son will be here within the next fifteen minutes. That's how I found out he… was… a… boy," she looked down at Karma and recognized something was seriously wrong. "Wait," she paused while summoning up her thoughts. "He's…a…she. And…I…you…said…I…had…ok something is definitely not right here." Karma suggested unwrapping Kenise. "Are you sure this is my baby? I most definitely had a boy."

Meanwhile, Kwame, Kenise and I seemed to be trying to figure out what planet she had traveled to and where she believed what she says happened…happened. Kwame and I were both there and I remember distinctively her being cut and the gagging feeling I felt afterwards.

Kenise started blowing bubbles at Kwame and he smiled saying, "Yeah. I know. That didn't happen. Not at all. Did it daddies little princess? Yes you are," he baby talked. "Daddies little girl." He kissed Karma and told her to relax until they were discharged. She's had a very long past few days and would need as much rest as possible and that he would do all the necessities of taking care of Kenise."

Just as Karma did as she was told Kwame tapped her on her shoulders very lightly asking, "Are you still breastfeeding?"

"I could have answered that question for her. If I knew my friend and I knew my friend although years had been lost, I knew most definitely she wouldn't have had it any other way but for Kenise to be breastfed."

"Of course I am," she snapped. "Why? Is there something wrong where I can't feed my baby?"

"Of course not. I just wasn't for sure. That's all."

He called the nurse and asked if it was ok for her to breastfeed their baby being that she had medicine in her system? That he wanted to make sure the medicine wouldn't be harmful to Kenise. And Kwame made a good point. One I wished I had thought of. Being unsure of the medicine given would be a price to pay had it been harmful but Kwame was paying attention. That's how I knew he was the one for my best friend. The one for her to marry of course.

"Did you attend the wedding?" Mrs. Williams asked.

"Are you kidding me? Of course I did.

"What was it like?"

"Beautiful."

"Describe beautiful to the court room. What made it beautiful? Was it the fact that your best friend was getting married? Was it their vows? The ceremony or reception? What about her wedding made you describe it in one word…beautiful?"

"I was her bridesmaid of course. She wore the classiest gown. It was simply gorgeous. A white dress with a red bow placed in the mid section. Red ruby ear rings with a matching necklace and bracelet. In her hair was placed a white Lilly because it was her favorite flower.

"Do you think he'll like it?" she asked.

"Kwame? Girl please. Kwame wouldn't care if you came out with a t-shirt and some pajamas. As long as you say "I do," that man will be happy."

"You think so?"

"I know so. It sounds to me like you're getting cold feet."

"Not really," she tried convincingly. "Ok...ok...a little."

"A little huh?" I crossed my arms. Standing her up and guiding her towards the tall mirror I said "Look at you. You're beautiful. Any man would be crazy to not want to marry you. Not to mention Kwame has always been crazy about you. You'll make a great wife. Now go out there and kiss your husband," I finished placing the tiara on top.

She did as was told but nervously. Her father greeted her as their song; You're Beside Me, by the Isley Brothers played.

"That's your hint baby girl," he said placing a kiss on her cheek.

Tears of joy began to fall down my face as I couldn't help but to feel so joyful for her. She deserved everything she was getting. A good man, beautiful baby, wonderful family. Karma had a good heart.

"It's time for me to let my little girl go," I overheard Mr. Gentry whimper.

"Daddy, I will always be your little girl. Nothing's going to change," she reassured him.

He hugged her one last time and wiped his eyes, "This is our secret right?"

"No, cause I saw everything," I tried to cheer him up.

"Of course daddy," she teased waving me off. "But you might want to wipe your eyes again cause I think you missed a spot," she teased.

"I love you baby girl," he said hugging her tightly

"I love you too daddy," she returned the hug.

Cleaning his face once more Mr. Gentry said, "Ok, we have to go. Kwame is going to start to think I kidnapped you," he took in deep breaths. "Ready?" he asked as the doors to the altar opened.

"Ready," Karma said standing in confidence.

She walked down the isle and saw Kwame looking so handsome. He wore a smile from ear to ear. The blue tuxedo with a white dress shirt and a red handkerchief hanging out of his breast pocket matched with Karma's dressed. The red shoes went well with their wedding colors; red and blue.

Above him was a projection screen; pictures were being shared as they captured their most loving moments together starting from teens up until this very point. The minister spoke of brief detail within each one. The last photo was the one of their daughter Kenise being born. From there, the minister spoke and they were married.

Kwame bent her over his lap to kiss every detail of her lips. It was very passionate and she enjoyed every moment of it.

"Did Karma ever tell you what caused the two of them to fall apart?" Mrs. Williams asked.

"Objection your honor. Here say," Mr. Ohio retaliated.

"I'll allow it," Judge Lanai Brown motioned. "Denise, you may answer the question."

"I believe it started about four or five years into their marriage. Kwame had lost his job and became extremely depressed. Distant, angry, easily jealous, possessive. Just completely opposite of what Karma and I was used to seeing.

Once, we were together; him, Karma and I trying to place Kenise into school.

"I think this will be a good school," I said to them as we walked the halls of Orion Academy.

"I think so too," Karma smiled.

Kwame didn't say anything. Do you know he actually tried to pull a cigarette out during our walk of the school and while school was in session. He had totally gone from good Kwame to terrible Kwame. A man no woman who'd ever known him could have ever imagined seeing. Hell, if I'd saw some of the things beforehand that he would turn out to be I would have never supported their marriage. But just like the good friend I am, I helped Karma to pick up the pieces.

Anyway, we had viewed the classroom and saw the things the teachers would be teaching and we; Karma and I felt very strongly for this school. This was the one. They had a lovely play ground, all of the teachers were warm and welcoming, their philosophy seemed fit...it was perfect. Not to mention they were a free Charter School. Most schools say free but with that comes a yearly fee per child. I think it's called school fees. But in Orion, there weren't any fees at all. No school fees, union fees, classroom fees, lunch fees unless your parents made too much. Everything was exactly free. Zero dollars.

After listening to the speech Mrs. Ballew gave we began to sign paper work; attempted to anyway. Out of no where Kwame had an outburst.

"What type of school is this again?" he asked.

"A Charter school," Mrs. Ballew responded.

"I don't want my daughter going to no damn Charter school."

"I'll give you all a moment to discuss things," she said walking out of the small conference room.

"What the hell was that?" I charged at Kwame. "I don't know what is wrong with you but you better check yourself real fast," I threatened.

"Let's just leave," Karma said embarrassed.

"Leave for what? Cuz he's being a asshole," I looked at him.

His eyes wore a tightened glance as if he couldn't see what was happening right before his eyes.

"Are you high?"

"Na...na...naw I'...I'm not...high," he slurred with a stutter.

I had noticed it earlier but because I've known him for so long I tried to give him the benefit of the doubt. But it was clearly noticeable now. He had to inject some heroin in his system, snorted it, taste it, he did something. Especially after the outburst for no apparent reason at all.

It didn't make sense to disagree with a man on drugs so the conversation wasn't continued. Karma became extremely stressed. It seemed as if she was holding on to a thin string that just happened to be attached to him. Every since he'd gone through these changes, she began to loose weight, quit caring for herself as far as hygiene and hair. It was as if she was letting herself go and Kwame, the man she fell in love with was so oblivious to this change that he couldn't see it. He was killing her without actually laying a hand on her. She was doing it all herself. Now that I think about it, I'm glad he's dead. When it comes to a choice of him or my best friend...it will always be her. Just look at her. Doesn't she look healthier?"

Karma
Point of View

An hour left before court start and I'm not sure if the jury is with or against me. My lawyer seems to be in good faith that we will win and I will get to go home. She is more than convinced that Kwame didn't intentionally kill his self; nor did I help him to do so.

We've overcome so much. Love was just a single word and could never express the way I felt deep down in my heart for him. His drug addiction would have never allowed me to leave though I did threaten to. He was simply too irresistible.

As I laid in bed, the correction officers opened the gates of hell.

"Mrs. Woods, RISE," they threatened unaware that I was already awake. "It is time," they mentioned placing handcuffs on my arms and feet as if I was a threat to them as well as myself.

They escorted me down the long halls, through one gate after another.

I was placed into a black and orange van with the word SHERIFF written on it. Bars covered the windows that looked jammed in pace.

"But why? Why do I have to travel with these cuffs and in that van" I thought to myself. "I'm innocent."

The vehicle begun to float about the streets. There were police cars in front as well as behind us to help ease traffic to a stop or allow us to pass prohibited. When we arrived the court house had at least two dozen protestors outside of it with a picture of me saying I was guilty. The people began to throw items at the van forcing us to use the back entrance. Problem is when we parked, out of no where came more inhabitants who wanted to see justice for Kwame and NOW! They said I was a horrible wife for allowing him to use drugs and not getting him help. As a wife there's also only so much I can do. It's impossible to try and babysit an adult. A male adult at that.

The officers pulled their weapons out and asked them to step away. That if anyone so much as took justice into their own hands, they would pay for it. I guess the look in their eyes was serious because the citizens begin to disappear one at a time.

I was jerked out of the van and guided in the direction of the courtroom. My lawyer was sitting in front of the witness stand well prepared.

"Are you ready?" Mrs. Williams asked as the handcuffs were being taking off.

"I think so," I said nervously.

"NO! You will tell me you are ready because I didn't come here to loose a case," she looked me square in the eyes.

"I'm ready," I told her as boldly as I could stand.

"Good, now take a seat," She ordered. "This will be the last seat you'd have to take after today," she promised.

I sat there staring at the empty chair realizing that soon I would be in that very seat to tell my version of our life before being judged by the jury. As the court room began to fill I couldn't help but to feel as vacant as my soul had felt the moment Kwame deceased.

The bailiff spoke, "ALL RISE....JUDGE LANAI BROWN IS ENTERING THE COURT ROOM.

Judge Lanai Brown said to the peers in the courtroom, "You all may be seated. We are here today for the case of Karma Woods VS. The State of Kentucky. She's here in arraignment of murder, wanting to defend her relationship with her husband; proving that he did not and would not have committed suicide; because it just wasn't in him to do so. Mrs. Woods further states that while she knew of Kwame taking drugs, that he indeed **was** the perfect guy. We have been told through other testimonies that Kwame was madly in love with Karma and likewise she with him.

I'm going to ask the court room to remain silent as our first testimony from Karma is heard. If anyone shall get out of order, you will be kicked out of my court room NO QUESTIONS ASKED!" she threatened. "Karma, you may begin your story."

I asked with my head down, "Well where would you like me to begin?"

"Begin where you feel fit to. Remember, it is you that have to prove to the jury as well as myself the type of man that Kwame were," Judge Lanai Brown said with encouragement.

Nervously, I lifted my head and responded.........................

Blooming Flowers

The year was nineteen ninety seven when Kwame and I met. I was to be fourteen in two days and was at my very first job. I was excited because I could finally buy the clothes and shoes that I liked; or that my mother approved of anyway.

That day was June 14th and it was very hot outside. I wore a light green dress and never knew just how good I looked until I saw the twinkle in his eye. Light caramel complexion, with hips; more ass and breast than needed for the age of fourteen. Light brown eyes that looked like sunrise, and a shoulders length of hair.

It was love at first sight (as he said) when he saw me that day. I on the other hand had a different opinion. Always being told "The only things boys want is to get between your legs," begins to leave an impression. Beside the point, I had on a dress that went to my knees and revealed my full figure. *What else could he have wanted with me?* Teens my age were already having sex. I just happened to be in the ten percent crowd that wasn't.

Anyway, on that very hot day, I caught the bus to work. Nervously, I walked down Park Town's Driveway in search of the Management Office. This was my first job after all and I was worried. *Do I have on appropriate clothes? Will I like the job? Will I fit in and make any friends? What if my boss is an asshole?* What I never once thought of, is meeting the love of my life.

There weren't any signs down the pathway that I was on. Not even an address to at least give me some kind of notice that I was in the right area of the apartment complex. The only thing that stood out was a set of steps leading to the inside of what looked like an abandoned building. I entered the old ragged door that set in place and it croaked. *How creepy?* A blanket of relief wrapped around me as I walked and began to see faces. Approaching two teenaged boys that were cleaning the hallway was unusual for me. I never thought I would see boys working; I always thought they ran the streets. You know, sold drugs and pimped out prostitutes of some sort. At least that's how it's showed on television and even in some books I've read.

One of the guys stopped the other guy from working. They stared as if they had seen an angel. Maybe they did," I smiled to the courtroom while recalling that day mentally.

One of the guys asked politely, "Can I help you?"

Overwhelmed by the deepness of his voice I stood still as if I was ordered to do so. It made my heart tremble in an unbelievable way. My lips became extremely shy and didn't know what to say. I never had a boy talk to me before that made me feel this way.

The guy that spoke with such authority was six feet five, dark chocolate skin and beautiful bedroom eyes.

He asked while walking towards me, "Miss Lady is there something I can help you with because you look lost? Are you sure you're in the right place?"

Noticing the clock in the corner showing I had five minutes left before my shift starts I overcame this feeling.

As I spoke, a part of me emerged "Yes, I'm looking for the management office. Do you guys know where's it's located?"

"Yes Miss Lady. You want to continue walking down this hallway till you see a pair of steps that sits on the left side. Go up those steps and that is the management office. I can take you there if you'd like but first I would like to know your name?"

"My name is Karma and no thank you I have the directions now."

We departed and I went on my way. The other guy stared with his mouth opened as I walked passed. That's all he seemed to be capable of doing at this point in time. He was five foot four, dark, lovely and dimples that would never keep a secret. Continuing down the hall, to the left were the steps, just like he said there would be. Sensing I was being watched I stopped then turned around. My sixth sense was correct because *I was*. As I continued to walk away I felt his piercing eyes reading my soul. *Oh brother if you only knew!*

As I kept thoughts undisclosed while walking up the stairs I was greeted by a woman who nearly startled me. She was short and I couldn't help but to focus on how long her hair was. I was in awe by the beauty of it. She continued to explain the job and how she will be there to help. Her name was Carol and for me to call her CC. Carol showed me a stack of papers, and the filing cabinets than told me to file them. I immediately begin to do so while smiling. *My very first day is easy. Filing papers, that's it. Wow.*

It took exactly two hours and forty two minutes to file the large stack of papers. Miss Carol asked if I wanted to take a fifteen minute break or go home. She said she didn't have anything else for me to do today and that I would just be sitting around waiting for the time to pass. I told her I would rather go home. Miss CC told me she understood and for me to come back tomorrow at the same time. I smiled while walking out of the door.

As I started down the stairs, the two young men from earlier were walking pass. I slowed down a bit to thank them for giving me directions again. The short conversation ended in us walking together. No one wanted to play follow the leader. When we approached the doorway that led to outside we stood there as if not knowing what to do.

One of the guys said, "You can go first."

I responded before leaving, "Thank you and may I have your names too?"

"My name is Bryant and this is my brother Kwame."

Walking down the long alley that led me to the bus stop seemed just as long and eerie as it did earlier. If it wasn't for the two brothers being behind me I probably would have ran instead.

They sound like they were arguing but I couldn't make out what they were saying. All I could make out was that it was a bout a girl. Little did I know, *I was that girl*. When I approached the sidewalk to the busy street I had to cross, the very polite guy from earlier, took me by the hand. I felt shy and awkward because things like this just didn't happen to me. I will be in the ninth grade this fall and have never experienced something this unique. Not to mention there was a warm smile which seemed to be within good intentions.

Finally the street cleared and Bryant took off running without giving me notice. When he ran, he jerked my hand forcing me to run as well. I guess that was the signal that the coast was clear. Once we were across the street the quiet guy motioned to his brother. Kwame walked over to Bryant and they both continued to disagree and motion back and forth. Again, I couldn't make out what the conversation was about. He walked towards me as we engaged in stares while Bryant stayed behind.

Nervously with his hands in his pockets he said, "Hi, how are you doing?"

I responded in my sexiest voice, "Fine."

"How old are you?"

I smiled and responded, "14."

Kwame asked while staring into my eyes, "Do you have a boyfriend?"

I said while crossing my arms with attitude, "No. And if I did?"

He said while stepping back, "I'm sorry. Maybe a little too personal. Can we start over?" He held his hand out in hopes of me meeting him half way with my hand and said, "I'm Kwame. The guy back there is my brother Bryant. What is your name again?"

"My name is Karma and yes that is my real name."

Kwame chuckled, "Karma is different but pretty." Than asked, "When is your birthday?"

"June 17th."

He said with excitement "You're a Gemini! Cry now; laugh later. Sign of the twins.'

I said loudly "Yep. That's me."

"Would you believe if I told you I am a Gemini too?"

"No way!"

Kwame said while looking down the street and noticing a bus coming towards us, "Well it's true. I am. June 3rd to be exact. What bus do you have to catch?"

I responded while looking in the same direction, "The 27."

"Well you're in luck. It's on its way."

"What bus do you have to catch?"

While digging in his back pocket, he said "I'm catching the same bus. Hey, where do you live?"

"You're asking a lot of questions. My dad always said to never tell someone you don't know, where you live."

Kwame mumbled, "Do you listen to everything your dad tells you?"

I overheard him and replied, "Yes! Why wouldn't I?"

Bryant started to walk our way still carrying the same warm smile as he and Kwame allowed me to get on the bus first. Sitting in the front seat closest to the bus driver seemed like the best option given the situation. Kwame and Bryant sat in the back near the exit. Laying my head against the walls of the bus and closing my eyes for only what was supposed to be a second turned into something much more than.

I must have fallen asleep because when I opened my eyes the bus was very loud and crowded. I looked to see what location we were at and was glad I had awaked when I did. My stop was next. The thought of being this tired from filing papers made me imagine what life is like in my parent's shoes. It must be really hard and stressful.

I ranged the bell and stood up. The bus driver stopped too fast causing me to fall. Only thing was Kwame slid as if he was playing baseball and was trying to get a homerun; catching me in his arms. It was the sweetest thing that could have ever happened to me. Blushing because my buttock was in his hands, I looked down at him who had seemed to already snapped out of the fact that he caught me and what he was actually holding on to.

"Uum...uumm...I apologize. I didn't mean to catch you in that form," he said giving me a boost with his hands. My bottom if you will.

"Thanks," I motioned now looking at the driver.

I was upset but was taught to never disrespect my elders. *Mommy always said if I want to go to heaven, I have to learn to bite my tongue.* In this case, I bit my tongue *real* hard.

Standing up then dusting his self off Kwame asked, "Will you be at work tomorrow?"

"Sure," I blushed.

"Than I'll see you tomorrow," he waved.

"I guess you will," I smirked again. Turning my attention back to the driver as I walked down the steps, "Thank you," I said cynically.

The doors closed and I could see Kwame in the window with his eyes fixed on mine. As the bus drove by I grinned again while signaling him goodbye. His face reddened so dark that the windows began to sweat.

The run home was swift as I couldn't wait to tell my parents how my first day at work went; minus Kwame and Bryant. They would never approve even though nothing has even happened. Just a sweet wave.

I opened the door and walked inside yelling "Mom…Dad…Mom…Dad," but didn't get an answer.

There was a note on the refrigerator door that read "Your mother is at an appointment and I will be home late. See you when we get back."

I thought to myself while fixing a glass of orange juice, "They're not expecting me home until 3pm. It's only 12:15pm. COOL!"

I went into my room and laid in bed. Staring at the ceiling, I put on my headphones and began to listen to Bob Marley. My favorite song was "Natural Mistic." As the music begun to play I closed my eyes and fell asleep.

It's dark out and I'm not quite sure why I'm walking. I just am. A noise sparked from behind so I turned to look. Surprisingly, there was nothing there; just voices. Continuing to listen, it sounds as if there are two guys arguing; *about a girl*. I wonder who it's about. I turned around and there were two guys standing right in my face. Ironically I heard the voices from *behind* me… Before now I thought I could see fine. And… they weren't there a minute ago. *Ok, creepy, It's time to go back home,* I began to think.

One of the guys approached me, "Miss Lady…Miss Lady…Do you need help?"

For some odd reason my sense of hearing wasn't working. There was an echo of what he was saying and I found myself lip reading. So I stood there.

Shaking me while yelling, "Are you okay?"

Slapping him, "Yes, I'm ok. What is wrong with you?"

Holding his face, "You have one mean hand."

Apologetically before screaming, "I apologize; I didn't mean to slap you. It's just that…**well why are you out here in the dark anyway? You scared me half to death!**"

Pointing to the inside of a building, "My brother and I work there. And we were cleaning the floors until you approached us and stood there as if you were lost. Then I asked if you needed help and you just stared at me."

"Oh," I said beginning to look foolish.

"So…do…you…need any help?"

Again I stood there feeling disoriented. Its dark out…I'm standing in front of two guys that came out of nowhere and he's asking *me* if I need any help. I don't know what I need.

I asked confused, "Where…are we?"

What seemed to be a nightmare shifted into another delusion.

I was lying in my bed with my blanket pulled over my head. Feeling as if I was going to suffocate, I continued to breathe heavily while pulling the blanket slowly down my face. Looking around an empty dark room I began to reach. The more I tried to grasp, the heavier my arms seemed to feel. Finally clutching what felt like a lamp, I played around the edges of it until I found the switch. Once the lights came on, I sat up and looked around a dimly lit room.

Going into shock while carefully examining every inch of the room, "Oh…my…gosh. This…can't…be…possible."

There were papers placed in rows and columns that were stacked to the ceiling. My eyes started to feel blur as I observed the room corner to corner, over and over again. Feeling dizzy while breathing heavy caused me to faint and I felt as if I fell into another dream.

Someone was yelling before taking me by the hand, "Excuse me! Excuse me Miss Lady! Do you think I can help you across the street?"

Nervous, but sarcastically speaking with a smile, "I didn't know I needed help."

The gentleman helped me across anyway. He stood in front of me while gazing into my light brown eyes as if he was falling in love. It appeared his body was shifting towards me. Continuing to look in my eyes, as if he was asking for permission, he placed his hands on my face and began to breath heavy. Tilting his head and closing his eyes, there was a whisper of space between our lips. Before going any further I forced my knee into his penis than pushed him away.

"What are you doing?" I asked.

Another guy joining the conversation also asked my male companion, "Yeah bra, what *are* you doing?"

He said speaking calmly while bent over, as if he had no intentions of kissing me, "I was just going to whisper in her ears that my brother wanted to get to know her," he choked, trying to catch his breath from the attack.

"So if this is true, why were your lips so close to mine?"

The other guy said jokingly to his brother, "You know you gone get it when we get home right? Well, maybe not. *Looks as if she did a good job handling you herself,*" he chuckled. "Hey Bryant, pick your penis up off of the floor; I think it just got jammed," Kwame laughed. Looking into my eyes as if caught under a spell while shaking my hand, "Hi, I'm Kwame. Sorry about my brother actions back there. You have a powerful kick. Can you show me that one day? Not as your victim, but maybe how to kick my knee out just right?

"Maybe."

And you are?"

I spoke while looking away, "Karma."

Kwame took me by the chin and guided me towards his eyes again.

He said while stepping back than forward, "You have some beautiful eyes. Well, by the looks of things, you're just beautiful period."

"Thanks. Is that all?"

Kwame chuckled, "How old are you?"

Becoming irritated I said, "I'll be fourteen Thursday. Why?"

"Really? My birthday was on the same day two weeks ago. June third to be exact. Looks like we both are Gemini's."

I said while putting my hands in my pockets, "Guess so."

Rocking back and forth, Kwame said, "So."

Looking around, I said "So."

There was a pause between us. We sat quietly as if the sun was coming down and rain would appear. Leaning back against the pole that displayed the bus stop I started to hear voices and a lot of banging. The voices sounded very familiar. Sounds…just…like…my mom.

I closed my eyes only to open them to a ceiling filled with pictures of Bob Marley and poems I had written over the years.

Now fully awake I thought to myself, "I must have been dreaming. Wow, some dream."

Following the voices into the hallway and peeking out the door I whispered; Mom. Just like I thought."

She was hanging a new picture and having a conversation with my dad.

Quietly interrupting the conversation while coming out of my room, "Mom."

She looked and said, "Karma."

My father interrupted, "How was work baby doll?"

I stood there in offense to my mom's response. She was a real bitch and we absolutely DID NOT get alone. My father on the other hand never understood the tension between us but tried his best to keep things calm.

"Work was fine but boring. I had to file papers. It seemed fun at first, then after the first hour, it wasn't any more."

Dad giggled and said, "I totally understand. Our job isn't fun either but we have to do it to get our bills paid and to support our family."

"Support our family? Dad please; the only one that supports anything dealing with me is you."

Usually my "mother" would say something but she rolled her eyes and kept attending to her pictures.

"Now, now Karma. Apologize to your mother."

"Apologize for what?"

"Karma!"

"No Gregg it's okay."

"What? She actually don't have anything to say?" I though to myself.

"Ok. Well just know that you are working to get your own school clothes; that we approve," he said looking at my mother.

She rolled her eyes and began to water her plants.

"Your own shoes, backpack, school supplies and etc."

Mom interrupted, "Don't forget to put some of your income in the bank. It's always best to save. Saving money is what I call having a backup plan. For example, if I was sick during my work week and know that my check will be a couple of days short, I will have the amount needed in the bank to cover my sick days."

I rolled my eyes at her.

"And don't think you will be calling off either. I've been your age before. You're going to go to work every day and get there on time," he looked stern. "I need to see that you're putting money into your account so you have one of two options. You can either bring home twenty five dollars out of your check for I to put in the bank for you. *Or*, you can do it yourself and bring home a bank statement showing the amount you placed in your account, and how much you have to date." My father put his hand on my shoulder and said, "And don't think of taking any money out because your bank statement will show it. If we see that you disobeyed us," he tried to include her. "And have been taking money out of your account anyway, you will be on punishment for a week and have to pay twice the amount of what you've taken out of your account. Understood?"

"Yes sir," I said with respect to my father.

Looking at my mother I let out an "Umph," as I walked passed.

She knew I didn't admire her so there was no use to thinking I would say "Yes ma'am."

"Karma get cleaned up for dinner. I smell it all the way up here. Um um. It's almost finish. We're having lasagna, garlic bread and salad; with a slice of apple pie. Um. Hurry girl, dinner's almost ready. Ski-daddle," she motioned.

"I'm not a dog," I retaliated.

My father hurried down the stairs while saying, Karma, do as you're told while I set the table. Can you at least do that? If not for your mom, than for me?" he pleaded.

"My mother replied, "Yea, you go do that," she said eyeballing me. "I'm going to the bathroom than I'll be down.

We departed. I went into my bathroom and took a quick shower. My mother hates for my father and I to come to the table without a shower first. Luckily for her I wanted to have my bath out of the way because I had to work again tomorrow. So this one time is considered me doing what she wanted because I needed to.

As I was putting on my clothes I couldn't help but think about the day that I had and then the actual dream.

I thought to myself, "What does it mean? Or does it mean anything?"

Than she yelled, "KARMA, LETS GO. NOW!"

"Some nerve," I thought to myself.

Because I was hungry and realized I hadn't eaten much today I hurried down the stairs nearly tripping on the last step. My mother looked at me and wasn't happy.

"Karma, what is the first thing we should do when we get out of the tub?

I thought out loud "Dry off.

"Well I think you better hurry and do so."

My father added as I looked at him, "Go on. You heard what your mother said.

I hate when my parents do that. They always took each other's side or opinion. *What if I was right for once? Would they take my side then?*

Holding Hands

Awaking to the music and rolling over onto my stomach I looked at the clock.

Thinking to myself while getting out of bed, "5:30am. I have enough time to shower and get to work early. I could walk around the neighborhood; get to know where the restaurants are and if there's a library…"

Thoughts of Kwame also crossed my mind *again*. I think I'm beginning to like him in an unusual way. He's my height, sexy and with a gorgeous smile. His personality is also very easy going but too easy going. I wonder what he's up to.

Getting on the bus and speaking to the driver, "Good morning. How you doing?"

The driver responded with a warm smile, "Good young lady. Do you need a transfer?"

Returning the smile I said, "No thank you sir. But thanks for asking."

The moment I turned to my left to take a seat I noticed the same two guys, Kwame and Bryant, from yesterday as well as from my dreams. Pausing as if I've seen a ghost I gasped for air. Suddenly I didn't feel so good. My heart was racing, palms were sweaty and I began to feel nauseated.

The driver asked, "Are you ok young lady?"

The bus seemed to be spinning around me. All the different faces were staring and laughing.

"Young lady, are you ok?"

Losing my balance, I fell backwards and by my surprise, for the second time now; into Kwame's arms again.

I remember hearing him so clearly even though I was unconscious for a bit. Hearing stories of folks as they were in a coma being able to capture the words and voices of things their loved ones would say caused me to become a believer after my own experience.

He picked me up, than spoke to the bus driver saying, "I will take her to that seat over there by the open window. She needs some fresh air. I know her, we work together. I can care for her from here."

Nervously and unaware of what to do the driver asked, "Are you sure? I can call an ambulance. She looks as if she needs emergency care."

Kwame said while sitting me in the seat where the window was open, "Yes. I'm pretty sure. Does anyone have a fresh bottle of water that's unopened? Some fresh air and nice cold water would probably make her feel better."

A lady passenger said, "I do. I have two of them. She is more than welcome to have one."

Taking the bottle of water from the nice lady, he said "Thank you ma'am. You will be blessed for what you just done."

The lady watching as Kwame pours water into my mouth; in return said, "No son. *You* will be blessed for what you are doing for this young lady."

Kwame turned a friendly smile as the other passengers watched in au. The driver continued his route but showed concern by watching in the mirror as often as he could. After about five minutes of coming to my senses, I opened my eyes. The cool breeze blowing through the window felt extremely good.

He put his hand on my hand while asking, "How are you feeling?"

Slapping him than crossing my arms; I responded "Why is it every time I look up I see your face? Yours and Bryant's that is."

Holding his face, he responded, "If it takes me to get slapped just to help you then I will take as many of them as you have to give."

The audience we have now created said "Awww."

Giggling and turning towards him to slap him again; I said, "I'm sorry. Maybe that wasn't hard enough. Here's another one!"

"Ouch! Now look missy, you are getting way out of line. I just helped bring you back to life and this is how you repay me?"

"I was never dead STUPID! I think I fainted. And I wouldn't have if I hadn't seen you two."

Mocking me in a mumble, "I think I fainted." Rolling his eyes, "Yeah; ya think?"

"Oh shut up."

Kwame said while protecting his face, "No, you shut up."

"You shut up."

"No you shut up."

Over hearing the argument the driver interrupted, "Why don't both of you shut up? And young lady, can't you see the young fellow has a thing for you?"

I looked at him and he looked at me. He gazed into my eyes as if he could see every star there ever was in the sky As if he could see every beat within the rhythm of my heart. As if he was watching all of my younger memories flash before him. Kwame continued to stare while sucking on his bottom lip as if imagining this was a first date; and at the end there was always a required kiss. *But he was unsure how to kiss me; without getting slapped again that is.*

On the other hand I was thinking of reasons to smack him allover again; though he couldn't tell though my disguise. Images of striking him for being on the same bus ride as me this morning and again for appearing in my dreams. And two more times for having to see his brother that tried to kiss me yesterday. Or was that a dream?

Together we looked at the driver and said, "NAH! IT'S NOT LIKE THAT!" Surprised we faced one another and motioned, "QUIT REPEATING ME! YOU QUIT REPEATING ME! WOULD YOU STOP! IT'S NOT ME! CUT IT OUT! "

We crossed our arms over our chest and our hands touched.

Yelling again to one another, "WOULD YOU STOP! YOU'RE DOING IT AGAIN! NO YOU'RE DOING IT AGAIN!"

Trying to calm myself, I spoke calmly to Kwame saying, "Can you please go back to your seat? I appreciate you *nursing* me back to health; but I'm better now. Is it necessary for you to **still** be sitting next to me?"

Kwame said while standing up and holding out his hand, "I can take a hint. Besides, this is our stop. May I?"

I turned up my nose and refused while looking away. Through the window I watched Kwame as he stood in position. He was serious in really wanting to help me off of the bus. A thought ran across my mind of a saying my father has always told me. *A boy will be a boy, a gentleman will always be a gentleman but a man… a man will always remain a man to the woman he loves regardless of the things he and she go through.* After thinking this to myself I started to feel sick again. *I hope Kwame don't have those types of feelings for me. I'm not even attracted to him. Or am I? I did dream about him.*

Interrupting my thoughts, the bus driver said, "Young lady, we don't have all day. Are you going to take the gentleman's hand or what? I have to get this bus going."

Unhappy with the bus driver, I stood up and Kwame made the decision for me. Surprisingly, we were holding hands. And I didn't let go. I felt like we were playing follow the leader and he was it. His dark brown eyes were full of mystery but they reassured me I was safe. Kwame walked down the steps then turned around to guide me as if I was of royalty. We went for a walk and the whole time I was still in au. As the sun rose the sky was a mixture of orange, blue and yellow. I really didn't know how to feel at this moment. I never felt this feeling of butterflies and loss of breaths as his eyes snuck peaks at mine.

Pointing down the street he convincingly said, "There's a Bagel Brothers there and they have some delicious food. We can stop in if you like? It will be my treat?"

"Umm. I'm not sure that's a good idea."

"Well you weren't sure taking a walk would be a good idea either but you came along anyway. One bite isn't going to harm anything. It's not like I'm going to poison you. *And*, we can still *pretend* to not like each other the moment we get back to work. Deal?"

"Ummmmm."

He literally sat there begging for me to take his offer while I thought on it.

Ok. Sure. But, this is not a date!"

"Fine. Not a date. Gotcha."

Nothing else was said until we got to the restaurant. There was a long line of customers waiting to be served. The aroma of the food smelled delightful. The sight of a clean atmosphere made me feel extremely comfortable.

Kwame turned to me than asked, "Would you like to sit down and eat? We will get served a lot faster?"

"Sure. Why not? I don't have to clock in till 8am. Its only 7:15am."

He chose a table by the window. Kwame said he love to watch the clouds move through the sky.

I spoke with a smile as he pulled my chair out from under me, "And here it is I thought you were trying to show me off. Good choice."

Kwame giggled, "I couldn't have said it better."

The waiter walked over and asked "What can I get you two?"

Looking at Kwame I said, "I will take an orange juice please."

The waiter than asked, "What to eat?"

"I don't want anything to eat. Thanks anyway."

Kwame interrupted saying, "Are you sure? The food here is excellent and always help me to start my work day."

"That's understandable but by the looks of the line and those folks that are standing over there looking at their watch repeatedly; I don't think we will be eating anytime soon."

The waiter whispered, "I'd take her advice. She's a smart gal. I'd keep her if I was you."

Amazed at my attentiveness Kwame said, "Ok, well I will have an orange juice too." Pulling the waitress in closer to him, he whispered, "She's not my girlfriend. Not yet anyway."

The waitress looked at me than looked at him and said, "Whatever floats your boat," as she walked away.

"What was that all about," I asked.

"Before I tell you should I expect to get slapped," Kwame asked.

I placed my hand on my chin, leaned in closer and said, "Hum, well that depends on the answer you give me."

"In that case, I'd rather not tell you."

"Don't tell me you're scared of being hit by a…by a…girl."

Kwame mumbled, "You sure don't hit like one."

"What was that," I asked.

"Oh I was just saying, how you're quite a girl. A girl indeed."

"Now I don't believe that's true. I'm…going…to have to hit you," I yelled.

He covered his face to protect it. I laughed and laughed. Kwame peeked through his fingers to see if I was serious or playing another joke. It took minutes before he uncovered his face. Watching me as I continued to laugh, he was in shock. He couldn't believe as mean as I had been to him that I actually had a sweet, charming side. Kwame also flashed back to our entrance just a little while ago into Bagel Brothers and how in less than five minutes I was able to tell how things were going in a restaurant I had never been to.

I only know this because he told me so. He also said he was truly amazed. All those qualities I possessed made him like me that much more.

Kwame continued watching me as if he just fell in love. Eventually I stopped laughing and noticed just how comfortable he had gotten. His staring at me started to make me feel nervous. I felt that feeling of butterflies again. Immediately gaining my composure I began to look out of the window. Through the reflection I was able to see Kwame, who was still staring at me. It was beginning to make me feel uncomfortable.

Like I was backed into a corner that I couldn't get out of; or as if I saw someone that I seriously disliked.

Turning to Kwame," Can you stop?"

Looking innocently, Kwame replied, "Stop what?"

"Staring."

"What's wrong with me staring?"

"It's rude," I snapped.

"What's rude about me starring at you?"

"It makes me feel weird?

"Weird like how?"

Becoming irritated with the whole ordeal I said, "Why is it every time I ask you a question you ask me one back?"

"Well…truth of the matter is…you make me nervous too."

Glancing pass him, towards the waitress that was coming our way, I said, "I bet you say that to all the girls?"

"Nope. Just you," he said as the waitress got between us securing him from me.

Placing our drinks down she said, "Here is your orange juice," as she served me my drink. "And here is your orange juice and bill," she said while placing it in Kwame's hand, as she smiled at me as if saying, *I got your back.*

Kwame laughed saying, "You females sure do stick together."

The waitress winked her eye as if to say, *you can take it from here* as she walked away.

Smiling at Kwame, I agreed, "Yes we do."

Gulping my drink and looking at my watch, I noticed it was seven twenty two. *Wow, time sure does fly.* I thought to myself.

Kwame than looked at his and implied, "Wow. Pretty soon it will be time to clock in. What do you say we go for another walk when we're done here?"

"Sure. Why not?"

Just as we finished our orange juice the waitress had returned.

"Is everything ok? Do you need anything else?"

"Everything is fine. Thanks," Kwame said as he pulled out his wallet. "Do I give you the money for our bill, or take it to the cashier?"

"I can take it for you; but you know that requires a tip," the waitress giggled.

"Good, cause I had planned on giving you one. I love your personality by the way."

"Thanks. I get that a lot. That's one of the glories of me being me."

"Yes it is," Kwame said as he stood up after pulling out a ten dollar bill.

"I'll be back with your change."

"No need to. Keep it," Kwame replied as he pulled my chair from under the table and guided me to a standing position.

Leaning over towards me the waitress said, "Girl you better keep him. Don't too many men offer to take on the responsibilities of paying a bill, let alone, give a tip. He's a good man. But I'm sure you know that already."

"Jennifer, I need your help," someone yelled.

"Welp, that's me. I really enjoyed being of service to you two and won't forget you. Yall have a good day as you have truly made mine."

―――――――――――――――――――――――――――――――――

Kwame reached out for my hand than led the way. Looking at his watch, we had thirty minutes left before our shift started. He opened the door for me to go through; than followed. We strolled down the street, hand in hand, swinging them back in fourth, sneaking smiles at each other intermittently. After hiking for five minutes, I spotted a park in the distance.

"Hey, there's a park ahead. Do you know if it has swings?" I asked Kwame.

"I'm pretty sure it does. Would you like to go take a look?"

"Would I? I love to swing. It's something about being so high up in the air," I said as I pulled Kwame in the direction of the playground.

Sitting down on the swing and looking at Kwame, I said "Aren't you going to sit down?"

Looking uncomfortable, Kwame answered, "Nah. I think I'm just going to enjoy pushing you.

I retorted, "Ok," as I began to move my legs back and forth.

There was silence after Kwame pushed me. The whole time I couldn't help but think *If he touches my butt one time, I am going to brake his hands.* But Kwame had some thinking of his own going. He was quiet, but I could tell something was on his mind.

Higher and higher I went till I was able to lay my head back and see Kwame behind me. This always made me feel so dizzy. Also frightened me too but I still loved to do it. Checking his watch as I went up into the air he said we had about ten minutes left. He told me he was going to help me stop my swing and for me not to hit him. Of course I laughed and told him that depends on how he stopped me. Chuckling too my swing was captured and held on to. The speed of it dragged him so many feet backwards before finally coming to a complete stop. When it ended, Kwame was holding me in his arms, or at least it felt that way. His body was next to mine. I could feel his heart as it began to beat fast. Could smell his sweet cologne and even the soap that he used. What than felt like I was daydreaming brought me to reality causing me to jump out of the swing as if I had seen a ghost.

"What's wrong," Kwame asked as he walked towards me.

"Nothing. I just got dizzy, that's all. I'm ready to go to work now. To go file some papers and…um…" I said refusing his hand as he held it out.

How could I hold his hand when my palms were sweaty? I was extremely nervous; feeling worst now, than I did when I had butterflies. What is that feeling? I wondered.

When we arrived at work, Kwame gave me a hug and told me to have a great day. He also said how much fun that he had and he would love to do it again if we could. I countered, maybe, as I was uncertain about anything towards the future.

Discipline

Another short day at work as I finished my assignment early. The whole time I couldn't help but to think about Kwame. It felt as if he was becoming an everyday routine. I've only known him for two days and the past two days seems like an eternity. First I fell into his arms, then there was the dream, next being resurrected from a fainting spell followed by breakfast and the park. Way too many encounters for me and in just two days.

On the way home I was convinced to have a talk with my dad. *I wouldn't dare talk to my mom. She wouldn't understand.* My dad and I always had a close relationship. The saying is girls are more attached to their father's than they are their mothers and likewise for boys being more attached to their mothers. There's also another saying that the reason in being so is that on an intimate level they want their mothers or fathers without knowing. Not sexually, but attention and affectionate wise. I don't know how much I agree to that. I couldn't imagine wanting my father. Yuck! He is not my style. Besides the point, he was so soft hearted and let my mom wear the pants in the house. *When will he ever wake up*, I asked myself in thoughts. I'm not saying to beat my mom or slap her around. I'm not even saying to be rude and disrespectful to her. I just wanted him to put his foot down sometimes and let her know when he disagrees with her, mainly because she *is* wrong. What high hopes do I have? He'll never do it. What a loser!

During times like this I wished my mom and I could have had a better relationship. Mainly so I can ask her things such as what does that butterfly feeling mean? And why did my hand become sweaty and I kind of felt weak in the knees when he was holding me?

These were questions meant strictly for mothers because fathers just wouldn't understand. My dad and I might have gotten along but I don't think he would like the fact of me and Kwame spending time together; then again, who knows.

I knew at some point in my life I needed to forgive her, I just didn't know when that time would have been. There was so much that she could have told me from a woman's point of view but neglected to. All this time I've been pretty much raising myself or listening to the advice my daddy gave. I wished I could have got into her head so I could understand why she was the way that she was. *Did she always have to be so mean? Is it necessary to be so controlling and clean all the time? Why she never wanted me? Etc. etc.* I wanted to gather my pride and talk to her but didn't know how to approach my mother. Maybe I will just talk to her instead of my dad when I get home. See if we can start over and begin a new chapter in our life. Got to start somewhere.

Gasping for a breath of fresh air I begin to think about Kwame again. So far he had so many qualities my dad would want for a boy to have when it comes to me. *His princess*, I smiled. I know he will be pleased. Like I said Kwame was polite, respectful, a gentleman, romantic in a way and sweet. Then again, I really didn't know how he would feel. I wasn't even fourteen yet and felt like I've found the boy of my dreams. I've heard a lot of grown-ups say that every boy is made for a particular girl. In hopes of that particular girl being me, I sighed as I fell asleep.

When I awoke my watch read one fifteen pm. I looked out the window and did not notice the location we were in. Dang it; where was Kwame this time when I needed him? I bet he wouldn't have let me overslept and I'm almost positive he knows the stop I enter and depart. Looking in front of me, the doors on the bus was closed and the driver wasn't anywhere in sight. Beginning to feel my heart beat fast I laid my head back against the walls of the bus and relaxed. *Maybe I am still asleep*, I thought to myself. As I began to calm down, I heard a jerk of the entrance in front of me and quickly sat up. The bus driver entered with a Snapple in his hands, looked at me and nearly jumped out of his skin.

"Hi little lady, you nearly caused me to piss my pants," he said shifting over to catch his breath. "Did you pay your fare?"

Confused, I said, "Pay my fare? I fell asleep on the bus and missed my stop."

Taking a seat behind the wheel while conversating through his mirror, he said, "Oh...That's right. I had forgotten all about you. This is what I'm going to do. Usually, when fare is paid to ride the bus, you would have to exit the either before lay over, or at the time of lay over. But because you and I are the only two people on the bus and I'm sure you're not going to tell anyone, we'll pretend like you've already paid. Ok?"

"Yes sir. Thank you."

Turning around in his seat with a reflection of his eyes on me in the mirror, he asked, "Now you're not going to tell anyone right?"

Nervously, I responded, "Yes sir...I mean no sir. Un un. Not a soul."

At this point in time I didn't know what to think. Rather to be thankful that I didn't have to pay fare again or run scared. My heart began to beat faster and faster as I continued to think about what just happened. *If he wanted to hurt me he would have did so,* I mentally bargained with myself. *If he…wanted…to hurt…me…he…would… have…did so,* I said with a panicky whisper as I breathe in and out between each set of words while my eyes were closed. *If he wanted… to hurt…me…he would have…did so,* I continued almost relaxed. *If he wanted to hurt…me…he would have did so,* I repeated in a soft, calm, whisper. Feeling the sweat that had formulated dripping down my face I wiped it away. My heart had finally slowed to its normal beat causing my chest to stop hurting and my breathing to remain customary. *If he wanted to hurt me he would have did so,* I softly said as strong and mighty as ever.

After overcoming this small incident the bus began to slowly switch gears and move. Walking towards the driver, while looking for a schedule, I asked him when we would arrive to Washington Lane. The driver said within thirty minutes. That was all I needed to hear. Thirty minutes away from my stop with no book to read, cell phone to use or Kwame to talk to. Wait, Kwame to talk to? We weren't that cool yet; were we?

Pacing back to my seat I decided to look out the window and wait patiently till it was time for me to ring the bell. I was actually glad I did; there were tons of things for teenagers to do that I was unaware of. Not that I went any where but maybe one day when I had nothing else to do, I could get out of the house and check it out. Ooh, and there goes a Busken Bakery. My favorite cookie is the sugar cookies with the yellow icing and the black smiley face on top. They are soooo good. Thinking about them made my stomach growl, which also made me think about my favorite doughnut, which is the long, glazed one with maple icing on top and maple filling inside. Imagining the taste of it caused me to slobber a little. Deciding to sit back in my seat I held onto my stomach. I couldn't wait to get home. Within the same breath I went from feeling hungry to feeling home sick. Nauseous as if I was going to hurl any moment now. Becoming dizzy I laid my head against the wall of the bus and closed my eyes.

My eyes were closed but I could hear the voice of the bus driver very clear. He continued to call for me and what felt like I was asleep became reality as I awoke.

"Young lady," The bus driver said as he was trying to get my attention from his seat. "Young lady, I believe this is your stop," he said while pointing out of the window. "Washington Lane," he continued as I laid there unable to remember my exact location.

Nearly crawling out of my skin, I jumped up out of my seat and got off of the bus while telling the driver thanks. He beeped as he pulled off to send the message that I was welcome. The streets were busy causing me to have to wait to cross. Getting home couldn't have come any quicker. In the back of my mind, I had the strength I needed to talk to my mom and dad. Once the streets finally cleared and the thought went across the brain to cross, my leg went up but came to a complete halt. My parents saw me as they turned the corner and pulled over suggesting for me to get in.

"Hey mom, hey dad," I said while placing a kiss on both of their cheeks.

My mother was totally astonished at the fact I'd just called her mom. I don't know what came over me or what caused me to say it, I just did. She couldn't drive off without looking at me through the rear view mirror.

"What's gotten into you," she asked. "Or should I say who?" I overheard her mumble.

Bitch, I wanted to say but I wasn't that disrespectful.

"Well….since you asked and we're all here, I'm going to tell you," I said while sitting up close with my arms on both the passengers and driver's seat. "I met a boy."

She had just begun driving before screeching our tires to come to a complete stop. Her and my dad just looked at each other. For the rest of the ride home no one said anything. I didn't know what else to say after the quiet treatment. This was unlike *them*. Well maybe not her but most definitely my dad. She tried to be strict, bossy and evil when it came to certain things but I never listened. My dad on the other hand was a different story. He always said *something*. It might have been in a calm tone but it was enough for me to feel disciplined in a way.

I am getting older and boys are going to be a part of my life. We'll go to school together, sit in the same class, walk pass one another, work and play on the playgrounds together; it's impossible for me to avoid a whole race of teenage boys. At some point in my life they are going to have to let me grow up. I understood that I was their only child but they needed to understand this is my social life. This is what I want and am going to do. Maybe not than, if it's up to my father; but eventually.

Sitting back in my seat imagining all of the awful things the two would have to say once we got home, I couldn't help but to roll my eyes. The way they were reacting was pathetic, but I dare not speak it aloud. After a five minute drive we were home. My mother jumped out of the car while it was still in drive and told my father to handle me. My father infuriated by her actions, put the car in park just before it crashed into our home. He chased after my mom and slammed the front door behind him. I could hear them arguing and for the first time my dad was wearing the pants of the house. He finally came back to reality and told her a few things she needed to know about herself. She *stinked*; bad and have been for quite some time now. Moments later, my father came back to the car and said we were leaving for a while. Just he and I. He told me to get into the front seat and buckle up.

A part of me wanted to root him on and tell him how happy I was that he finally fixed the winch who stole Christmas. Knowing that my dad wasn't his self though I did as I was told. No questions asked.

We must have road around for hours. He seemed to keep circling a particular street. Eventually I got the courage to ask him why.

"Dad, this seems to be a nice street."

"Yeah, I know," he said with a scratch in his throat.

"We've road around this same block for at least the past fifteen minutes. And you keep looking at a particular house," I said as we were beginning to approach it again. "That house right there," I pointed. "What's up with that house? Why do you keep looking at it?"

"Don't worry about it honey. It's nothing; really. Just a bunch of old memories is all," he said as he finally drove off.

We drove five minutes down the road before pulling into a park. My dad switched the gears to the car and asked me to get out.

"Why?" I asked.

"BECAUSE I SAID SO," he shouted! "I am sick and tired of you and your mother going at each other's throats daily for my love and attention. She is my queen you are my princess. The two of you will never become any more or any less than the other. So....STOP IT."

I was completely speechless. My father never raised his voice at me. He may have disciplined me emotionally or mentally but raising his voice was something he just didn't do.

"Honey I love you. And I love your mom. This park is where your mom and I met. I guess I didn't realize that one day my little girl would grow up," he said with a teary eye. "Your mother and I only want what's best for you. You're not even fourteen yet. Haven't had a job for more than a couple of days but you've already met a boy that you really like," he announced while looking out of the window. "Do you know how hard it is to except something like that?"

I continued to listen with my arms crossed. I was beginning to feel disgusted by the conversation. After our *long* father daughter talk he drove us back home. While turning the ignition off my father said for me to go to my room for the night. When we walked into our house it was full of smoke and candles were lit everywhere. Making my way up the stairs I noticed my mother sitting on the couch smoking a cigarette.

Running down the stairs, I screeched, "Mom, what are you doing?"

"Smoking. What does it look like?" She responded with arrogance.

"You're smoking?" I asked with a lot of questions going through my mind.

"You're smoking?" She repeated. "Sister it's a lot you don't know about your dear mommy."

At that point my father stepped in and took the cigarette out of her hand. Than he looked at me.

Walking away, "I know, I know. Go to your room."

He continued to watch me as I watched him anxiously awaiting the results for my mother. I couldn't believe how she behaved. And what did she mean by *it's a lot you don't know about your dear mommy?* I entered my room and attempted to crack the door. My father shouted for me to close the door all of the way. Once he heard my door click into place I assume he began to talk to my mom quietly. For the longest I listened but couldn't hear anything. No voices, movement, not a sound. Becoming restless I laid in bed and looked at my ceiling as I always do. Eventually I fell asleep.

Change of Plans

It's the day of my birthday and I have been having a wonderful week minus yesterday's wild evening. I started my first job Monday. Tuesday I got treated to breakfast. I wonder what today has in store. *Hopefully nothing dealing with my dad*. No wild surprises. No goofy birthday cakes. No *stupid* kiddy presents.

I was running five minutes behind and knew there was no way possible I would make the bus. Kwame and I agreed yesterday to catch the same bus together this morning. Hopefully the bus is running late, I thought to myself, as I ran as fast as I could. Recklessly I continued until I saw the bus past me by. The light up ahead was red. Mentally I saw myself flying. Felt myself move swift but without my body doing any work. Before I could grasp a breath of air, I was at the front door of the bus. The driver looked at me, than looked at the light which had just blinked green. She paused as the passengers waited anxiously for her decision. Would she allow me to board the bus, or will she be a no-heart having, self-less bitch and pass an innocent teenager by? She looked at me one last time while saying, "I'm sorry," than attempted to drive off. Because her thought process took so long within her decision, the stoplight turned yellow causing her to have to wait for the next green light. As my adrenaline began to increase more, first by trying to get the bus and second by the broken heart I felt, I darted across the street to the next bus stop that wasn't too far away.

I can't miss this buss I pleaded with myself using every ounch of strength I had left.

It seems as if the red stop light waited exactly until I got to the bus stop before it turned green. The closer I got to the stop the more my heart felt it was going to burst through my skeleton than pass my skin like in the movie Alien. Now standing at the bus stop I was beginning to huff and puff trying my best to capture air and hold it in. My chest ached horribly as the pain was unbearable. A horrible cough had come across and I knew without a doubt in my mind I was having an asthma attack.

At least that's what I thought at that point in time before I ended up in the hospital.

Before I knew it, my body begged for breath one last time and I was on the ground without remembering how I got there. After about ten seconds, I was unconscious; never seeing if I made the bus.

As I was under, or asleep if you will I dreamed of meeting Kwame. For some reason my body attempt to tell me my location; which was on the bus, when I knew that wasn't true. My last memory was of me falling down to the ground and seeing the sight if the bus await for the light before reaching me.

Anyway, he greeted me on the bus and was extremely happy to see me kissing my lips. *Whoa, when did we start kissing?* My conscious began.

"I'll be paying her fare," he told the driver.

The funds were administered with a smile and we took our seats.

"I'm glad you were able to make it? I haven't been able to sleep all night?"

"Yea, neither have I," I said looking out of the window.

"What's wrong?"

"Nothing. Just nervous I guess."

"Why nervous? We're not doing anything we haven't already done."

What did he mean by that? What did we already do?

"I know," I said kissing his lips.

He returned the favor by placing his tongue into my mouth. Excited I allowed it to enter and fight with mines. We tongue wrestled until he placed his hand on my chest cupping my breast.

"Wait a minute?" I motioned.

"What's wrong? I always do this when I kiss you," he alleged with his hand still in position.

"No, no. That's not what I'm talking about. My chest had begun to hurt a little bit."

"Well what did it feel like?"

"Like someone was pushing into it."

"Baby," he smooched between words. "You...don't have...anything... to worry about. I...am what...you need...to focus...on right...now," he bite into my bottom lip gently.

Wait, he is overstepping his boundaries. Why didn't I slap him by now?

Kwame climbed on top of me and began to unbutton my shirt. Tongue kissing my neck than moving up and down my chest. Looking out of the window things suddenly shifted from day to night. It caught my attention but I was so wrapped in what Kwame was doing it was impossible to stop.

Uncovering my right breast he begin to nibble on my nipple. It made me extremely excited as I begin to feel moisture against my legs. Unstrapping my braw then removing it completely from my body he just stared at my nudity.

"Damn girl you are so beautiful," he taking his shirt off. "Stand up."

I did as was told and he pushed me up against the back door of the bus. Kissing me ever so seductively as I fell victim to his demands. Kwame turned me around then brushed his body up against mine.

"Ouch," I screamed.

"What's wrong this time?" he begin to become impatient.

"I felt that pain again except this time it was much sharper than the last time."

"Oh you about to feel some pain alright," he said grinding his jewels up against my ass so I could feel how excited he was.

"Daaammmn. That feels like more than I can take."

"Oh you gone take this," he said unzipping his pants and pulling it out for me to see.

"Dadammmnnn. Un un Kwame. I can't do this."

"You did it before and took it just fine. I didn't even make you squeal the way I would have like to," he suggested pulling my pants off.

Turning me to face him as he placed the condom on he smiled.

"One could never be safe."

Putting my hands over my head he licked my lips. Than pulled my hair as he gnawed at my neck and breast. Looking me into my eyes he picked me up and held on to my ass as I wrapped my legs around him. Slowly and gently placing his gems inside I moaned. Teasing me inch by inch while tenderly caressing my pussy he took his sweet time. Damn he felt so good as my body showed through vibration.

"UNH," I moaned tilting my head back; except it wasn't for Kwame.

The pain had returned feeling as if I was electrocuted.

"OK I NEED EVERYONE TO STAND BACK! I CAN'T TAKE A CHANCE ON HAVING TO HELP SOMEONE ELSE DUE TO CARELESSNESS. UNDERSTAND?" I heard someone say out of no where.

Kwame pound harder and harder as my body went up and down. Kissing at my breast, biting my lips and neck became a habit. His head kept going back, forth, left and right as he made faces of pleasure. He walked me up and down the aisle of the bus as it drove. Getting the hang of things I begin to ride him as hard as I could take it. He became weak in the knees as he took a seat on one of the side benches.

"IS EVERYONE CLEAR?"
"WE'RE ALL CLEAR!"

I heard the noise again but could not stop. The quivering of my body wouldn't allow me to.

"Oh shit…Oh shit…ohhhh," Kwame continued. "I told you, you could take this dick. Take this dick…ohhhh shit….yea ride that dick just like that…um…" Kwame continued in total excitement.

"Ohhhhhhh shhhhiiiittttttttt," we said on the verge of climaxing.

"OHHHHHHHHHHH," I shouted.

My vision begins to clear as I coughed and gasped for air. Looking straight ahead I could see people surrounding me and a helicopter. From that point on I don't remember what happened because I blacked out.

My stay in the hospital lasted about a week. Things could have been worst then what you've already been told about our encounters but I was actually thankful for the accident. Because of it, Kwame and I didn't have to sneak around and my parents became closer than ever.

They were able to communicate about the time that Kwame and I had spent together for breakfast without one belittling the other. They said I was growing up and trusted me to make mature decisions. Due to their trust and their support for Kwame and I, we began to tell them any plans that we wanted to complete.

Following my accident, my mother began to take me to work and pick me up, *when I was ready*. My father straightened her out real well and became the man of the house. After meeting Kwame and seeing what type of guy he was my father respected him a lot. He said that Kwame was an old soul in a young mans' body because there weren't anyway, these young boys around here knew anything of how to treat a lady. My father also said that no ordinary young man would stay in the hospital as long as he had to assist in taking care of me. The longer our conversation lasted, the more I was beginning to seriously like Kwame. *It was only natural for me to, right?* A father knows best, as I always say.

July 13th marked our one month anniversary. Kwame and I have been closer than ever; but, *still* friends. Daddy always said, *the way to a man heart is to make him use his imagination.* I guess in this situation he's using his thoughts because I know he want me to be his girlfriend. And as long as I keep him waiting, he will respect and appreciate me more when I finally do tell him that I'm ready for that. Which in this sense, I'm only fourteen. A boy is the last thing on my mind. I like having Kwame as a friend but I'm not ready for a boyfriend type of a friend yet. I mean, what type of things do you do with boyfriends that you can't do with your regular boy friend? Why do we have to put a title on our friendship anyway? That's just ridiculous. Nothing would change between us and I think he knows that deep down. That's why I believed he agreed to take his time with me. Cause daddy said, *if a man only wants to get between your legs, that's all he's gone be good for, is getting between your legs.* All of daddies saying have truth to it. But Kwame works too hard to please me so obviously he don't want that down there. *Do he?* Well, I'm sure one day he would like to. Maybe even I would like to.

To celebrate it, Kwame bought me a total of six Lilies. Four for each week we've spent together and two for the close calls we encountered. I thought it was the sweetest thing. Because we stayed in the same neighborhood and I discovered the movie theater close to us he treated me to a show of *Northern Lights* where a guy died leaving things to unfold amongst the friends. It was extremely good.

Holding the glass door as I walked through, he said, "What movie would you like to see?"

"Something romantic."

"You…a romantic watching movie girl. Yea right," he spat.

I giggled because he caught my bluff.

"You know me entirely too well. I'm actually a horror fan."

"You don't seem like that type of person either. More so like a person of comedy, suspense, action or thriller. How are you a horror fan when you're not easily scared?"

"Don't know, just am."

We made it to the front desk and he ordered two tickets. Than we walked hand in hand to the concession stands; ordering a bucket of popcorn, a box of sour patch kids, two hotdogs wrapped in pretzels and a huge cup of Dr. Pepper to drink.

He truly was a charming boy.

Walking down the halls to the room that our movie would be showing Kwame saw an acquaintance.

"Whoa, Kwame who is this," he asked shaking Kwame's hand.
"This is…" he said kissing my hands "Karma."
"Dag Karma you got it like that?"

I smiled at Kwame and allowed him to speak.

"Yea she does," he blushed.
"Ok well I'll let you two go than brah."
"Yea you do that; and make sure when you walk past that your eyes stay ahead of you."

Recalling that moment made me smile because he took a stand for his woman; telling his friend not to be disrespectful by checking me out.

"Thanks," I kissed his cheek.

His face flushed as he continued to walk.

"Thanks for what?"

"For what you said back there."

"I was serious," he laughed. "And he knows I was; that's why he walked without looking back."

"So Kwame is big man on campus, huh?"

"Naw not really. Kwame just goes after what he wants especially when he thinks it's worth it," he smiled.

"Jerk. You are such a suck up."

"I know. Did it work?"

"No," I paused. "Well maybe a little. Let's just find a seat," I suggested as he guided me through the dark aisles.

"Where do you prefer; front, back or middle and which side?"

"Wherever you want to sit; it doesn't matter. Long as I'm not too close."

"How about here," he directed sitting in the middle of the mid section.

"Hungry?" he asked handing me the hotdog.

"Sure," I countered. "Starving actually."

"Let me know when you're thirsty. I'll provide moisture to your lips."

"And how do you plan to do that?"

"Like this," he said placing the cup of Dr. Pepper to my mouth.

I thought he was going to kiss me but I was wrong. It actually hurt my feelings that he didn't; at this point I've been hovering over those sexy brown lips of his. Maybe he feared one kiss would lead to other things that he just wasn't ready for, I tried to think outside of the box.

He had no intentions in doing so at all. The whole time he was very respectful and asked for permission to even hold my hands during the movie. We giggled at the funny parts and shoved each other back and forth. By the time the movie was over he planned to take me out for ice cream. Pizza and ice cream that is but if you ask me I think he wasn't ready to let me leave just yet.

Kwame led me to a pizza restaurant titled Mama Yum. He said she had the best Pizza throughout the state of Kentucky and could make you an ice cream cone that would make you want to slap your momma. Not literally, but figuratively speaking.

"Two seats please," he said to the waitress who had her back turned against us from a distance.

"Follow me," she said before turning around to see who her customers were.

She eyeballed me then looked at him. I could tell by the look he was giving her back he was becoming uncomfortable.

"Follow me," she stated again but in a different perspective.

"I know her," he stopped in his tracks." She's probably staring because I used to date her. Only difference is, we didn't do the things you and I do. I didn't even talk to her on the phone. She was just a name; my girl friend at the time. You on the other hand will be my girlfriend; the one whom I'd continue to take on dates. Continue to buy Lilies for…Call every night, twice a night or more if I'm able and so much more."

I didn't know what to say so I didn't say anything. Hearing about him dating another woman just to have the title made me feel a little uncomfortable. How did I know he wasn't going to do me the same way? Just because he say's things are different don't mean that they really are. Right?"

"Are you okay," he asked.
"Yes, I'm just feeling a bit dizzy."
"Well how about I go head and get you home," he suggested calling me a cab.
"Are you sure? What about you?"
"I'm more concerned for you. Besides the point I plan on getting

in the cab with you. Not to follow you home or anything, just to make sure you make it in safely."

"I don't think that's a good idea Kwame."

"Yea, maybe you're right. How about I allow the cab to take me home, then you'll know where I live and have the taxi take you home afterwards?"

"That sounds better."

"Fine. That's exactly what we'll do," he placed my head on his shoulder as he carried me outside.

We Meet Again

It's the evening before our last night of seeing each other. Hoping one of us would do the honors was impossible. We both feared rejection; madly in love with one another but afraid to say so. The kisses I'm sure we both foresee haven't come. Even when we hug it's from a distance.

Admitting that Kwame does something more than making me weak in the knees was harder than anticipated although I think he knew. He'd touch my hand and I nearly shiver as if cold. When our eyes met it was like a mother seeing her newborn after birth. Kwame filled my soul with joy. Something that I never knew existed. So naturally there's no way I could get any sleep with thoughts of never seeing him again on my mind.

I've never had sex but he made me feel so comfortable that I wanted to. Not to mention the dreams that I had of us doing so; which seemed so real. It's hard to explain where those unconscious thoughts came from being that I've never watched anything like so or experienced it for myself. My thoughts just seemed to takeover leaving the rest of oblivious.

I was asleep for maybe five minutes when my cell phone rung.

Wait a minute? I have a cell phone? When? How? From whom?

The song, Could This Be Love by Bob Marley was playing indicating that the caller was Kwame.

"Hello," I answered in a tired voice.
"Hi sleepy head."
"Hey baby what's up?"

Wait a minute…did I just call him baby? When did we start this? And he let me?

"I wanted to know if I could come over? I missed you and needed some of your sweet everlasting kisses. The ones from earlier must be wearing down."

And he's been to mu house? No way. Did he just say we kissed? What was it like?

"Sure, just climb up the ladder like you usually do."

Am I allowing him to sneak into my bedroom or is it okay for him to be here?

"In that case here I am," he said looking at me through the window.
"Dang it Kwame! I told you about doing that you scared the crap out of me!" I said giving him a hard slap to the face.
"Oooh," he moaned. "You know I love it when you're feisty. It gets me hot; see," he said looking down at his jewels.

Naturally my eyes followed towards the direction he was looking in. His dick was sticking straight out and when I grabbed it he tilt his head back in a moan.

"Do we like that?" I tugged bringing him closer to me.
"Uumhum."

Kissing his lips than moving my tongue up and down his neck I pressed my body into his instantly becoming wet.

"Is this what you want?"
"More than anything," he mumbled.

Kwame gave me a rough kiss suggesting he's going to take things from here. He picked me up and began to nibble all over my chest before lying me down on the bed. Standing over me with his eyes doing the undressing he climbed on top. I was wearing my pink and white pajama dress that had "Kiss Me" written over the shirt and on the back of my buttocks.

"So you want me to kiss you huh?" he asked reading my shirt.
"Uumhum," I begged like a puppy dog.
"What if I wanted to do more?" he closed in on my face just a whisper away from my lips.
"More like what?"
"I don't want to tell you. Just go with the flow," he smooched me. "You can trust me. I'd never…" he spoke between words tongue kissing me. "Do…anything…to…hurt…you."

The last kiss was the most seductive. My heart unraveled beneath as he gently guided me into a lying down position. With his teeth my dress were pulled up above my waist line.

"No panties on huh?"

"What?" I responded nervously before catching on to what he was saying. "Oh, that's right. I never wear them when I go to bed."

"Never?"

"Never."

"Hum, looks like I'm going to have to start coming over here more often," he suggested circling around my navel.

Getting on his hands and knees he began to kiss circles around my tummy. I pulled his hair with each intense nibble. Lowering his tongue until he's at my thighs I began to moan uncontrollably.

"You like that?" he asked with a whisper. `

"Uumhum."

"Can I take it further?"

"Yes…wait. What are you going to do?"

"You trust me right," he asked sucking on my inner thigh that was closest to my vagina.

It felt so good that I couldn't stop moaning to answer his question. He continued nibbling and biting causing my body to tremble. Pausing to allow me to catch a breath I felt his breath against my gem. Blowing against the lips of my essence his tongue entered slowly causing me to scream loudly.

"OH SHIT."

Kwame giggled flickering his tongue inside of me. Mind you this was the first time I ever experienced something so extravagant. In and out, tickling places that I never knew existed; licking the very inner part of my lips around my clitoris. Moaning out of control as I pulled my hair I felt a tingly feeling.

"Kwa…meeee," I moaned.

(Beep…Beep…Beep) I heard a noise vibrate.

"Keep going," he licked between words.
"Are…are you…sure?"

(Beep…Beep…Beep) it continued.

"Release it."
"Ooooohhhh. Uuunnnnnh."

(Beep…Beep…Beep) I rolled over to hit the clock that interrupted my focus. Looking down at my pillow that I chewed was a simple indication I was dreaming. Searching my room with my eyes in hopes of continuing what we started was a drag.

"Stupid clock! Stupid, stupid clock. I didn't even get to finish."

There was a pause as I attempted to go back to sleep. Unfortunately it never works that way and all I could recall was the last bit of the dream. Screaming Kwame's name and feeling my body shake uncontrollably.

"Our last day of being together and this is how you REPAY ME!" I sat up and yelled.
"Babydoll are you ok," my father asked after knocking first.
"Yea dad I said trying to hide the mess on my bed."
"Is it okay for me to come in?"
"NO…I mean, it's just that I was in the middle of getting dressed… getting dressed," I whispered to myself looking at the clock. "I GOTTA GET DRESS!" I yelled in an outburst again.
"Okay honey I'm coming in."

I ran to the bathroom grabbing anything to throw on as quickly as possible out of my closet on the way. My father was snooping around but I guess he didn't find anything because he was quiet. My bedroom door clicked closed, or so I thought, until I opened the bathroom door and saw my father sitting on my bed.

"There you are Princess," he said. "Well you look okay. Want to tell me why your bed is wet?"

"Damn it!" I mentally sighed.

"I had an accident dad. It's a bit embarrassing. Can you PLEASE not tell mom?" I asked with my lips poking out.

That always worked with him.

"Fine. Just make sure you clean it up before you go to work. Wouldn't want your mother coming in after me to find what I found," he suggested leaving out of my room.

"Damn Kwame," I pouted. "This is your fault. I don't even know what happened to me last night. I do remember how good it felt," I smiled laying back in bed.

"Karma, are you ready?" my mother asked with a knock.

"Just a few more minutes," I suggested caressing over my bed.

"Okay. I'll be back in five minutes exactly."

"Yes ma'am."

There was a pause.

"What did you say?"

"I…just said yes ma'am," I repeated just catching on to what I had done.

My mother had worked so hard at giving me respect that I felt comfortable enough to respond to her with respect now. I knew she understood what had just happened and didn't want to overstep her boundaries. Her shoes shown beneath the door indicated she was lying against it.

"Five minutes."

"Ok."

My day dragged at work. This was the first day all month I was needed for a full shift. I had gotten used to getting off early and wasn't in the mood to be here today. Thoughts of Kwame troubled my mind. He was the real reason to why I didn't want to be bothered. Today was the day; the last day we'd spend together. No more gifts or being token out on dates. No more phone calls or sweet surprises after work. No more breakfast and lunch. No more Kwame period.

After I was finished I grabbed my things and waited for my mother outside at our destination. Fifteen minutes later someone grabbed me by the waist and I stumbled into their arms.

"Are you okay?" Kwame asked helping me to a standing position.

"Okay?" I asked with an angry look. "Yes. I'm fine...thanks," I said dusting myself off. "What are you doing here?"

"Uum...I work here too? Or at least I did being that today is our last day."

The both of us became emotional. It would be impossible to live without Kwame. I was beginning to have strong feelings for him. Love type of feelings.

From behind his back he pulled out a dozen of Lillies, each one in a different color.

"Awww, thank you," I responded; giving him a kiss on his cheek.

"That's a first," he mentioned gently caressing his cheek that was blushing. "I'm really going to miss you."

"Yeah...me too."

"Where's your mom? She's late isn't she?" Kwame asked looking at his watch.

"Yea she is. I wonder what's going on?"

"I have a hunch," he shrugged.

"Oh really…spit it out."

"What would you say if I told you I called your mom and asked if I could spend time with you ALL of today and brought you back home tomorrow?"

"I would say you're lying."

"Well, you wouldn't be wrong," he laughed. "But…I did ask if I could bring you home later than usual tonight and at first she became quiet. Your father actually suggested things would be okay."

"So?"

"Soooo, you are mine for the next," he said looking at his watch. "Eight hours I believe."

"No way?"

"Yes way. Oh and I apologize for being late I wasn't expecting to be needed as long as I were."

"That's ok. It was worth it."

Kwame smile became huge.

"First things first," he mentioned rubbing his hands together sneakingly. "We are going to my place."

"What? Wait a minute? Huh?"

"Yes Karma, my place. For there," he sanged in a sexy voice, "I have a gift especially for you."

"Really?"

"Yes ma'am. And I believe this is our driver rented for the whole day."

A Black Lexus stopped in front of us and the driver rolled down the window.

"A Mr. Wood I presume?" the driver said with a butler type of voice.

"Yes ma'am that will be correct."

"You may enter sir."

Kwame pulled the door open as always and buckled my seat belt. The lady driver smiled as she watched enthusiastically.

"Where to sir?"
"1511 London Lane please."
"Yes sir."

"How did you afford something like this?" I asked Kwame.
"I will tell you all of that at the end of our day; but for now, home we go."

It felt weird knowing Kwame lived just around the corner from me. I was beginning to think that was the only way he was able to pull something like this off.

"We are here sir; 1511 London Lane."
"Thank you madam," he said with a bow.

His house was gorgeous. It was three times as big as mine. They had two living rooms and dining areas, five bedrooms, four bathrooms, one huge kitchen, a balcony with a sofa set, a basketball court, tennis court, swimming pool, sauna and hot tub. It was the perfect place for anyone to ever want to live.

I was led into his bedroom which had a large box placed on top of his divan. It was wrapped in red and pink wrapping paper with a white and pink poky dot bow.

"Aren't you going to open it?" he asked in a charming voice.
"Open it? This is your house. I can't just come barging in and opening your things.
"What if I told you the gift was for you?"
"You're bluffing."

The look in his eyes suggested he was telling the truth.

"You are aren't you?"

"Bluffing? No; it's really for you. Open it."

I looked at him with huge puppy dog eyes while unwrapping the gift. It was draped so neatly. Everything was in perfect place. After taking the lid off I removed the pink tissue paper that covered what I had yet to find. Inside the gift was a beautiful spaghetti strapped orange and brown gown. It was long in length with flowers embedded all throughout.

"Do you like it?"

"Like it? I love it."

"Good. Dig further, there's more."

Removing the dress and placing it on the bed I saw red tissue paper. Once eliminated, there were two packages of earrings, a necklace and a small box.

"Oh my gosh they are beautiful," I smiled holding the earrings in my hands. "Why two packs?"

"Because I couldn't make up my mind on which one to get you so I got you both."

"That is so sweet. Thank you Kwame. I really appreciate all you have done for me though out the summer season. This has truly being the best summer of my entire life."

"Thank you and I'm not through yet. The day is just beginning. Why don't you open the box?"

Confiscating the box into my hands I lifted its lid. Underneath was a beautiful pink-gold ring with three diamonds on top.

"I wanted you to have something to remember me by," he said while I was choked for breath.

"Kwame this is beautiful but I can't accept this."

"Why not?"

"I don't think my parents would approve."

"Don't worry about your parents. I've already told them of everything I suggested on doing today and they were ok with it. Even us having sex."

"WHAT?"

"Just kidding," he chuckled over and over again. "But they do know of our plans and of the things that I bought you," he continued laughing. "You…should have…seen…your…face.

"It wasn't that funny. You better be glad this is our last day together or I wouldn't be so nice," I watched as he laughed nearly in tears. "Did they agree that I can take this?" I asked looking at the ring.

"Yes…here…let me place it on your finger."

Gently taking the ring out of the box he placed it onto my ring finger. It slid on without any indications of ever falling off.

"Isn't it bad luck to place a ring on your married finger if you're not married?" I asked looking at the ring.

"Well possibly; but in this case…no."

"Why not in this case?"

"Because I plan on making you my wife."

"Your wife! I'm too young to get married."

"Not now silly; but when we are able to. Like maybe eighteen," he said lying in bed.

He became so quiet that I could tell he was thinking about what he had just said. Marriage? Already? Wow. My life flashed before my eyes as well. Angels floating back and forth through out the room, pink and white roses displayed all over. Pink and white candles placed on each table. Large ones on ours with a lot of pink and white Rose pedals.

"Well I'll leave you to get dress," Kwame stood up.

"Wait a minute; what about my shoes?"

"Oh, I apologize. In the restroom that is through that door," he pointed to the left side of his room. "Is two pairs of dress shoes; again I couldn't make up my mind and some perfume. There's five bottles of it because I never smelled any scent on you and didn't know what you liked so I picked one of each smell but all different; totally different scents," he said grabbing his nose.

"Thank you," I responded in my sweetest voice.

He closed the door behind him than knocked.

"I'm not going to open the door; don't worry. I forgot to tell you no one's here. I didn't want you to have to worry about anyone barging in on you."

"Oh...ok. Thanks for letting me know."

His footprints that showed underneath the door way had now moved. It was safe to get dress. I felt so comfortable that I didn't bother locking the door. My clothes were pulled completely off. In the bathroom like he said were my shoes and the different scents. There was also a washcloth and towel. Taking a shower never felt so good at this point in time. Besides, I was eager being that he had a huge shower stall where I had plenty of space. There were two heads as well; maybe Bryant took showers here too? I also saw the extra bed in his room that could have also been for Bryant.

As I finished my shower and dried myself off the towel felt so warm and cozy. It was very fluffy and felt as if I was being hugged by a teddy bear. Walking into the bedroom I could smell a strong aroma entering underneath his doors. It smelled so lovely as my nostrils seemed to do little dances. After slipping into my dress, placing on the orange and silver earrings that made me look like a Goddess, stepping into the brown flats, and spraying the perfume titled Precious, I was on my way downstairs when suddenly Kwame knocked at the door.

"My lady are you ready?" he asked without turning the knob.

"His lady?" I whispered. "This evening couldn't get any better," I thought to myself. "Why don't you come in and find out?"

He opened the door and I gave a slight bow bending my knees. Kwame stood there as if his heart was stolen from his chest. His eyes went up and down my body and I could see the drool he attempted to wipe away.

"Wow, you look…you look…Wow!"
"I'd take that as a compliment."

Guided down the stairs I could see he was cooking in the kitchen.

"What are you cooking?"
"It's a surprise. When it's finished I am going to blind fold you and take you to a part of our house that is made specifically for events like this."
"What type of event is this?"
"Shhh…shhhh. In due time…in due time."

The clock read 4:45pm. I couldn't believe how fast time was going. Walking around the living room looking at pictures of him and Bryant when they were younger brought back memories of my own. They had the most beautiful family. His mom was gorgeous. Continuing to stare at the picture I couldn't help but to remember the familiarity of her. The more I concentrated on where I saw her; the more Kwame had his eyes on me. He looked a bit nervous as if there was something to hide.

"Is everything okay?" he hesitated.
"I saw this woman before. Is she your mother?"
"Her…uum…yes…yes she is."
"I've seen her; I don't know where but I have."
"Well we do live pretty close to you. Maybe that's how?"
"No…no. I've seen her…I thought…today."

"Foods ready," he said hoping to steer me in another direction. "I'm going to put this black blindfold around your eyes than lead you to a sacred place."

Kwame did as he said he would causing me to feel nervous and completely taking my mind off of his mother.

Feeling my knees buckling he asked, "What's wrong?"
"Nothing. I just never had an experience like this...that's all."

The room became quiet as I felt his body next to mind. He was embracing me in his arms as I started to become extremely panicky. I couldn't help but to think about the wet dream and how we were alone. All alone in this huge house. Unaccompanied and able to do whatever we liked.

"Now what's wrong?"
"I'm sorry...I'm just extremely anxious."
"And I'm not?"
"Well?"
"I am...very edgy. I thought if I hugged you it would make me feel better...as well as you."

We walked down some stairs and he guided my hands to the right side of the banister. Feeling the walls once we were down the steps he continued on our journey. It seemed as if we had walked for ever before finally reaching our destination.

"You may now take off your blindfold and look before your eyes."

Removing the blindfold was like walking into a room of flowers. The vision of everything was well thought. There were red and pink scented candles displayed all over the walls, tables and floors. Red and pink rose pedals were distributed on the table, chairs and around our seating area. Above the arrangements, red and pink lights were placed displaying a well beautifully lit room.

I took so much time in absorbing the beauty of his creation that he was able to gather our food and set the table.

"May I do the honors of seating you madam?" he asked in lure.
"Yes…you may."

Dinner was one large bowl of spaghetti and meatballs, one large bowl of salad with home made chopped bacon, shredded cheese, sliced carrots, onions, and fiery diced tomatoes. A plate of garlic bread also accompanied the meal.

Kwame and I took turns feeding each other the spaghetti and salad. When we got to the last strand of spaghetti it was super long. So we decided to share it by placing one end in his mouth and the other into mine. Sucking and slurping until our lips met we stopped as if not knowing what to do. Kwame looked at me for reassurance but the dream I had the night before caused me to do something different. I wasn't ready for sex and I didn't want things to get out of hand so I bit my piece of spaghetti and left Kwame to slurp the end on his own.

Looking at me with understanding eyes, he said, "Time for dessert," and clapped his hands.

Moments later the driver from earlier pushed a cart into the room with a lid covering a medium sized plate.

"Dessert is ready," she announced than left the room.
"She looks so familiar? I just can't seem to place it," I followed her with my eyes.
"Don't worry about it. Let's just eat our dessert."

He removed the lid from the plate and discovered a strawberry cheesecake swirl with a bowl of ice cream and smothered in cherry cordials.

"Oh…my…gosh…Tell me that's not cherry cordials on top of that ice cream?"

"That wouldn't happen to be your favorite…now would it?" he teased.

"You know I get out of control for some cherry cordials. And with vanilla bean ice cream?"

"Wow you're good. How did you know?"

"That's the best ice cream to eat with the cordials of course. Only a girl would know so."

The thought of Kwame's mother and the woman I just seen again seemed to make sense now. They both were the same person; his mom. Kwame saw the furious look that I was given him and knew it was time to confess.

"Karma…I need to tell you something."

"Too late," I suggested giving him the hint that I already know.

"Can I speak first?"

"She's your mom?" I asked enraged. "Your mom Kwame? Your mom?"

"Eehum…uumm…yes. She is; but I can explain."

"Explain…explain…you could have did that a long time ago."

Kwame clapped his hands signaling his mother to join us. That might have been the best thing for him to do at this point because I was becoming angrier by the moment. She came around the corner and smiled eager to finally get introduced.

"Karma…this is another beautiful woman in my life; my mother. And mom, this is the beautiful woman in my life; Karma," he tried to suck up.

At that point all I could do was blush. Not because I wanted to but because Kwame was in trouble when this was all over. I couldn't believe she was in on it the whole time and even willing to give up her home so Kwame could make this evening romantic. My parents would have never did such a thing. I'm lucky to even be here right now.

We shook hands and suggested how nice it was to finally meet each other. Kwame waited till things became calm and signaled her to leave the room so that we could talk. She was well prep as she knew exactly what to do.

"Karma I have something to tell you. Well…two things to tell you," he said turning to face me and holding my hands.

I remember thinking, "Oh boy, here we go again."

"To start things off, I can not cook. Well I can but not what I had prepared tonight; that was all my moms' idea. She knows how I feel about you and was willing to do so to help me please you more. So while you were showering and getting dressed she snuck back into the house and cooked this meal for us while I prepared our room."

"You said two," I mentioned sternly.

"Ok," he swallowed. "The second thing is I…I've been borrowing funds from my mom to get you some of the things that you have. Of course I will pay it all off and my mom knows this, that's why she agrees every time."

"Wow," I said snatching my hand from him. "You just gave me a hard pill to swallow. Are you sure that's everything? You didn't leave anything out?" I asked with my hands now crossed.

"Yes I am," he spoke in confidence. "You don't know how hard it was to keep something like this from you."

"Oh I can imagine," I motioned sarcastically.

"So Karma," his mother said walking into the room. "How did everything taste?"

"It was delicious Mrs." I glared at Kwame for not telling me her name or what to call her.

All I knew was that she was his mom. A damn good mother at that who wanted the best for her son and was willing to do whatever it took to make sure he got just that; the best.

"Mrs. Woods. But you can call me Momma Woods."
"Ok...Momma...Woods."
"I also spoke with your parents on Kwames' behalf so that is why you get to stay a bit longer."
"Is...that...so," I looked at Kwame with a *I thought you said that was everything* look.
"Well I'll give you two some time to get to know each other," he suggested feeling the vibe I was sending his way. "It's getting stuffy in here," he said walking out of the room trying to avoid looking at me.

In the end everything was well worth it. Kwame, his mother and I talked and laughed throughout the evening. She even had me show her how I kicked Bryant when he came in. Bryant was so pissed. He said he thought that day would have never returned and here he is reliving it and in his own house. Bryant became so disgusted that he went to his room and slammed the door.

Of course Kwame went to talk to him and we all apologized...after laughing once more. He wasn't happy but we were repaid for what we did. Bryant challenged us to a game of UNO. In their house he was known for kicking ass when it came to this sport. Everyone knew of it except for me so when he dared us I took him on. Because my big mouth didn't object to his challenge, Kwame and his mom also were forced to play.

"I hope you know what you're doing?" Kwame sat down to the right side of me at the table.

"She would have found out sooner or later," Mrs. Woods said to

Kwame. "Lets just enjoy a few rounds and we'll leave the rest of the evening to you two."

That seemed to make Kwame feel a lot better. We really haven't had much time at all together today. Everything couldn't have gone as planned. Bryant ended up winning a total of fifteen games straight. Every time I came close to winning it seemed as if I had the whole family against me. There would be a Draw +2 here, than someone would play a reverse and either Draw +2 me again or I would have to Draw +4 more cards. But I still had fun and it was worth the experience. Plus Bryant had a huge smile on his face and something to hang over my head for the rest of our life; calling us even.

After the game and finally telling everyone goodbye Kwame and I went for a walk in his backyard. He took me to a spot that was surrounded by flowers and had a swing.

"You are so sneaky," I said while sitting on the swing facing him.

"What?" he smiled with his arms extended on both sides. "What did I do?"

That was the very first time I thought we were going to kiss but things ended up happening differently.

"You know what you did," I climbed down and walked towards him seductively.

Kwame stood there and allowed me to get but a breath a way. He wasn't even nervous as we continued to gaze in each other's eyes. There was a full moon and the weather was just right. It wasn't too hot or too cold at all due to the season being summer. It was actually warm and in an unusual type of way.

I pulled Kwame by his shirt close to me and he placed his hands on my hips. Some lights from the first floor of his house came on causing both of us to look in that direction. It was but a glance; a quick reflex before we were looking intently into one another's eyes. His face began to get closer and closer to my lips as I was also meeting him. I wanted this…yearned for this moment…dreamed of this. Before I knew it my eyes were closed and my lips puckered. The thoughts of the dream last night struck me again as I opened them to see Kwame just staring at me.

"What?" I asked.

"You…are…so beautiful. And as much as I would love to kiss you," he hugged me placing his nose into my hair and my neck. "I know that deep down…you aren't ready for that. And it's nothing to be scared of because neither am I. I want to take my time with you and wait. The more that I wait for you the more comfortable that you will become when I do kiss your," he said tracing my lips with his fingers. "Precious…lips," he stopped than allowed space between us.

I could see his jewels getting hard and why he decided it was best for us to have some breathing room. He had a lot of control for a boy his age. Completely quiet and just listening to him was like listening to a bedtime story.

"I want to ask you something but I don't know how you'll take it," I said as we sat on the sofas near the hot tub.

"Ask me anything you'd like."

"How do you feel about sex?"

Surprised by the question he began to choke and his jewels were put away. I could tell I possibly made him uncomfortable.

"I'm sorry," he gasped. "I don't think I heard you correctly."

"How…do you…feel…about…sex?"

"Oh my…she really did just ask me that," he said to himself but I overheard.

"What's wrong with that?"

217

"What's wrong with it? You are only fourteen and I'm fifteen. That's what's wrong with it. We're too young for that."

"Well your dick didn't seem to think so?"

"It does that a lot when I talk to you. I…don't even know what that means when that happens."

"What if I told you I had a dream?"

"You…had a dream?"

"Yes. About us having sex and I dreamed it last night."

"Karma look. Don't take this the wrong way. I like you but I'm not ready for that and I know…I know…you aren't either."

"How do you know I'm not?" I asked standing up pulling my straps down.

"Oh no you don't. I think it's time for you to go home," he suggested putting my strings back on my shoulders.

As he touched my shoulders his jewels became hard again.

"See, I told you," I said pointing to his gem.

"No…" he looked down. "Never mind that. It has a mind of it's on."

"Oh…does it," I suggested walking towards him."

"Karma…stop," he motioned stepping backwards.

"Why stop when you want to? You want to…I want to. Let's just do it."

"Okay Karma. It's really time for you to go home now. Maybe too much spaghetti and garlic bread I don't know but you have to go. This isn't like you."

"Please Kwame. Please. I really want to experience this with you."

"Are you sure?"

"Yes," I said nibbling on his ear.

He looked me into my eyes for confirmation. It was most definitely there. Guiding my face to his our lips touched and he pulled us apart.

"Mom," he yelled seeing her walk out of the back door. "It's time for Karma to go home I think," he said as he walked towards her dragging me by the hand. "It's getting late and she's tired; real tired."

"She looks fine but you are right. It is getting late and I did promise to have her home by a certain time so Karma if you'd like to change before you leave that's fine or you can wear what you have on"

"I can go home like this. Thanks for asking."

Kwame ran in the house and allowed his mom to take things from there. I was rushed home without a good bye. No hugs, I'll call you to make sure you made it home okay, I'll miss you. No nothing and all because of my stupid hormones.

It's been exactly two weeks since I last saw or heard anything from Kwame. After the performance I gave I was beginning to think he was no longer interested so I began to forget about him. Or at least try to. With school starting tomorrow I'm sure there'll be more boys to be entertained with. None no where near close to Kwame but it would have to do. Anything, anyone to help me get over him.

It was funny that I felt this way because we ended up falling into each others arms the first day of school. If you ask me our parents handled some things behind our back so we could continue where we left off at. Maybe not exactly with the unknown, but with being in love; realizing that we are each others destiny.

I enjoyed high school very much. Relished having a best friend that had my back and to share my deepest darkest secrets with. Being an only child wasn't any fun at all so when Denise came along I was able to have sleep overs; cause you know my parents would never approve of me going over her house. Their favorite saying was *we weren't born yesterday*! They made me so sick sometimes but looking back on things I'm glad they were as strict as they were. I wouldn't have had it no other way.

Kwame and I spent just as much time in school as we did when we worked. Minus the performance I gave on our last day of work. It was never spoke of and I never thought twice about coming on to him again.

We volunteered at the Free Store Food Bank every Saturday. Often times, Denise volunteered with us. She would call me just at the last minute to ask if she can tag along but we never cared. Kwame liked Denise. He said she was funny and always made our day.

"Mrs. Woods, we were told By Denise of how honest she was. You never had any weird feelings with her always wanting to be around you and Kwame?"

"Denise? No not at all." So you're telling the court room that Denise was that honest about wanting to sleep with both your father and Kwame as well?" Mrs. Williams asked me.

"Yes she was. She never held back on anything that crossed her mind. If she thought of it, you better believe I knew about it. Good thing no cops were involved," I chuckled. "I'd be going to jail for conspiracy without proper knowledge to the situation."

Mrs. Williams smiled.

"And even though you had knowledge, you and Denise," She looked at Denise who was in the court room as well. "Are still friends till this day? Best friends am I right?"

"Yes."

"Were you ever nervous with her around you and Kwame?"

"No, not at all. Denise was crazy but I guess it just wasn't in her to cross me. Not to mention," I said bending down towards Mrs. Williams ear. "Kwame only had eyes for me. Trust me. A woman knows these things."

"Your honor I'm going to ask for the witness to repeat that last statement. No one else heard it but her and Mrs. Williams. Need I to remind Mrs. Williams, she's on trial for the murdering her husband," Mr. Ohio demanded.

"Mrs. Woods, please repeat to the court room *loudly*," Judge Lanai Brown Brown said while giving a shy smile to Mr. Ohio. "So that everyone can hear, what was just said."

"Kwame only had eyes for me. I didn't have a need to worry about anyone else."

"Will there be anything else Mr. Ohio?" Judge Lanai Brown Brown asked.

Mr. Ohio didn't say anything. The judge than looked at Mrs. Williams as if to ask the same question.

"Mrs. Woods, how did you feel when Denise was taken away from you?"

"I was devastated. That night after we did the ritual I couldn't sleep. Couldn't imagine what high school would be like once she was gone. We were only in our freshman year; and though I had Kwame, it wasn't the same as the friendship Denise and I had.

I'm at school and am in a hallway with about five other teens. Digging in my locker for books or something I continued to look around with an eerie feeling. Why is everyone watching me? To my left and to my right all eyes were on me; whispering. Holding my hands against my face while taking a breath to clear my thoughts, I pulled myself together. The moment I closed the door to my locker the lights in the hallway burst one by one. Immediately looking around I noticed no one was

there. But what happened to the other teens? The ones that was just…
here? Something was behind me because I felt its presence. Instead of
trying to look at something I could not see I dropped my things and
ran. It seemed like the more sensible thing to do.

"KARMA," someone yelled from behind me.

I wanted to stop and turn around because that voice seemed familiar
but I was too scared.

"KARMA WAIT," the voice yelled again.
"I CAN'T," I yelled back.
"WHY ARE YOU RUNNING AWAY FROM ME?"
"I'M NOT RUNNING AWAY FROM YOU…I THINK.
SOMETHINGS BACK THERE!"
"THERE'S NO ONE BACK HERE SILLY"
Still running, I turned my head to take a peek. The moment I looked
I didn't see anything. Not even the person speaking to me. Because I
was still scared and my adrenaline kept me moving I ran to the nearest
exit but it was locked. Going from door to door I tried to open it as to
hide or at least jump out of the window but nothing would budge. Alone
in the dark was the worst thing to happen to me at this moment. I can
remember thinking "If only I had Denise." Than poof, just like that she
was standing in front of me.

"Where…am…I?" she asked.
"In my dream…I think," I said confused. "It's dark and I'm alone.
I was scared and thought about you except you…well the moment I
thought of you, you appeared."
"Like that?" she snapped her fingers.
"Just like that but faster."
"Wow."

Till this very day, I never knew what the significance of that dream meant. But what I did take in was even though my best friend would be far away, she'd be right there with me when I slept. And I was happy with that.

Sexual Essence

It's August 16, 2001. I missed Denise dearly but had to move on with my life as I knew she would do hers.

Kwame and I have known each other for over four years now. We both graduated from high school and are beginning college. Since we have been the best of friends for so long, we decided it would be best to become roommates. I trusted Kwame with my life; especially after my accident. At least I know he'll be there when I need him the most. I do know that much. Agreeing to be roommates, we both suggested picking and choosing bills to pay.

"I'll always pay the rent to our apartment," Kwame said standing tall and strong with his chest poking out. "That is something a man does, *even though we're not together*," he mentioned.

I was glad he mentioned the part of us not being together because his saying *that's something a man does* sure did feel weird. It sent shivers through my spine and had me seconds away from changing my mind of us being roommates. He sure did know how to make a girl nervous.

"I will also pay for food and our gas and electric bill. That leaves you with," Kwame stated before being interrupted.

"That leaves me with shopping."

"Cute," Kwame chuckled. "But you're forgetting the phone bill and cable. Every once in a while I like to watch ESPN," Kwame said hoping the sports channel wouldn't be heard.

"ESPN huh?"

"That is ok isn't it? It's every once in awhile."

"Every once in a while huh?" I teased as if he was in danger zone.

Kwame didn't know how to answer so he just starred at me. It was so hard not to laugh. I stepped closer to him and he began to shiver while attempting to block his growing and face. Hilariously he kept switching from his face to his jewels. He was unsure of where I'd strike. *If* I was going to strike anyway. Finally, I couldn't control my laughter anymore. I laughed so hard that it caused me to run to the restroom because I had to pee.

"I nearly pissed myself Kwame," I continued to giggle.

"Ha ha ha. *Ha.* I'll show her," I overheard him mumble.

Things got quiet in the other room; as if he were no longer there.

"Kwame?" I spoke out than turned my ear towards the door.

I held my breath but didn't hear anything. Not a whisper or movement. At least two minutes had passed and he still didn't answer.

"Kwame, are you out there?"

Still sitting on the toilet I continued to stretch the sound of my ear.

"Kwame if you're out there than say something. This isn't funny."

He continued to not answer. Beginning to panic I cleaned myself than washed my hands. While the water was running, I heard a bump in the other room.

"Kwame if that's you quit kidding around. This shit isn't funny anymore! I'm really scared."

Continuing to listen and hope that Kwame would acknowledge I had been speaking, I finished washing my hands. As I was drying them on the dry towel there was three hard, heavy knocks at the door. Knocks that sounds more powerful than what Kwame was capable of. Hesitantly, I rushed forward to try and lock the door. As I placed my hands on the door, the knob began to slowly turn. The door pushed forward just as I was turning the lock. Screaming, I placed my back against it and forced it closed. Before I could turn the lock again, the door flung open. The strength of the door caused me to fall into the tub while pulling the shower curtain down. I hid my eyes; peeking as to not have been seen, except nothing was there. Not even a sound again. Waiting for time to pass and for my heart to slow down I finally climbed out the tub while trying to make as little noise as possible. Pulling down the shower pole I walked towards the door with it in my hand as if it was a baseball bat.

"RAH!" Kwame screamed while jumping out of no where.
"AHHHHHHHH!" I screamed while beating him with the pole.

I kicked and hit him over and over again until realizing it was Kwame. By the time he had finished oohing and ouching I hit and kicked him again for scaring me half to death. Not to mention on our first night of living together. That's all I needed was to be scared to be home alone now. I was so outraged that Kwame stood on the floor covering and blocking any area of his body that was exposed.

"I didn't think that shit was funny Kwame! You scared the hell out of me dammit. I could have killed you stupid! You're such a jerk!"

"Is it safe for me to get up now?"

"Kwame I can't believe you," I said while walking towards my bed. "I'm going to sleep. I need it after the way my heart nearly exploded."

"I'm...sorry," Kwame mumbled feeling the after affects of my pain. "I guess I shouldn't have taken things that far," he whispered to himself.

"Yeah, well I guess not dick head."

"I'm sorry Karma but you started it."

"I didn't scare you; big difference."

"You did scare me. And for a person so tough I didn't think what I did would even make you bark."

"Oh so I'm a dog now? That made me feel much better. Thank you Kwame; AKA, asshole."

"No, that's not what I'm saying. Not at all. You're like the toughest girl I ever met. I didn't think you feared anything."

"That's just it. I'm still a girl. *Tough* and all," I proclaimed beginning to calm down.

"Yea I here you. I think we both have had a long day. I am going to get some rest too. I can use it. Especially after the beating I just got," he chuckled.

I couldn't help but to laugh too. I guess I did beat him pretty bad. But what would you have done if it was you?

Kwame laid in bed every night glad to be watching me sleep. He watched me read, study and even relax. He was beyond in love with me. Each year that I have been a part of his life has been another happy memory jogged. I really had no clue just how happy I made him. Being able to watch me sleep was a breath of fresh air for Kwame. Even when we moved into our dorm Kwame had no complaints. There was little dispute at all as far as where to put our personal belongings; who's television to watch; who got what side of the closet and etc.? Kwame loved me so much he didn't care where things went as long as we got to sleep in the same room. As long as he got to see me awake every morning. As long as he was able to continue to be a part of my life.

One day Kwame was lying in bed imagining how things would be if he'd had the courage to ask me to be in a relationship. I saw him completely daydreaming and decided to throw a pillow at him.

I smiled while saying, "Snap out of it. You were over there drooling all over yourself. Who do you be thinking about all the time? She must be special."

Deciding to express his feelings, Kwame responded, "She is; very much so. She just doesn't know how much I love her. You probably wouldn't believe me if I told you who I been in love with since the first day I laid eyes on her."

Feeling a bit jealous that he was in love with someone else, I demanded jokingly, "Maybe; maybe not. So tell me who?"

Kwame rolled from his back to his stomach and said, "You," finally while feeling butterflies in the pit of his stomach for him to go ahead and share how he truly felt. "I've been in love with you since the day we met. You are so beautiful to me. You have the most hypnotizing eyes. Your smile sends out rays of sunshine to my soul. My heart aches of joy every time that I awake and see you laying across the room from me. We've been friends forever it seems and I can't imagine life without you. Without kissing your sweet cheeks. Without smelling your gratifying perfume. Without getting slapped or kneed in the growing by you every once in a while. " Kwame chuckled as he got out of bed and walked towards me holding my hands in his. "I love you so much. You don't know how much you mean to me. How happy I am just to be sharing this room with you. My life revolves around you. When I am daydreaming, it's of you. When you're asleep, I can't sleep because I'm watching you. Sometimes I even want to hold you," Kwame let my hands go and started to shy away. "But I don't want to make you feel uncomfortable. I love you Karma. I…love…you."

All the feelings from the past immediately arose as we had placed them on hold I guess. I fell in love right away. By hearing everything Kwame said I knew that he was the man for me. I always did. Any man that met my father and was able to live and be granted another day of life was *the* man for me. Beside the point we were friends for over four years and haven't even kissed lip to lip for the first time. Kwame always respected me as a woman and respected my parents as well. Even when I had to slap or kick him on the occasion; he always took the sting and never ever hit me back. Not that I'm saying I wanted him too. Just letting you know the type of man that he was. He never even tried to touch me inappropriately. Our conversations were always appropriate for the occasion.

I looked at Kwame who sat on his bed embarrassed. He really didn't know what to expect or how I would react. Should he take cover by blocking his face, or should he cover his penis. Kwame continued to watch as he waited for a response. He began to sweat as time went on. I walked over to him and gave him a hard slap in the face.

Holding his face Kwame said, "Ouch woman! What was that for? Well, I know what that was for because I came at you incorrect. But hell, they say the truth hurts, and I'm willing to be slapped, punched or even kicked to continue confessing my love for you. You've never seen me with any other woman. I'm always available for you. I participate in events with you just to be with you. I would sit through a singing at the opera just to be seen with you. Just to be next to you. Just to smell your scent; to look into your eyes and see that you're enjoying this just as much as I. To see your dazzling smile; to feel your soft, soft hands."

"Wow. I never knew just how much you cared for me. Well, maybe I did but was too afraid to say something or acknowledge that the chemistry was there."

"Maybe," Kwame chuckled.

There was a moment of silence as we locked eyes. Kwame begin to move forward towards my face and I felt my hand tempting to rise. He was moving too fast for me. I still needed time to process everything that had just happened. Everything that was just said; his true inner feelings. This was no longer Kwame, my best friend. He was now, the Kwame. My knight in shining armor. My king. The man I would live the rest of my life with. Get married to and have children by. The... Kwame.

He went to place his succulous lips onto mine and the wall that was once built collapsed as I fell into his arms. We looked at each other. That same look we shared once before the day we met. Except this time my heart raced and my body said to kiss him back. Or at least allow him to kiss me repeatedly. This wasn't a practice test or a thought, this was going to happen. With the chemistry that was flowing at this moment it was only natural for us to kiss. At this point there is no turning back. My heart is his and his is mine.

Kwame kissed my lips ever so softly. He stepped back to look at me. My eyes were still close as I froze. *Wow! My first kiss. And it only took for me to be eighteen before I received it.* Kwame cupped my face into his hands than kissed my lips again. Smooch after smooch while saying how much he loves me.

He than looked down at the floor and said, "So."

"So." I repeated perspiring.

"Shall I continue? Are you ok with that?"

"Yes, you shall," I said as I guided his chin towards mine so that he would look me in my eyes again, just like he did when we met.

A smile followed by another peck was administered.

"Your lips are causing me to feel tired. Maybe...you...can hold... me... while I sleep?"

Still looking in my eyes, Kwame replied, "Are you sure? Cause I don't want to get slapped again." He chuckled.

"I'm very sure."

Deciding to cut the light off than join me in bed he held my hand. Wanting to be comfortable he laid down first than put his hand out to help me into bed. We laid there snuggled and fit. It felt good to have him hold me. His heart raced extremely fast. I thought he was going to stop breathing any moment now.

I asked nervously in a whisper, "Are you awake?"

Knowing what I wanted to experience was easier to edge into little bits at a time. Kwame just wasn't that type of man and after my last seduction years ago I didn't want to get rejected again. I knew what I wanted.

He responded anxiously, "Yes. What's wrong?"

"Can you rock me until I fall asleep? Sometimes I move my body back and forth till I fall asleep. But of course you know that because you watch me."

Kwame laughed while beginning move, "Yes I do."

He began to hold me tighter than ever. As if he was keeping me from falling over a cliff.

Fifteen minutes had past when Kwame asked, "Are you asleep?"

I mumbled in return, "Un un; a little. Why?"

"I was thinking about our first kiss and how exciting it was. I've always wanted to kiss you. And now that you gave me the chance I would like to kiss you again. May I?"

I jumped up out of bed while saying, "Woe. Woe."

231

My hormones were going a mile a minute but I didn't want to rush into it.

Before I could say anything else Kwame jumped as high as I did and landed with a kiss to my lips. To my surprise I actually liked it. Again! Even though I was giving him the signal to slow down and he did it anyway. Even though he did it and my brick wall was put up before I got to knock it down to accept his quick kiss. Even though he moved sooo fast that it was hard to keep up with his next move which normally would have caused me to slap him. Kick him too, possibly. But I liked it. I actually liked it.

He had the softest lips I've ever felt. Well, the only lips I've ever felt. And was so gentle about how he kissed me although he moved with the speed of lightning. It almost felt as if I had gotten struck. It was just smooches; no tongue. He placed his hands on my face and continued to peck me. Kwame than moved his hand through my hair releasing it from the pony tail it was in. He watched as my hair came down in a relief to be freed. He looked at me again and pulled my hair behind my ears. As he rubbed his index finger moderately over my lips before kissing me again I became timid, allowing him to lead. I watched his every move as he took his time in appreciating me from my head to my toes. He laid me down onto the bed. I was extremely tense but certain that I was ready for what we were about to do and finally.

We were about to do…it, I think. It certainly felt like it. The pit of my stomach was full of butterflies. The heart that once had a slow, steady beat felt as if I was having a heart attach; its rhythm was off. The blood flow going through my veins seemed to stop. Beginning to feel dizzy, I decided to think of my happy place, Bob Marly, and closed my eyes. My hands were so sweaty that it leaked like a faucet. Even with my eyes clothes I could hear the drips of perspiration. By the time we came around to taking off our clothes I'm sure my body would look as if I'd been sprayed with a water hose. And so would the bed. Kwame continued to kiss my lips, than my forehead and moved down to my neck. The aroma of my perfume made his eyes roll in the back of his head. He then continued to kiss down my chest that was slightly available before reaching my breast. Removing my shirt he rubbed me down from my neck to my belly button repeatedly.

Kwame jumped out of bed, "I can't do this."

Uncertain of why the mixed feelings I asked, "Can't do what?"

"We shouldn't do this. I feel like I'm forcing you"

I sat up covering my chest, "Kwame this is my first time too and I'm just as scared as you but..."

Kwame interrupted, "No. We shouldn't do this. You said years ago that you wanted to wait until you got married. Let's just wait."

I kissed Kwame admiring his ambition to wait. "Yes, I did say that. But lets not forget the day that I tried to seduce you behind your house. Truth is, I love you too." Holding Kwame hands, "I feel the same way about you that you do about me. That's why I asked you to hold me. I wanted to be embraced in your arms. I wanted you to love me more. So please, let's just try this." Kissing Kwame, "I love you and you love me. There's nothing wrong with that."

Fretfully Kwame laid me down again. "Let's start over. Turn over onto your stomach."

I did as was told. He began to massage my shoulders, than my back and moved down to my feet removing each clothing item but my panties and braw as he went alone. I was so panicky that the massaging actually helped to cool me down.

It felt as if I was a Goddess, wearing a white robe running through a field of Lilies. Not too far away was my king, wearing his strong, golden crown in the form of a lion that is stalking his prey.

"Turn over onto your back. I want to look into your eyes," Kwame spoke to me.

Quietly and still imagining that I was his Goddess, he kissed me. This time it was very different. It made me extremely nervous but passionate. I think I almost called for my daddy, that's how excited I've became. We kissed, rubbed and grind even. This was both of our first occasion. We were sure that it's to be one we'll never forget. Not knowing what to do or how to start, our night stretched. It was as if we were placed under a sex spell. The feeling we felt was remarkable. We were in love; always have been. I guess I was too stuck up to admit it. Even so, the feeling of rejection isn't one that I liked so much.

Kwame kissed me on my neck while he removed my braw. Continuing on, he kissed me down my belly and onto my hips. Kissing and kissing as he pulled down my underwear.

"Unh," I moaned out in ecstasy.

The way he kissed me; *there*, you know? Right there on my feminine essence sent thrills threw my body. I felt as if the world had picked a part of my body to tickle and I couldn't keep from laughing at the feeling of it. Wow, what a gratifying emotion.

He noticed that I became extremely anxious and decided to sit up and take his shirt off. The whole time I couldn't help but to want him to kiss me again. *Kiss me again, **there please**, would you? Please*. I begged silently while moving my body blissfully in bed. Kwame continued removing clothes as he watched. He wanted to give me some time to regain my composure. As he kissed me again, I threw him on top of me and kissed him in return placing my tongue in his mouth.

"Woe," he said.
"Woe," I chuckled. "Now I have you saying woe," I mentioned as I overthrown him and climbed on top.

He removed my bra and kissed me from my neck down to my belly button; every time when reaching creating circles around it. I looked at him and liked what I saw. He was dark, lovely and full of muscles. I rubbed my fingers up and down his chest and arms. Over throwing me he kissed down my chest while taking my panties off. My heart was beating so fast I thought it would explode. I closed my eyes to think of a happy place and couldn't. It was happening right now with Kwame. Before I opened my legs I saw my King's jewels and became aroused but timid at the same time.

As he placed his self on top of me he asked nervously, "Do you want to use a condom?"

"Of course. I'm not ready to be a mother yet."

Luckily there was a condom machine in our dorm for nights like this and on our floor. Grabbing a robe he mentioned to return within five minutes. While he left I went to freshen up followed by posting sexy in bed.

Returning with a kiss he asked, "Are you ready?"

Apprehensively, I replied, "Yes."

Kissing me again, Kwame said, "I'm going to take my time. I can't imagine hurting you and I won't be able to make love to you if it hurts. So if it does let me know and I will stop," he pecked. "I love you"

"Love you too."

Continuing to kiss me without a given notice of when he was going to place his jewel inside of me helped to keep me relaxed. He stroked my sandy brown hair over and over again while rocking back and forth. Than he looked in my eyes and I knew it was time. He placed his jewel at the lips of my essence. Kwame pushed a pinch at a time while watching and feeling my body expressions. I closed my eyes again and held him tight. I thought of the day we first met and all of the memories we had up until now. After the third jog down memory lane I felt a feeling that was painful but I was happy it was with him. Opening my eyes and gasping for air I pushed up on his chest and looked at him.

Kwame asked while shivering, "What's wrong? Are you ok?"

Removing my hands and holding on tightly I responded, "Yes."

Still shivering as he pushed his self in and out very slowly while saying, "Yes it does. It feels real good," he moaned.

He continued to kiss me while making slow passionate love. I held on to him as tight as I could. The feeling of making love was amazing. I began to moan a pleasurable moan. Kwame stopped but still was shivering as if he was cold.

"Are you ok? Am I hurting you?"
"Yes I'm fine. It just feels so good. It truly is remarkable."
"Do you want me to stop?"
"No Kwame. Please don't stop. Keep going."

Continuing his pattern up and down, up and down his head kept moving back and forth. As he tried to reach the ending of my essence the pain was unbearable and I bit my bottom lip as I scratched his back.

Kwame removed his self slowly from where he was positioned to a more comfortable position.

"I'm so sorry baby. I didn't mean to. I was in the moment. The deeper I got the greater the feeling felt. Do you want to stop?"

Looking at him with my arms pressed up against his chest again, "No. I actually don't; just don't go that far again. That really hurts."

Looking into my eyes he said, "Ok. I won't. Tell me when you're ready."

I took a few deep breaths, and then said "Ok. I'm ready," while removing my hands.

Kwame continued his pattern but slowly than ever this time. We kissed over and over again. Twenty minutes later we climaxed. It was the greatest feeling ever. We both moaned and yelled out during the period of excitement while holding on tightly to each other. Kwame climbed over me and held me from behind and kissed me one last time while finally rocking me to sleep.

Black love

It was about four years after we broke each other's virginity that things began to change. Lately we haven't been intimate at all. Kwame has been distant with work and I have been busy with my last semester of college at Wilbur Force. I never thought things would come to this. When I walked into our apartment Kwame was laying on his bed flat on his back. Once he saw me come in, he turned over onto his side and faced the wall. I didn't know rather to leave and find somewhere else to go or to continue on my mission into our house. I stood in the doorway for nearly five minutes contemplating in thought if I should tell him what I'm about to do. Should I tell him I'm about to take a pregnancy test? Should I wait until I find out the results and only tell him if it's positive?

Having his arms wrapped around his body Kwame said to himself, "I love her dearly but she has been getting on my last nerves. Lately things just haven't been the same. I try talking to her and she gets an attitude. She complains about everything. *Why isn't your bed made? Oh I see you been sleeping in your bed while I'm at school, huh?* I don't understand what's wrong with her.

After overhearing this I decided to step into our bedroom. After all I've had a long day and was extremely tired. In the mood for a hot bath, I took off my backpack and removed the pregnancy test from the side pocket. Feeling the need to pee causes me to rush and kick off my shoes than run into the bathroom. That's when the nervousness began. Once I finished peeing on the stick, I stood on my tippy toes while looking into the mirror to see if I could see any signs of pregnancy. My stomach was rounder than usual.

Thinking to myself, "When did this happen? And how? I know I'm not…Nah; couldn't be. There isn't no way in hell I'm pregnant. Guess I just gained a little weight. Nothing the good ole gym can't fix," I laughed to myself as I left the restroom.

Looking straight ahead I noticed that Kwame was no longer in the room. He had up and disappeared while I was in the bathroom.

I thought to myself while crossing my arms on my hips, "That little son of a bitch. Oh well, I needed some time to myself anyway," I said as I fell asleep.

As I was resting I overheard Kwame enter the bathroom. It didn't take long before he exited quickly.

Yelling as he entered the doorway "KARMA! KARMA!"
"WHAT! WHHHHAAAAATTTT!" I yelled impatiently.
Kwame places the pregnancy stick in my face and ask "What is this?"
"What does it say?"
Quietly he says, "You're pregnant."
"And?" I said impatiently.
"What do you mean and?"
"I'm not ready for a child right now and I'm still in school."
"Well what do you want to do?"

"I only got two decisions. Abortion or adoption."

"Karma, you're saying you don't want a family with me?"

"Not right now! I'm not ready."

"Then you're not ready for me," Kwame said as he left the house.

I was so hurt that I cried myself to sleep.

At this point Kwame and I begin to hug one another. Kwame lifted my chin and stared into my eyes. He always did that and seem to go unconscious.

"Karma, we need to talk and I want you to just listen before you say anything," he began while rocking us side to side.

I followed his lead and acknowledged by saying, "Ok."

"I talked to my mom this morning and," Kwame stuttered. "And… well…umm…You Know how we were intimate and then we became less intimate; then you became moody and quit liking me as much?"

Stepping back and looking at him more seriously I said, "Kwame what are you trying to say?"

Scratching his head while backing up to avoid getting hit, Kwame replied, "You're pregnant. There I said it. My mom and I think you're pregnant. I mean look at you. You picked on some pounds and your stomach is rounding out like a balloon. Don't tell me you didn't notice?"

I was speechless. Continuing to look in his eyes to see if this was a joke I sat down. I started to feel nausea. My life flashed before my eyes. College graduate, marriage than possibly kids; this is not what I planned. How could this have happened? How could I have let this happen I thought over and over again? Lying down in bed with my back turned away from Kwame caused him to lay down with me. Just like he did our first night. It used to help calm me *but not this time*.

Kwame said calmly while rocking me back and forth, "What do you want to do?"

With arrogance I said, "What else can we do? It's not like we have a choice."

"Ok well as of right now let's pretend that you're not pregnant. Why don't we take a test and see what the test says? I will go pick it up myself so you won't feel embarrassed. How does that sound?"

"I'm not sure. At this point I really don't care. What am I going to do with a baby?"

"But you're not by yourself. I'm here. So the question should be what are we going to do with a baby?"

Turning towards Kwame, I looked him in his eyes and asked, "Are you sure you want to know? Are you sure you can handle the truth?"

Kwame kissed me on my lips, and then said, "I'm as sure as knowing that I'm only in love with you. As long as I have you and our baby or babies in our life I am a very lucky and happy man."

Teary eyed I said, "Ok. I will take the test."

Kwame stood up and walked towards his jacket, "Good cause I already bought one. That's what I went to do while you were in the restroom."

"You jerk! What if I would have said no?"

"I had other arrangements made but now that you are willing to take the test, there's no need for them. So, let's get started.

Reading the directions one step at a time with one hand as he held the cup for me as I urinated in the cup with the other was not the most romantic move. It felt awkward but I didn't want pee on my hands so it was a better choice than if I would have had to do it. Once I was finished Kwame said it would take exactly ten minutes before we knew the results according to the directions. I was so nervous I didn't know what to do. We sat in the bathroom awaiting the results like vultures awaiting their prey. After five minutes the wait became unbearable. I told Kwame I was going for a walk. He said it would probably be best if we both went to get some fresh air.

We held hands the entire time. Never once did we turn to look at each other to talk or to kiss like we usually did. I couldn't help but to think about how Kwame was right. My attitude has changed; appetites, weight, even the shape of my stomach which I hated that he noticed. Today was an exceptional day. The ending of what was and the beginning of what we'll become.

Our walk lasted exactly forty-seven minutes. I believe we both stalled on getting back home to finding out the news that we already knew the answer to. There was no doubt about it.

I yelled, "PREGNANT! ARE YOU SERIOUS? HOW? WHEN? WHERE? WHY? WHY NOW? WHY NOT LATER IN LIFE? OH LORD, WHY? PLEASE TELL ME WHY? WHY ME? OH LORD WHY ME?"

Kwame kept his distance while saying, "Honey I have your back. You have nothing to worry about."

I walked over to Kwame and begin choking him. He put his arms around me and repeatedly said he loved me and that I have nothing to worry about. I could trust him. When I feel pain, he will feel pain. When I get sick, we both will be sick. When I need his help to go to the bathroom he will be here to help me. When I need a massage he will be here to rub me down. Everything sound so reassuring but I just wasn't ready to become a mother.

Decision Making

The next day I awoke still feeling the same. Even though it hurt Kwame I just wasn't ready to become a mother. At the age of twenty two; *What could I possibly do with a child? These things just don't happen that way nowadays. I had to be wise and think smart* as my daddy always said.

OMG! WHAT AM I GOING TO TELL MY PARENTS? My mom is going to kill me. Maybe they both will kill me? Maybe dying won't be so bad after all? My father is going to disown me and he won't believe I carelessly got knocked up. Some luck I have because I know a person who has been fucking since eleven years old and they are the lucky ones! Maybe I should have started early too.

The more I thought of things dealing with this baby, the more irritable I became. I sat down at our computer desk and typed in Planned Parenthood. I saw things for adoptions and abortions. Adoption wouldn't seem so bad if I didn't have to carry a baby for nine months before having to give it away. Why couldn't I just take the baby out of my womb now, by surgery or something and place it in someone else's womb to carry? I'm not sure if I would want to give my baby away after carrying it for nine months. That's nearly a year. I'm sure my baby and I would have some kind of attachment by than.

Planned Parenthood seemed like the best choice. It was another option that was placed at the bottom of the screen, except I didn't know what it meant. When I clicked on it, it said Planned Parenthood: Abortion. There is no way I can kill my baby without Kwame knowing. He already knows I'm pregnant. Even though this was the best option for me, I'm not sure how Kwame would feel about this. This is our first child. He seems pretty happy about it and he's kept his word about everything since I've known him. Ugh! I'm so scared. I don't know what to do. Clicking on the site says that it is safe and legal. But how on earth am I going to convince Kwame to agree to this as well. He does have a choice in the matter too, *doesn't he?* Who makes the decisions in situations like this? Me or him? Ugh! Getting even more frustrated I scrolled down the page and noticed there's a pill that I can be prescribed. I'm eighteen and legally grown. I don't need parents consent so no one will know about this but me and the doctor. This might be the route for me," I continued to think while twirling my hair. It said I can be prescribed it up to sixty three days or nine weeks after my last missed period. PROBLEM, I sanged. How the hell many weeks am I? The pregnancy test doesn't state all that. And I sure as hell don't know or could possibly guess, could I? No, that wouldn't be a good idea. What if I'm too far along and the abortion pill doesn't work causing my baby to still be born but deformed? How can I ever forgive myself? How can Kwame ever forgive me? And what if this baby is meant to be born?

I drifted into a dream that Kwame and I was still together. He was wiping the sweat off of my forehead as I went into labor with our child. The doctors took a sonogram of our baby before they were born. Wait a minute! They? I'm having twins? Twins. We're having twins, a girl and a boy I hope. We wanted it to be a surprise so we won't know the sex until they are born.

The contractions started to increase and hurt like hell. Kwame was holding my hand with teary eyes.

"Dr. is there anything you all can do to ease the pain? She's in so much pain and I can't take it anymore. I can't be strong for her. Not knowing she's in pain."

"Well sir, she said she wanted to go natural. Pain is pretty consistent with natural birth. When a woman decides to have a baby natural, there aren't any drugs available to them. Now a while back she could have gotten a epidural but because she's so close with her contractions and is nearly eight centimeters dilated, by the time we get the anesthesia team in here your babies will be born. She doesn't have much longer to go. Her breathing is not a concern nor is the babies. Just keep comforting her."

"Dr. I think she's ready to push."

"See what I mean," The Dr. said to Kwame. "Ok team, you know what to do. Lets get those babies out, cleaned, wrapped and into their parents arms."

"AHHHHHH," I began to scream while pushing.

"Well that was fast. We have a boy!"

The nurses rushed over, sucked the blood out of his throat, wiped him down than wrapped him while the doctor continued to deliver our next baby.

"AHHHHHHHHHHHHHHHHHHHHHHH," I screamed in agony while pushing.

"He's six pounds six ounces," the nurse shouted out.

"Here is our last baby. It's a girl! A beautiful little girl. She's a chunky one too. Probably the most dominant twin."

The nurses placed our son into my arms. He didn't even cry. He just looked up with those big eyes and I could tell already they were mine. I could feel it. He was gorgeous; perfect in every way.

"Um, Doctor," I said while placing the baby in Kwame's arms. Doctor; DOCTOOOOOOORRRRRRRRRRRRRR!"

"I see another head!" Yelled a nurse.

"ANOTHER HEAD," everyone repeated in question.

The doctor ran over and had to immediately grab the baby because she/he was making their entrance in the world and fast.

"Ok, our princess here weighs eight pounds three ounces," a nurse yelled from across the room.

"AHHHHHHHHHHHHHHHHHHHHHHHHHHHHHHHHH HHHHHHHHHHHHHHHHHHHHHHHHHHHHHHHHHHHHHH HHHHHHHHHHHH!" I yelled till I was nearly blue in the face.

"Hi you. Where were you hiding in there? Huh little fellow? You all, I have here in my arms, yet another baby. It's a boy! A beautiful baby boy. They are all identical and he is also a juicy one. I think he's the bigger of the two. Woman, where were you storing these babies? By first glance it looked as if you were only carrying one child. Basically mom, you looked good to be carrying twins."

"Thanks doctor."

"He is nine pounds five ounces. He is a big baby," the nurse yelled from across the room. Speaking to the last born child, "Where were you hiding in there huh little man? Where were you hiding?"

"DOCTOR, please tell me there are no more babies coming out of me? I still feel like I have to push."

"Well this time it should be your placenta sliding out of you, though some women does say it feel as if you have to give it a little push. But being that you surprised us all tonight, or shall I say this little fellow surprised us all, I am going to sit here just to make sure."

"Thank you doctor."

"Oh, don't thank me yet. I SEE A HEAD!"

"WHAT!" I screamed out.

"Just making sure it was your placenta I saw that's all. See," he said while showing it to me."

"You son of a bitch!"

"Well, I've been that before," he laughed off. "Plenty of times in my days. You mommies tends to get that way during labor. I should know. I have twelve kids of my own.

Hearing the comment of the doctor having twelve kids caused me to snap out of it. Even though I saw how handsome my little boy was I still wasn't convinced that being a mom was the thing for me. And aren't you supposed to turn dreams upside down? I don't know what to do.

Looking for advice I decided to contact the clinic. The least I could do is listen to what they have to say; right? I'll just keep this our little secret and not even let Kwame know what's going on. Than if I go through with it, maybe I can lie and say I miscarried or something.

"Thank you for calling Planned Parenthood where the decision is yours. How may I assist you today?"

"Um, hi," I said.

"Hi. How are you doing today?"

"I'm confused."

"Oh, I understand how confusing pregnancy can be. I'm sorry, are you pregnant?"

"Of course I'm pregnant! What type of dumb question is that?"

"I'm sorry ma'am. I wasn't trying to offend you in any way. How about we set you up an appointment for you to come in for a consultation? That's where you come in, we show you around, where you'll get to see the tools used, medication given if that's an option and meet some of the doctors. Does that sound like something you would like to do?"

"Um, sure?"

"Ok, to give you more time to think about your given situation I am going to schedule you a week from today. Is that okay?"

"Sure, I guess."

"The only reason why I'm doing so is because we like our patients to feel as if this is the decision that's best fit for them at that they aren't rushed into or coerced into doing something that's going to stick with them for the rest of their life."

"I guess that makes sense."

"Ok sweetheart, so I'll see you one week from today at 9:30 am."

"Ok," I responded not happy at all about having to wait a whole week while this baby is growing inside of me.

"Bye honey."

"Bye," I sighed.

Shortly after our phone conversation I laid down and went back to sleep.

Confessions

As I drove to Planned Parenthood, my eyes watered. I never could have imagined doing something so horrible to myself and to someone I love. Kwame and I haven't talked in weeks and I regret having to do this to him.

The parking lot is full and I'm wondering if this is a sign. *Could this be a coincidence?* With no other choice I parked on the street and thought I spotted a Blue Escalade a street over. Shaking my head to clear the thought, I got out the car. Walking into the lobby Kwame stopped me.

"Hey Karma, how is your day going," he asked while trying to hide a bag behind his back.

Trying to hurry to the elevator I stated, "Fine I guess."

"How are my two queens doing?" He asked while getting down on his knees and talking to my stomach.

"We're fine Kwame, thanks," I said sarcastically.

He gave me a look of disappointment .

"Kwame, would you just stop it!"

"Whats wrong? You know you can talk to me?"

"I know I can Kwame, I just…have a lot on my mind. That's all."

"Well, this might cheer you up. I talked to my mom today. And,"

"YOU DID WHAT!" I yelled while standing up.

"I talked to my mom today and,"

"And what Kwame? And what? Let me fucking guess. She wants me to come over for dinner so she can say *just how happy she is that we're having a baby together*. Great Kwame. That's just fucking great."

"Well, it was something to that nature. It's not like you haven't met her before. It won't be any different than the first."

"It won't be any different than the first," I mocked in disappointment.

"Trust me. She's liked you since day one. Every since I told her how you kicked Kwame in the balls."

"You told her that?"

"Sure did."

"What did she say?"

"She laughed and laughed."

"My type of woman," I chuckled. "Maybe it won't be so bad after all."

Of course that was the thought for the moment. Once I realized what I had been planning just moments ago, I felt sour all over again.

"So whats in the bag?"

"Oh, *now* you want to know what's in the bag. Well let's see what's in the bag, shall we?" Kwame walked over to the bag and picked it up. "Hum, I wonder what we have in here."

"I know I know," I said while trying to be jolly for the moment.

"Well, I have some booties," he said while pulling some infant shoes out of the bag. "And I have an outfit for either a boy or girl. A cautious dad already. Here's some socks to go with the shoes. And a cute little baby hat to protect our little one from the sun. Oh, I almost forgot. Here's our babies first blanket too. What do you think?"

"What do you think I'm here for?"

"That's it. You're still going through with this? What can I do to make you change your mind?"

"I always knew when I would have a child I'd be married. And not because I was pregnant but because I was his queen and he was my king," I became teary eyed with a trembling voice.

"Well," he said getting on his knee.

Presuming to pull out a ring box he proposed and asked me to be his queen. The ring was a sapphire with one carat diamonds surrounding it. Looking into his eyes I noticed the same expression he gave me the first day we met and the first time he confessed his love to me.

Beginning to cry, I was asked my name before I could respond. "Are you ready to see the doctor?" The nurse asked.

Turning to Kwame I responded "YES KWAME!"

We went home and immediately became intimate. As he slowly caressed my body he paid special attention to my abdominal body. He was being extremely cautious due to the baby and he proceeded to make sweet passionate love to me as we began our new lives together.

That night I awoke feeling extremely sick. The toilet was begging for me to come by. My stomach hurt so badly. While running I began to feel the vomit exit my throat and enter into my mouth. My hands began to over flow with bile as the bathroom seemed to travel away. Before I knew it the unimaginable happened. I was barfing all over our hallway floor. Kwame ran from the bedroom and grabbed the trash can.

"Are you okay honey?"

"I will be, blaaaa, after I'm done, blaaaa."

"Awww. My poor baby."

"Shut up Kwame!"

"I'm sorry baby. I didn't know what else to say."

"Blaaaa. Try saying nothing."

"Okay. I can do that."

He sat down back against the wall and rubbed my back until I was finished. It seems as if it went on forever.

"What is this?"

"Morning sickness darling. Well at least I think it's still considered morning sickness being that is so early in the morning."

"And I have to deal with this for the next six months?"

"Some women do and some women don't. Maybe it will go away eventually. Ask your mom how was her pregnancy when she was carrying you. I'm sure she can give you a thing or two of advice."

"Yeah, I'm sure too," I replied sarcastically.

Kwame and I sat with our head tilt backwards into the wall. For the first time since we found out about our baby, I saw distress in Kwame's eyes. I don't know what was quite going through his mind, but it was enough to signal me that he too don't think we're ready for this baby.

"Here," Kwame said taking me by the hand. "Lets get the two of you back into bed and I'll clean this mess up. Unless you want to see your vomit and barf again, that is?"

"Un un. No thanks," I waved my hands. "I'll accept going to get into bed over cleaning up that mess any day."

"Good, than I'm glad we have a deal. I'm going to hold you in my arms until you fall asleep. Is that ok? I can touch you right Miss Meanie?"

"I am not mean," I protested.

"You have been lately. Snapping at me, don't want to be touched, kissed or caressed," Kwame said while lying me down in bed. "Um.

Come here my queen and let me hold you," he said while placing the cover over me.

The next day, I awoke with my stomach in my hand. It scared me half to death. I'm not used to my belly being this big. *Could I be farther along than expected?* Moments later, Kwame awoke saying

"Good morning Beautiful," as he rolled over to kiss me.

Well, that was till he looked down and saw my stomach.

"Woah! What is that? What…is…that?" He asked jokingly. "That's…our baby? Mine and yours? That?" he asked while pointing to my stomach.

"Yes. That. Silly. This is our baby," I said while placing his hand onto my belly while laughing.

"Is it safe to touch her?"

"Why do you keep calling it her? How do you even know it's a girl?"

"Well usually when women say they know something I believe you say something like this, *it's a mother's instinct.* In my situation, I'm going to say, it's a daddies instinct. I just know."

"Really?"

"Ok. Well we'll find out…eventually."

"Yes we will."

Test of Loyalty

Kwame walked out of the house saying "I'll be back later. I'm going to spend time with Bryant?"

"Bryant?" I thought to myself. "When did you start having time for him?" I yelled after him as he approached the stairs.

"I do now," he exclaimed while looking at me one last time before walking down the stairs.

After he left my conscience began to play tricks on me. I felt guilty about the thought ever crossing my mind. I mean, what was I thinking? Was I really willing to kill my child? Could I have actually gone through with it? The thoughts from earlier reproached me. *I told you not to do it. Didn't I? I told you, you have a good man, or should I say had, now that he knows you were going to kill his baby; his first born child. How dare you when he's been nothing but good to you? How dare you? Guess it's too late to think about those consequences I warned you of, huh? Was it worth it?* Continuing to think without moving my lips I saw the unexpected. Kwame was going out with Bryant; only the brother that's always been jealous of our relationship. Bryant probably is going to have some little sleazy slut to seduce him and he's going to end up cheating. That's how life always happens. I can't allow Kwame to be seduced. He has to be stopped!

Grabbing my things to leave out, the phone ranged. To my surprise it was Bryant.

"What!"
"I just called to let you know not to expect Kwame home tonight."
"Why is that Bryant?"
"I told you, you should have been with me," he slurred.

Immediately after hanging up the phone, I ran out the door after Kwame. Thoughts crossed my mind as I thought of the sluts that would be all over him. Entering my car felt like a heat stroke had taken place. My palms were sweaty, my hair became moist, and I became sick again; dizzy and extremely nausea. There was no way possible I could continue my journey under these circumstances. It was as if something or someone was trying to get me to stay home. Even with an unsettled stomach I couldn't allow another woman to tear apart our family. Quickly placing the seat belt safely across my belly and lap I placed the car in drive and began to search all of the local bars. His car was parked outside so I know he had to walk; but there weren't any signs of him. Even after five bars and at least every street close to home and in the following neighborhoods. It was as if Kwame disappeared; *or didn't want to be found.*

Not knowing what to do next and feeling extremely tired I decided to go home and lay down. At this point the least I could do was take care of my baby. From the way things were going, I was going to be one of the sick, pregnant mothers. The ones that stays hurling and queasy and fussy; extremely fussy throughout their pregnancy.

By the time I had made it home I was bent over the toilet. It was than that I wished Kwame was home. I managed to get puke all over the walls, toilet and floor. ***Thanks a lot baby***, I said to my stomach as I looked for a clean rag to wipe away my mess. ***It's your fought you know*** *that I keep managing to get sick. I didn't experience these things till I found out about you I said while wiping around the toilet.*

Extremely tired I looked at the clock. Two thirty p. m. ok, I have plenty of time to take a nap and relax. Placing my foot in bed never felt better. The moment my body was under the blankets I was more diminished than ever and fell asleep almost instantly.

My vision is blurred as I open my eyes. For whatever reason it is now dark in my home. Looking at the clock that shows eight thirty p.m. doesn't even register with my brain. *Eight thirty is fine*, I thought to myself. *I'll just do some work on the computer; eat dinner and...EIGHT THIRTY! HOW LONG DID I SLEEP? AND WHERE THE HELL IS KWAME?* I looked outside to see if his car was still parked but it wasn't. Selfish cunt, I thought to myself. He didn't even bother waking me up to let me know that he'd at least stopped home before leaving out again. I tried calling his phone but kept getting his voicemail. After the fifth attempt flashbacks approached o some sleazy helfa on my man. Except this time, I wasn't going to look for Kwame. *If Kwame would allow some woman to please his vunerableness right now than so be it. Hope it's worth it 'cause we won't be together anymore. AND I HOPE YOU CAN HEAR ME TOO,* I screamed out. *WE WON'T BE TOGETHER ANYMORE; wherever you are!* Following my outburst I fixed a cup of honey lemon tea and sat in front of my computer screen. *You did this you know*, I rumored with the computer. *Being as smart as you are; you had to suck me right in huh? Couldn't just leave me alone? Now look at us. We're both stuck here together with no Kwame. And I miss him so much,* I said beginning to cry. Out of the many things I've done to him he's never been this mad or naive. I've kicked him in the growing, slapped him on numerous occasions and who knows what else. I guess you don't cross a man and his child.

The clock ticked countless minutes as time passed. Waking up at eight thirty turned into four o'clock a.m. I was devastated. I wanted to break every bone in Kwame's body. I wanted to set his hands and feet on fire so that's he'd never pull a stunt like this again. I even thought of giving him sleeping pills and making him sleep away the amount of time he had me wait for him to come back home. Especially being how inconsiderate he is knowing that I'm pregnant. Doesn't he know I can have a miscarriage from this kind of stress? Men! Ugh! After a long evening and semi-morning I decided to go back to bed. There weren't any point of staying awake.

The sunrays entered through my window and knocked on my face. I could tell today was going to be a hot one. Still no sign of Kwame. Not even a missed phone call, unanswered voice message or text. Not even a letter on our kitchen table of bedroom dresser. No signs that Kwame even existed anymore besides the clothes, shoes and other miscellaneous item's he's left behind. *He could have been more of a man about the situation,* I thought to myself. *It is my body; no one else! All of this because of a thought about an abortion. It's so petty. But…I can also understand why he's mad. I did make a decision without involving him. I even was secretive about the decision I had made. Pretending to be happy about this baby when deep down I was plotting to get rid of it and pretend that I miscarriage. Wow! I guess I owe it to myself. Kwame has been being a man; since I've known him. I guess I been taking him for granted and not appreciating him like I should have been. Starting today that's what I'll do. Appreciate my man a little better than what I do.* With that being said I decided to give Kwame a call. It rung and I actually thought he would answer but I was wrong.

"Hello?" A lady answered from the line that I dialed which I thought was Kwame's phone number.
"Um, I'm sorry. I think I have the wrong number." I suggested.
"That's ok. Bye."
"Bye."

Looking at my phone in search of the number I just dialed it showed that it was Kwame's line. *Ok, maybe something weird happened and the wrong line got tapped into. Let's try this again. I know he isn't that bold and crazy.* The phone ranged and once again the same woman picked up his line.

"Hello?" She said in an intensified voice. "Didn't you just call here?"

"Well yes I did. Is this three one seven, sixteen fifty three?"

"I'm not sure what the number is exactly. I just met him yesterday."

"Hold up, you just met who yesterday?" I said with my heart in my stomach.

"Kwame. That is who you're calling right?"

Everything in my heart and soul melted away. My tongue couldn't move as my eyes filled with water. Every memory there ever was between us had shattered in the blink of an eye. Every memory there would have been; marriage, our child, watching him bond, doing things as a family had burned before my eyes. Been completed tourn apart; shredded. I wanted to kick Kwame's ass. Fury filled my kindness.

"Hello," the lady continued to ask while I became an emotional wreck.

"I'm here," I said barely able to speak as hearing her voice took another shot at stabbing my heart. "Is…Kwame with you?"

"Yes he is. He's in the shower. Hold on while I get him."

"He's in the shower," I cried to myself. *"So cheating was that easy?"*

My heart wanted to hang up the phone and leave but my soul and spirit wouldn't let me believe that Kwame was there with this woman; and in the shower! I wanted to believe that she found his phone. But that couldn't be true because she knew his name. Tears filled my eye socket but I refused to let them roll down my face. I held them in as tight as I could because I needed to hear his voice. "That's not my Kwame. I know it's not!"

"Hello," she answered as I was hoping she had things wrong.

"Yes," I replied.

"He said he'll be just a minute. Hold on."

She placed the phone down and I was able to hear the conversation amongst the two of them.

"Hey Thickness, can you help me with my shirt please?" I over heard Kwame saying to the woman.

"Sure, why not? There's no harm in helping you with your shirt right?" she responded.

Kwame giggled. I wanted to jump through the phone and rip his tongue out. Then tell him *laugh at that*. And ask, *Do you think that's funny you peace of shit?* But of course this wasn't television and I had to continue listening with a broken heart.

"Thanks Thickness. I have to go home. I know my girlfriend is worried sick."

"*Ex-girlfriend*," I said while listening.

"Oh, Kwame," She yelled after him. "Your phone! Don't forget your phone and someone's on it. She's been waiting awhile now."

"Did you say…she?"

"Yes; she. What's wrong?"

"Hello," he answered remorseful.

"Yeah, darling. **I know**. I know that you're a deceitful bastard who can't keep his dick in his pants."

"Wait a minute baby I can explain!"

"Explain! Explain! How can you explain? Go ahead and try it. I'm just curious what the hell you have to say for yourself."

"Well for starters,"

"Let me guess. It ain't what you think? Was I right?"

"Well, yes, but no. "

"Really? Well which is it Kwame? It ain't what I think or it's exactly what I think?"

"Um…can we just talk about this when I get home?"

"Home? Are you fucking serious? There is no home! There is no you and me! There is no us! Don't be surprised if when you get to the place you call home, that I'm not here. Cause this isn't my home. Not anymore," I said while hanging up.

My mind couldn't have been more made up. He cheated and it was obvious. I had the evidence. The woman's voice was heard and he had just gotten out of the shower. What more did I need? It was over. My bags couldn't have gotten packed sooner. Exiting the door that I was once so happy to walk through I took one last look. Walking through it felt like relief after the stress I've been through in the past half hour. I called my parents but of course no one answered. *Just like them* I thought to myself. Good thing I know where the spare key is. After placing the suit cases into my trunk I got in my car and drove as fast as I could away from our dorm. The gas tank beeped for me to get gas which was the last thing on my mind. But being that I was pregnant, the last thing I wanted to do was be stranded, sick and hungry. The nearest gas station was just a few blocks away. Once I got there I was glad I stopped. Being pregnant causes you to need the toilet a lot. Either you're running to it because you have to pee and feel incompetent or you're running to it because you have to puke. And that's only if you make it. In this case I had to pee; and really, really bad. My stomach felt like it was going to ring every ounce of liquid out of me and force it to travel through my bladder. That was so not a good feeling. While I was using the toilet Kwame called me. Of course I didn't answer. Why should I have? Aren't I the same pregnant woman he left home alone and all night? He wasn't thinking of the baby and I when he had his pants down, was on top of the other woman, her on top of him, or however it was. My phone ranged and ranged until someone in the next stall became irritable.

That's when Denise and I ended up finding each other again. At that point in time she was very much needed as she helped to take my mind off of Kwame because we had maybe seven years of catching up to do.

Naturally I went back to her place and we did a lot of girl things. Mainly talk, talk and more talk. Even though I spent nearly the whole day with her it didn't help my dreams.

Images of Kwame and the woman he cheated on me with kept appearing. How they met? How the conversation went? What happened after their conversation? Did they jump straight to sex? How long did they talk before sex? Did he hold her like he did me while they slept? Did he caress her the way that he did me while we made love? Did he make love to her the way he made love to her? Was their kiss the same as ours? Was she better looking than I?

"So what's your name?" Kwame asks the woman behind the bar as she wiped empty shot glasses dry.

"Kwame," he responded slamming the empty shot glass on the counter. "Another shot please," he demanded from her.

"Did you drive here?" the bartender asked.

"What does it matter?"

"It matters because as a bartender I am held accountable if I allow those that are under the influence to operate a motor vehicle. So again, I will ask…did…you…drive?"

"Yea, but so what. I'm not drunk."

"Didn't say you were."

"So are you going to give me another shot or what?"

"Or what?" the bartender repeated sarcastically with a smile.

"I'll give you a good tip if you do," Kwame begged drunkingly.

"Honey, you've had twelve shots of Suicide drinks. I think you've had plenty."

"Just one more. One more won't hurt will it?"

She walked away to help other customers at the opposite side of the bar. By the time she had returned, Kwame climbed over the countertop and began to help his self to another shot of Suicide.

"WHAT ARE YOU DOING?" she yelled. "Sir, I'm going to have to ask you to leave. You are wasted and I have other customers to serve. I can't babysit you," she said impatiently. "Look…you're not a regular so obviously you're under some stress. Do you want to talk about it? I have time until the next paying customer requests a drink."

"I don't want to talk about it," Kwame slobbered.

"Look at you. You look disgusting. You're making a mess just slobbering all over yourself. I'm sure you'd feel a lot better if you talked about it. So go on…talk."

"My girlfriends pregnant," Kwame said trying to get his self together."May I have a bottle of water? I'm so thirsty."

"Now I'm definitely convinced that you are not a alcoholic," she laughed. "A bottle of water…coming up," she said delighted to give him something other than alcohol. "So your girlfriend's pregnant huh? Ouch! I guess that's something to drink to…or against," she said confused.

"Well her being pregnant isn't the problem," he said taking a sip of water.

"Well if that isn't the problem, than what is?"

"She doesn't want the baby," he uttered while sucking down half the bottle of *water*.

"Double ouch."

"Tell me about it."

"Does she have any other children?"

"Nope, none, nada; never even a pregnancy."

"Well do you have any other children besides the baby she's carrying?"

"Nope," he said drinking the rest of his water. "I never laid eyes on anyone but her."

"Aw. That's sweet."

"Sweet but true."

"So what's the problem? This is yalls first child together. And you've only been in love with her. I don't understand why she would pass that up? Good guys don't come by the dozen."

"Tell me about it. And I do everything for her. Cook, clean, rub her feet; and after I get off of work. Can I have another bottle of water please?"

"Sure. So you're a good man huh?"

"Yes ma'am."

"Well, if you were my man, I'd treat you like you deserve to be treated. Sounds to me she's taking advantage of you."

"Oh really. So tell me…since she's taken advantage of me, what type of things can you do to take advantage of me right now? Especially being that I'm drunk?"

"Are you sure you're ready for what I have to give cause I don't think you are?"

"Sure I am? Why wouldn't I be?"

"Um, because you're drunk and I'd be just taking advantage of you since you can't think clearly."

"But I'm not drunk!"

"If you're not drunk, how many bottles of water have you had?"

"That's easy. Five."

She looks at him with a told-you-so look as she dried the last pile of glasses.

"Ok. I was playing. Four or maybe three. No four for sure. Yea, four."

"Darling, I'm going to tell you this. One thing's for sure is you're drunk. Secondly, I can't allow you to go drive like that. Where do you live? Maybe I can *call a taxi for you.*"

"Uummmmm. I…can't…seem…to remember," Kwame said before passing out.

The bartender took him to her house. Some customers helped him to her car so that she can leave work on time. When he awoke, he was laying in her bed with his clothes stripped off.

"Where am I? And why am I naked?"

"You passed out in my bar," she said while in the bathroom. "I wanted to go home on time which meant you had to follow. Especially being that you couldn't tell me where you stay. Beside the point, you seem like a nice guy. I feel safe with you here."

"So I take it you live alone?"

"Yep, just me and my cats, Skitzy and Buttercup."

"Any children?"

"Nope, and never wanted any."

"Why not?"

"Never met the right guy."

"Wow."

"Yeah…tell me about it," she pronounced while opening the bathroom door.

Kwame immediately became aroused as he saw her standing there with a black slip on that had a split on the right thigh. He admired the way it was placed onto her leg and rose close to her hip. As she walked towards the bed he began to shake nervously.

"What's wrong?" she asked.

"Nothing, nothing's wrong."

"Than why are you shaking?" she asked while climbing into bed.

"I never have been with anyone other than…her."

"Who said I was going to sleep with you?"

"Well, you are…aren't you?"

"No," she giggled while turning out the light. "I was just messing around."

Reflections

I rose in bed in a complete sweat. Glancing over at Denise who was sound asleep than outside the window I could tell it was raining extremely hard. Could even hear so. Lightning begin to form shadows as thoughts flashed of Kwame and I cuddling and making love to the sound of the rain drops. Everything about him was so gentle from his sweet caressing down to his soft lips. Reminiscing while lying in bed never felt better. Dreaming of him flirting with other women was ridiculous. Even though I knew the truth. He cheated and there was no way in hell I could let that down so easy. My father always said *a man only gets away with what you allow him to get away with.* I wonder what he would say about this situation? Am I running away from our problem due to the fear of letting him get away with cheating? Lord knows I love him. And I am still young and able to make mistakes. I just don't want it to be a mistake that's going to cost a big change in my life and for as long as Kwame and I are together.

Lord give me the strength to deal with this problem. I don't pray as much as I should but I think I pray enough for you to listen to my cries tonight. Lord I'm stressing. I'm pregnant…and as far as I know my man has cheated on me. Even though I keep forcing myself to believe he cheated, deep down in my heart I'm in disbelief. After the dream I had tonight, I'm almost positive that Kwame would never do anything to hurt me. Yea he didn't come home, but I guess given the situation I could understand why. I've always been told that you speak to us through our dreams. In my dream tonight, Kwame didn't cheat. He was going to, but didn't. As a child, I was always told to turn my nightmares upside down. And in this case, Kwame was in the bed with another woman. Should I look at things as he never made it to bed with another woman? He never cheated on me? He didn't go to a bar last night? How should I look at things father? Only you and Kwame know what happened last night. Lord, I pray that you shed some light on my situation. I also pray that you help me to accept this child I am carrying. Amen, I said as I rolled over and closed my eyes.

The next day Kwame asked if we could talk and we did just that. Well not exactly in the beginning. Denise took me over to our place and I guess things became too steamy because she left. Obviously she knew he was in no harm else she wouldn't have left.

"Looks like it's just you…and me," I said frightening to Kwame.

"Wait, before you kill me I need to tell you something," Kwame said taking steps back.

"Go on," I said stepping forward.

"Um," he said tripping over the coffee table. "Um, the girl Thickness. Baby…sweetheart….snookums….pookybear…she's my cousin."

"Why have I never heard of her?"

"There's a lot of my family you haven't heard of," he said boldly. "She's from California," he startled again.

Picking up the phone, I said "Prove it."

"Fine, I will. I'm calling my momma."

"Why are you calling her? She can't help you."

He replied while listening to the phone ring in his ear, "Because that's where Thickness is at crazy woman. Hey mom how are you?"

"I'm fine why does your voice sound frantic?"

"Because," he said as I took the phone away from him. "KARMA IS TRYING TO KILL ME," he yelled hoping she would have heard.

"Hey mom."

"Hi darling. What did Kwame just say?"

"Oh Kwame," I said looking at him with threatening eyes. "He's just babbling. You know Kwame," I chuckled.

"Sounds like he said something about someone trying to kill him."

"Kwame…please," I chuckled. "Not sweet, dear ol Kwame. Who would ever want to hurt him?" I asked giving him a slap in the face.

"Mom," he howled quietly.

"Look, we don't mean to take up much of your time. I need to speak to Thickness."

"Thickness? Well what on earth do you want with her?"

"Well I've never heard of her and thought we can meet and have girl talk."

"With Thickness? She just arrived in town. I don't think that will be a good idea so soon."

"Well why not mom? Are you hiding something?"

"From you? No darling, you can't be serious. It's just that Thickness traveled here," she mentioned from being interrupted.

"From California, I know; I've heard."

"She's been through a lot. Kwame haven't seen her but once his entire life. The other day when he was home they had a lot of catching up to do."

"Yes mom. I couldn't have said things better. Well I have to go. Nice talking to you."

"Anytime honey. And Karma," she said before placing the phone on the hook. "Don't hurt my boy. I know you're pregnant and experiencing hormonal changes but he's telling you the truth. He's never cheated on you and never will. It isn't in him to do so. Kwame's been in love with you since he's first laid eyes on you. You're the first and last woman to ever capture his heart. Besides the point…I know where you live," she threatened.

"Thanks mom. I look forward to it. Bye."

"HELP! HELP! SOMEBOFY HELP ME!"

"Ah shut up. Sit your dumb ass down. Had you came home like you usually do none of this would have happened anyway."

"So…you're not going to kill me?"

"And risk raising this baby by myself. Um…no."

"Thank you Jesus she's calm," Denise said cheerfully walking through the front door.

Kwame and I looked at her surprisingly.

"What? I was scared of what she might have done so I stuck around; just in case."

We continued to look at her astonished.

"You don't know what's she's capable of being pregnant and all. Have you seen the things she can eat?"

Kwame looked at her as if he could choke her himself.

"Well since things are calm around here I guess I'll go home and leave you two love birds here to patch things up," Denise said walking towards the front door again.

"Thanks girl," I said hugging Denise. "I appreciate it. I may have needed someone to keep me off of him," I told her while giving Kwame a eerie look.

Kwame and I had a very long discussion. I thanked him for not cheating on me but there were consequences for him not coming home. No bad habits were going to begin within our relationship. Not if I could help it. He said he admired that about me and wouldn't dream of beginning any new habit *without* my approval. Especially since he thought I was a crazy woman.

First Come Love
Than Come...

"Mrs. Woods fast forwarding past Kenise being born and the complications with your labor; tell us about...the day you and Kwame got married. Well...that had to be the happiest day of your life. You had an extraordinary man. Loving...kind...respectful...faithful. How did your wedding day go?" Mrs. Williams asked.

Kenise was a little over one when Kwame and I became one. The ceremony was exquisite with about one hundred and fifty people that attended. I couldn't have asked for any more or any less.

I wore a white dress with a red bow placed in the mid section. Red ruby ear rings with a matching necklace and bracelet that of course Denise did the honors of helping with. In my hair was placed a white Lilly; only the loveliest flower in the world. And of course sense tonight was going to be a wild night; my hair was cramped with spirals placed at the end.

My father walked me down the isle. Kenise had just got finish sprinkling red and blue lilies. She wore a white dress with a blue bow and a red Lillie in her hair. I remember seeing Kwame's face; a huge smile was worn ear to ear. He wore a blue tuxedo with a white dress shirt and a red handkerchief hanging out of his breast pocket. His shoes were red to match the handkerchief as well as our wedding colors. Above him on a projection screen; pictures were being shared as they captured our most loving moments throughout life. The minister spoke of brief detail within each one. The last photo was the one of our daughter Kenise being born.

"It takes a real man to step up and know that what he has in front of him is all he'll ever need. Can I get an amen?" the minister said in excitement.

"AMEN!" the crowd roared.

"I said can I get an AMEN!"

"AMEN!"

"Let's be on with it. Dearly beloved…we're gathered here, in the sign of God to join together this man and this woman in holy matrimony. When the couple came to me and suggested that I be the one to ordain them, there was no way I could confuse. Look at the two of them; happy, in love and in unison.

If any person can show just cause why they may not be joined together…let them speak now or forever hold their peace."

There was a pause. The crowd became anxious and began to whistle and root in enthusiasm.

"Marriage is the union of husband and wife in heart, body and mind. It is intended for their mutual joy and for the help and comfort given on another in prosperity and adversity. But more importantly it is a means through which a stable and loving environment may be attained.

Through marriage, Kwame and Karma make a commitment together to face their disappointments, embrace their dreams, realize their hopes and accept each other's failures. Kwame and Karma will promise one another to aspire to these ideals throughout their lives together through mutual understanding, openness and sensitivity to each other."

There was another pause.

"We are here today…before God…because marriage is one of His most sacred wishes…to witness the joining of Kwame and Karma into one soul. This occasion marks the celebration of love and commitment with which this man and this woman will begin their life together. And now…through the power invested in me…He joins you together in one of the holiest bonds."

There was a pause.

"Who gives this woman in marriage to this man?" The minister asked the crowd.

"I do. Michael Gentry," my father answered as he walked towards the alter to stand.

"And who are you in regards to Karma?" the minister asked my father placing a hand on his shoulder.

"I am her father; a very proud father."

"Amen. He said he's a proud father," the minister spoke to the crowd. "Aint nothing wrong…with being a proud father; a…men. You may have a seat if you please," he spoke to my father. "This is a beginning and a continuation of their growth as individuals. With mutual care, respect, responsibility and knowledge comes the affirmation of each one's own life happiness, growth and freedom. With respect for individual boundaries comes the freedom to love unconditionally. Within the emotional safety of a loving relationship, the knowledge self-offered one another becomes the fertile soil for continued growth. With care and responsibility towards self and one another comes the potential for full and happy lives."

There was a pause.

"By gathering together all the wishes of happiness and our fondest hopes for Kwame and Karma from all present here, we assure them that our hearts are in tune with theirs. These moments are so meaningful to all of us, for what greater thing is there for two human souls than to feel that they are joined together, to strengthen each other in all labor, to minister to each other in all sorrow, to share with each other in all gladness."

There was a pause.

"This relationship stands for love, loyalty, honesty and trust, but most of all for friendship. Before they knew love, they were friends, and it was from this seed of friendship that is their destiny. Do not think that you can direct the course of love, for love, if it finds you worthy, shall direct you."

There was a pause.

"Marriage is an act of faith and a personal commitment as well as a moral and physical union between two people. Marriage has been described as the best and most important relationship that can exist between them. It is the construction of their love and trust into a single growing energy of spiritual life. It is amoral commitment that requires and deserves daily attention. Marriage should be a life long consecration of the ideal of loving kindness backed with the will to make it last."

There was a pause.

"Now it is time...to exchange the vows. Kwame, why don't you take your bride by the hands...and speak from your heart. Why you're doing that I'm going to have a seat cause the way you're looking at her, I can tell...this gon be a while. Amen.

"AMEN!"

"I'm just kidding. How many of you ever been in love? It don't take a few seconds to say what you have to say. It takes an eternity. Am I right?"

The crowd roared in excitement.

"I'm just kidding young couple. It's an honor to be here this afternoon."

"Thank you sir," Kwame replied.

"Alright Kwame. Shall we?"

Kwame looked into my eyes. He had the same blank face as the day we met when I was lost; speechless. But deep in my heart, as well as in the heart of everyone else that was here, I knew he had so much to say.

Beginning to cry he said, "Karma...I have loved you from the moment I've laid eyes on you. I can't say it enough how much I love you. How much in love I am with you. There is no me without you. There is no I; hasn't been in quite some time now," he chuckled. "I knew I would love you," he said bending down on one knee. "From the first time you kicked Bryant in the growing. That was the funniest day of my life."

"Hey, I object!" Bryant shouted.

"Sit down Bryant," Kwame's and Bryant's mother said calmly. "Or I'll sit you down. And give her another shot at kicking you," I overheard the conversation.

"You wouldn't?"

Looking at him with devilish eyes she said "Are you willing to bet your life on that?"

Bryant did as he was told while mumbling "Kwame always got the girls."

Patting his leg their mother said, "Not this time. He has *the* girl."

The projection screen above showed a photo of someone portraying to be Bryant and I; and the way his face looked when I did it. Kwame was full of surprises I must admit and it was hilarious to see that moment rethought of in our vows.

"I loved you more when I saved you from fainting on the bus and we had an argument because we kept repeating the same thing."

A small clip was played reacting the scene that day. I believe he added a little more to it than what actually happened but I laughed as I remembered similar events.

"I loved you even more when you thought I cheated on you and threatened to kill me while my mom was on the phone. I must admit, you gave me quite the scare."

The projection screen showed me in the form of a Freddy Krueger mask chasing after Kwame. It was by far the funniest moment of the evening.

"And my love exceeded far and beyond the day you bore my daughter; our daughter. And for that I could never repay the traumatizing events," he began to cry. "That took place that day," Kwame said taking a deep breath. "Truth is I've always knew I would marry you. I wanted it to happen sooner but than we had bills and Kenise…everything I had planned just started to fall apart. At least that's what I thought. But… here we are today. Hand in hand; confessing our love for each other.

It couldn't have happened at a better time. I love you," he said kissing my hand.

"Wow. That was wonderful. A real man knows what he wants and goes after it…doesn't he?" the minister exclaimed.

The crowd roared and shouted.

"Kwame did such a good job I don't think we need to hear what Karma has to say; right?"

The crowd looked in disagreement. They including myself became confused.

"Just kidding. Ok, Karma. It is now your turn to tell your groom how much in love," the minister winked. "You are with him."

"I'd be honor to do just that," I said looking Kwame into his eyes. "Kwame, you can't imagine how much I love you. I know in the past I've been…what some would some say…abusive but my father always taught me to be tough."

"That's right baby," my father stood and shouted "And look at my little girl. She's getting married to the man she loves. Tough love gets you a long way!"

"Yes it does daddy. Now as I was saying…Kwame, I wish I had known sooner the way you felt about me. Truth is, deep down I've always been in love with you too. The way you made me feel was an experience within itself. How you stayed at the hospital with me when I collapsed; not caring about how my parents would take it. The support you gave me over the years as well as while I was delivering Kenise."

Kwame began to cry uncontrollably. Wiping away his tears I kissed him on both cheeks.

"I love you too Kwame. And I am honored to be your bride."

"AWWWWWWWW," the crowd said together cheerfully.

"Ok. I guess that is my clue to get on with the ceremony," the minister suggested. "Do you Kwame…take Karma…to be your wife? To live together after God's ordinance, in the holy estate of matrimony? Will you love her, comfort her, honor and keep her, in sickness and in health, for richer, for poorer, for better, for worse, in sadness and in joy, to cherish and continually bestow upon her your heart's deepest devotion, forsaking all others, keep yourself only unto her as long as you both shall live?"

"I DO…EVERYTHING," Kwame shouted.

"He said he does…everything," the minister repeated. "I don't think I've ever heard any groom get any happier than that," he said to our guest. "Karma you are a very lucky woman."

"I know minister. I know," I reassured him.

"And do you Karma, I love your name by the way, take Kwame… to be your husband? To live together after God's ordinance, in the holy estate of matrimony? Will you love him, comfort him, honor and keep him, in sickness and in health, for richer, for poorer, for better, for worse, in sadness and in joy, to cherish and continually bestow upon him your heart's deepest devotion, forsaking all others, keep yourself only unto him as long as you both shall live?"

"I DO," I shouted.

"She does," the minister said to our guest jokingly. "It is now time for the bride and groom to exchange wedding rings."

Bryant walked down with a small blue pillow with a red ribbon tied on top; that held both of our wedding rings in place.

"May these rings be blessed as the symbol of this affectionate unity. These two lives are now joined in one unbroken circle. Wherever they go… may they always return to one another. May these two find in each other the love for which all men and women yearn. May they grow in understanding and in compassion. May the home which they establish together be such a place that many are welcomed upon. Kwame…it is an honor to be the minister in witness of this ceremony."

"Thank you sir," Kwame said.

The crowd became extremely quiet and eager while looking forward to the kiss that secluded our bond.

"Kwame…you may now…kiss…your bride."

At this point I began to cry. Remembering everything that was said and had taken place through our wedding ceremony was too much to handle. I couldn't believe my Kwame was gone. I loved him so much and missed him dearly. If I could have him back I'd rather that be an option than to suffer this way. I needed him, we needed him. Kenise hasn't been the same since her father died. Now we have to pray on a miracle. A touch of GOD's light to restore my family. It's what Kwame would have wanted.

Our guest roared and stomped their feet as Kwame bent me over and kissed my lips. It was ever so passionate and very romantic. He truly had made me the happiest woman in the world.

The recession was just as romantic. Our theme was Hearts so naturally everything seen indicated some form of just that. There were blue chairs seated to red heart tables smothered with blue Lilies and red candles. The chosen dance floor was white and smooth. The lighting arrangements were a switch of our wedding colors. Often times my husband and I were placed in the spot light where we shared a kiss or some famous memory. Blue and Red Lilies hung from the ceilings and was embedded in our seat.

It was Kwame's idea to choose a mixture of reggae, R n B and oldies. My favorite songs of the night were the Cupid Shuffle and The BootyCall. Our first dance was very unique as we didn't do the normal slow dance that most couples chose to do. Instead, we did the Salsa followed by the Sugarhill Gang Apache (Jump On It). My gosh we had our guest completely in tears. They couldn't believe we actually thought of repeating the episode seen on Fresh Prince of Bel Air where Carlton and Will Smith were dancing on the stage. By the time we'd finished everyone was completely in tears. It truly was the laugh of the night.

Unplanned
Changes

Sitting on the couch and going through our photo album brought back so many memories. The day I married Kwame was the happiest day of my life. I couldn't have ask to been married to a better man. He was everything I have ever wanted.

Two years into our marriage we experienced a lot of turmoil. He became extremely depressed, jealous and distant after he lost his job. Said he wasn't the man of the house if he couldn't provide for his family. Trying to reassure him he was wrong just made things worst.

One particular night I went to a convenient store to get Kenise some pampers and wipes. I had a quiet thought to take Kenise with me but it was extremely cold outside. Beside the point I would only be gone for fifteen minutes. Thirty minutes tops, if there was a shortage on cashiers. So I left Kenise in the care of her seemingly depressed father. I thought this would be a good time for the two of them to do some catching up. Even Kenise liked the idea. She smiled as I walked out of the door.

On the drive to the store I felt at peace. No man to argue with, no responsibilities of caring for Kenise or household chores; just peace and quiet. It felt so good to be alone for once that I screamed to the top of my lungs. I never realized till now just how much stress I was under. I felt like a single parent on the road to divorce. How could things go so terribly wrong when they have gone so right up until now? Is this what I deserve? Did I do something God didn't like? Hundreds of thoughts crossed my mind but none of which made sense.

By the time I had finished crying and gathering my purse I had already been gone for an hour. Getting out of the car just to get the items Kenise needed seemed like the hardest thing I had to do. My body was weak. So was my soul and heart.

"Are you okay?" someone asked.

"I will never be ok again," I snapped.

"God only put on us what we can carry. He will never make you hold more than that."

"Thank you but I don't want to hear that shit right now," I excused myself.

"Did you ever tell Kwame about that night?" Mrs. Williams asked.

"With the things he was going through; heck no. I wish I could have though; at least as a good bye. Now I have to wait until I'm called home to reveal that to him," I sighed.

"I'm sure he's watching us and thinking "What a woman!"" Mr. Ohio suggested. "I just have one question. If you and your husband were so close, why didn't you tell him about the conversation you had in the parking lot?"

"I couldn't."

"You said you and Kwame were close; heck the best of friends. And the only excuse you have for not telling your husband was you couldn't?"

I didn't know what else to say so I kept quiet.

"You want to know what I think? I think the story you just shared with our court room is the story you want us to believe that happened. In reality, the truth of the matter is you were tired of Kwame."

"I could never get tired of Kwame," I interrupted.

He continued, "When opportunity came knocking you took it; beginning an affair."

Becoming frustrated, "An affair? I loved Kwame. I could never cheat on him."

Ignoring my comment, "Hoping this day would come. That your beloved husband would end up dead and you can begin to live your new life with the man you love. Isn't that right Mrs. Woods?"

"Objection!" Mrs. Williams shouted.

"No. That isn't right at all. I went home to my husband and child."

"Yeah and I went home to Janet Jackson," he retaliated.

"Your honor!" Mrs. Williams said. "He's badgering the witness."

"You're way out of line Mr. Ohio. Have you made your point or is there a point to be made?"

"No further questions your honor."

"Mrs. Woods you may continue from there," Judge Lanai Brown Brown said.

Once I pulled into the driveway, I could hear Kenise crying. Immediately running into our house to see what was wrong, I walked around to fetch her father. While she was crying he was taking a shower. I was so angry at him. I cleaned her face and packed our things. When I was finished I placed her into her crib and kissed her cheek. Then I went into the shower where her father had the nerve to be singing.

Pulling back the shower curtains I said as calmly as possible, "So I guess you didn't hear Kenise crying huh?"

Cutting the shower off and grabbing for his towel Kwame responded, "Yea I heard her cry; so what?"

Angrily I spoke, "So what? So what? I can't believe that's what you have to say for yourself!"

Looking me into my eyes Kwame said, "What do you want me to say Karma? Huh? Do you want me to say I enjoyed hearing her cry? Cause I didn't. I just wanted to take a quick shower and she would have been ok until I got out. That's till the bitch of the house came home."

Slapping Kwame in his face I walked away heading towards Kenise's room.

Walking towards me Kwame said, "Where do you think you're going?"

"I'm tired Kwame...tired! We're leaving."

"Oh you think you're going to leave out of this house that I paid for?"

Walking pass Kwame I responded, "Watch me!"

He grabbed me by my arm and told me I needed to think about what we're doing than flashed his hand in my face showing me his wedding band. I snatched my arm away and told him to throw the wedding band away; it means nothing to me anymore. As I attempted to take another step, Kwame pulled me by my hair and told me I better not drop his daughter. To protect Kenise I did as I was told. He guided me back towards her room and told me to place her in the crib. By this time Kenise began to cry. She could sense something wasn't right by the change in my heartbeat. For the first time in months, Kwame spoke to Kenise saying *that everything is going to be ok and that she didn't have to worry. Mommy and daddy are going to have a little talk and he had to show mommy who the man of the house was.* Of course he still had my hair in his hands so that I would cooperate; while having me to also reassure our daughter that everything will be ok. Kenise's bottom lip quivered as she knew this wasn't the end. She laid down and closed her eyes in hopes to be sleep. After seeing this Kwame had calmed down and let my hair go. I looked at him not knowing rather to defend myself or take him into my arms. He picked Kenise up and sat in the rocking chair sitting across from her bed. Kissing her lips while cradling her close he begin to cry. Looking at me than lip motioning, *I am so sorry. Please forgive me?*

I walked away and allowed Kwame to heal his bond with our daughter. His depression has caused him to miss out on months of our daughter's life, months that he can never get back. Fifteen minutes had passed as I laid in bed dreaming about the old times; memories of happiness and love that filled the air. The door creaked as Kwame walked into the room. Lying down beside me not knowing what to do or say, it seemed like days had passed before he finally spoke.

"Karma, I can't take back the pain I've caused my family. I can't even take back what I could have done to you tonight. If it wasn't for the way Kenise looked at me when you placed her in the crib I...I...I probably would have hurt you. And who knows; maybe even Kenise and myself."

I didn't know what to say as I listened to his spirit. A part of my heart was telling me to take Kenise and follow through with my plans to leave; while the other part was saying to work things out.

How can I work things out when I lost hope for him months ago? I still loved him dearly but things had got way out of control tonight. Who's to say that there won't be a next time? I have to think of Kenise and what's best for her. I wouldn't want her to be with a man that was on drugs, abusive and violent. Further more I don't want to become six feet under because the man I'm madly in love with is so depressed that he can't realize he's hurting me.

As thought from thought emerged I begin to get a headache. Ignoring Kwame, I turned onto my back and pulled the blankets over me.

Seeing that I felt uneasy about the conversation he asked, "Karma can you ever forgive me?"

Looking him in the eye I responded with a shy voice, "I don't know."

Beginning to cry he said, "Baby please don't say that. I love you and Kenise too much to lose out on a lifetime of memories. Please tell me you'll forgive me. Please?" He begged as he began kissing me.

Peck after peck and ever so gently. Responding slowly with a smooch in return he placed his hand on my face.

"I would never do anything to hurt you or our daughter?" He continued to kiss. "You have to believe that much. I know I've changed and been doing things you don't like but I'm still a good man."

Tears rolled down my face as we began to hug and caress. It had been months since Kwame and I have been intimate. Feeling his lips against mine sent shivers down my spine. He saw that I was getting aroused and begin to move his fingers up and down my body; stroking as he went along. Kwame climbed on top and began to kiss me from my lips down to my navel. I started to sweat in excitement. He took my clothes off and we began to make love. After what had just happened it was more than amazing and worth the making up. Like I said, I loved him and was willing to hang in there for the long haul.

While he was inside of me I kept toying between thoughts. I saw us on our wedding day, than envisioned our evening tonight. I saw the pain in Kenise's eyes and the lost soul in his. He had never grabbed my hair, that was knew. It only began with the name calling; bitch this bitch that but I didn't care. In my soul I believed he would change back to the man I was in love with.

As Kwame pushed deeper inside of me near climaxing I saw doves floating in the air. They were a pearly white and chasing each other around in circles. When the dominant Dove reached the other one they sung than kissed. Within the same breath they changed colors and were no longer white. The birds now became black crows and were hawking forcefully at each other.

I immediately attempted to return to reality and heard Kwame moaning within each push getting louder as he went. Turning my head caused the vision to revisit. There were no longer two crows but three and two of them were now chasing violently after the one. Finally the two went separate ways to trap the vulnerable bird and they broke his neck. Hitting the ground with a loud thud I felt Kwame jammed in position. Within a blink of the eye, as we both moaned our last moan of gratification, I saw death; myself lying in a coffin with my hands transverse across my chest.

Breathing heavy, I froze in place. Kwame kissed me one last time and hugged me tight. We cried in each other arms until we fell asleep. Only thing is he had no clue why I was crying.

"If Kwame was emotionally abusive and began to become physically threatening why didn't you just leave?" Mr. Ohio asked while walking over to the jury. "I mean why on Earth would someone want to stay in a relationship like that?"

"I loved him and as much as I wanted to give up I couldn't."

"You couldn't give up on a man that gave up on you and your child? A man that had a fist full of your hair tangled in his palms…in front of your baby girl? A man that decided to turn to drugs instead of getting another job like most people do?"

"The economy was low."

"The economy was low…you even have the nerve to take up for him."

"He's still my husband."

"Honey I don't know if you didn't get the memo but your husband is dead. You are now a widow being charged with his murder.

As emotionally disturbing as that was I ignored him. I know Kwame is gone and never coming back. But I wasn't going to allow him to say horrible things about my husband. Dead or not he will always and forever be the man I've been in love with since the day we met. No one could ever take his place or the memories we have together.

"Mr. Ohio are you finished?" Judge Lanai Brown asked.

"Yes ma'am."

"Mrs. Williams."

"I'm sure there are a ton of stories you could share with us about your husband right?"

"Of course. We've had just as many good times as we did bad…in the end."

"Like what?"

I'd say "Kwame, I just came from Winton Montessori and it's a really good school. The teachers are extremely qualified and it's tuition free, something we can afford."

"I've never heard of any school being free. What did you do to make it become free?"

"What do you mean?"

"Who…did…you…fuck…to get her in?"

"I can't believe you would disrespect me like that Kwame. What the fuck has gotten into you?"

"Naw the question is what's gotten into you and by the looks of things," he said looking at my gem. "Been in you."

It didn't make sense to argue with his so I walked away.

"Another time he actually slammed my head into the wall. Again, I had just gotten home and today was payday. Normally I'd pay the bills first before going home because having money around a drug addict isn't good for business.

What caused me to stop home was the fact I had left two or our most important bills on the dining room table. Kwame must have walked passed and noticed them than thought about my return home to get them; because when I got home he was ready for me."

"What you doing here?" he asked as if he didn't already know.

I didn't want to tell him the reason behind my presence so I lied. Well didn't exactly tell him why I was there.

"Ummm…I just stopped by to grab something," I motioned pass him.

"Something like what?" he followed.

"Just some paper work that's all," I said in search for the bills.

He continued to allow me to search for the bills as I hurriedly moved throughout each room.

"Looking for something," he suggested with the bills dangling from his hand.

"Yes…that's…exactly…what I…was looking for," I responded calmly.

"Now how did I know that?"

"I…don't…know," I hesitated. "May I have them please."

"Sure," he said politely.

The moment I stepped towards him he ripped the bills in half.

"Oops. I'm sorry baby. I didn't mean to do that."

"That's ok. Maybe they'll have an extra copy available."

"Maybe," he suggested walking to the front door.

"Alright then," I tried to walk pass him.

The moment my hand touched the door knob my face hit the wall. I don't remember what happened after that. My features hit the wall just hard enough to knock me unconscious. By the time I awaked, Kwame was gone; with my car and purse. Not only was I not able to pay any bills but was also late picking up Kenise from my parents.

"Why weren't you able to pay the bills?" Mrs. Williams asked.

"Kwame stole my money, purse, cell phone and car."

"Mrs. Woods, how do we know that all of this isn't made up? Or that maybe something close to this happened but instead of him stealing the money you spent it on your new boo?" Mr. Ohio intervened.

"OBJECTION!"

"Sustained. The witness will speak."

"First of all I told you I loved my husband and there was no one else; never will be. And second of all I didn't make anything up. It really happened. Pricks like you are the reason to why I didn't go to the police because I didn't want to be judged or belittled, " I snapped.

"And I rest my case. If Mrs. Woods is able to place harsh words so well together in a sentence like that over something as simple as what I said, who's to say she wouldn't have helped Kwame commit suicide?"

The court room became quiet. Some of the jury agreed to his little masquerade as they put their heads down to show so. Mrs. William began to write notes down and was the only hope I had left in winning this case. I didn't want to go to jail for a crime I didn't do and she was the only one as well as the judge who seemed to believe me at this point.

"Mrs. Williams," Judge Lanai Brown signaled.

"Mrs. Woods, please tell us the rest of the events that happened that night."

My cell phone was in my purse so naturally I had to use the house phone to alert my parents I would be later than usual to get them. Only problem was I didn't realize how late it had already been.

"Hello," I mumbled.

"Karma? Karma are you alright?" my mother answered.

"I'll be fine mom," I answered. "Has Kwame been by to get Kenise?"

"No he hasn't. We haven't heard from Kwame in quite some time now. Why? What's wrong?"

"No-nothing," I stuttered. "Is it alright if I took an extra hour to come pick her up?"

"Sure buy why? Karma I hear it in your voice that something isn't right?"

"Is dad around?"

"He's upstairs I think?"

"Kwame ran off with my car and some other things."

"Other things like what?"

"My purse."

"Well was there anything in it?"

"Yea mom. Actually…there was. Cash…lots of it."

"Why on Earth…never mind. I won't tell your father. I will let him know that Kenise is going to stay the night with us so you two could work some things out."

"Thanks mom, I really appreciate it."

"You're welcome baby. I'm still in debt to you so anything I can do to help is a pleasure."

"Mom you don't owe me anything. You've done plenty already."

"Thanks Princess."

"You're welcome mom."

"Love you."

"Love you too."

Now this conversation sounds as if everything was going to be okay. All I had to do was put some ice on my forehead and wait for Kwame to get home. The problem I was faced with was not knowing the whole time I was speaking to my mother, my father was on the upstairs phone; patiently and quietly listening to everything as well. When the phone conversation ended, he must have waited for the two of us to hang up before he did. Than knowing how my mother would be, to avoid conference he left their house another way.

After applying ice to my head I was extremely tired and fell asleep in the chair near the front door. I can't remember how much time had passed but I remember clearly the confrontation between Kwame and my father. The lights to my car flashed in the living room indicating he was home. He took a moment to come into the house as he was fidgeting inside of the vehicle. By the time he made it indoors out from behind me my father charged at him.

The only thought on my mind was *how the hell did he get in here?*

"Yeah, I got yo bitch ass huh," he snatched Kwame up from his standing position.

It happened so fast that even Kwame appeared to be in a twilight.

"So you been putting your hands on my mutherfucking daughter huh?" he asked while shaking him. "Answer me bitch," he motioned as he threw him down. "Yo bitch ass can put your hands on my daughter but can't fight me huh?" he kicked him in the ribs. "Don't just stand there; I want you to get up and fight me like you fight my daughter."

At that point Kwame stood up and charged towards my father with his head bent down. My dad took his two fists, placed them together and hit him in his back two times causing my husband to drop to the floor.

"Get back up bitch," he spat at him. "You a coward and if I known then what I…know…now," he kicked him again. "You wouldn't be with my daughter. Would of…never…married…her."

As this ordeal was happening I was bemused. I've never seen my father step out of line like this but then again I never gave him a reason to as Kwame was the only boy friend I ever had. And lets not forget I was an only child so no siblings, no issues with their mates either.

My husband stood to attempt to fight my dad again. Excited my father took off his coat and put his dukes up.

"Come on bitch...show me what you got," he swung out hitting Kwame in the eye.

His head cocked back as more blows returned to his eyes, nasal cavity, mouth, and abdomen.

"Oh...I guess you're tired from whooping my daughters ass huh," he drop kicked him. "Should...have...saved...some...for...me," he said while stomping Kwame's face.

Returning to reality and realizing that this is really happening I tried to pull my father off of him.

"Dad, you're going to kill him," I yelled.
"Relax baby girl. Daddy...wouldn't...kill...a...soul. But I...will... fuck...someone up...over my daughter," he said becoming tired.

My father looked at Kwame as he was arched over taking air breaks.

"And this...is for...my damn...grand...baby."

I watched my father who was now completely winded as he walked into the kitchen and washed the blood off of his hands. He than walked towards me and told me to pack some things for Kenise and I that we wouldn't be back.

"Was your father ever convicted for the assault?" Mrs. Williams asked.
"No."
"Why not?"
"I guess Kwame didn't press charges."
"Is it because he didn't want to or you didn't want him to?" Mr. Ohio rose from his seat.

291

I couldn't answer the question right away because I knew it would have just made me look guilty.

"Your honor," he said having her to overrule the decision.
"Answer the question Mrs. Woods."
"I don't want to."
"Do you know I can hold you in contempt for up to thirty days?"
"What difference will that make when I'm already incarcerated?"
"Are you saying you'd rather go back to a cell than to end it all here today?"

There was a pause as I didn't answer.

"We're going to take a fifteen minute recess; court is adjourned."

Judge Lanai Brown took me into her chambers and asked me to be seated. She stared at me over and over again causing me to look at the floor.

"Do you want to know why I'm staring at you?" she asked.

I said nothing, just continued to look at the floor.

"Because when I look at you I see a battered woman. A woman that's been through hell with a man whom she was madly in love with. The same man who raised his hand to bruise her beautiful face. The same man who stole the money for the bills to get high. The very same man who is now no longer here and have you being arraigned for murder. At what point in time do you get a break? When will you stand up and defend yourself girl?"

Everything she said made sense. I have experienced a lot of turmoil for him and now that he's dead and I have a chance to start over I was still hanging on to that misery. Still allowing him to control me from his grave.

"We have about five minutes left. What do you say we get out there and finish this trial?"

I looked at her and gave a shy smile that I was ready to do so.

"Let's go," she waved me off.

Entering into the court room I felt relieved. It was a lot clearer than before which gave me more time to take in deep breaths as I sat in the witness stand. Eventually recess was over and it was time to pick up where we left off at.

"Ok people, before our short break Karma; excuse me, Mrs. Woods, told the story of how her father brutally beat Kwame due to a misunderstanding.

Her lawyer asked "Was your father ever convicted for the assault of her husband?"

Mrs. Woods specifically said "No."

Than she was asked "Why not?" by the lovely Mrs. Williams again; by the way

Mrs. Woods countered "I guess Kwame didn't press charges."

And when I asked Mrs. Woods "Is it because he didn't want to or you didn't want him to?" she became quiet and could not or should I say refused to answer the question. "Again…Mrs. Woods…once more… Did Kwame not press any charges because he…didn't want to or…you didn't want him to being that it would have been against your dad?"

"I didn't want him to," I retorted. "Happy now?"

"You can bet your sweet ass," he started before noticing what he just said. "I mean yes I am.

"Because Mr. Ohio has chosen to be disorderly while court is in session I am going to ask the jury to forget about everything that was just said and have it removed completely from the manuscripts," Judge Lanai Brown motioned.

The court room became hysterical.

"If you don't agree with my decision than feel free to remove yourself before we go any further."

Everyone became quiet.

"Anyone," she waited.

No one stood.

"Good. We will begin from her answer to Mr. Ohio's last question."

"Were there any other things you and Kwame argued about?" Mrs. Williams asked.

"There was a disagreement on just about everything. How he wasn't able to feed and support his family, to send Kenise to a good private school just all sorts of things.

I'd say, "Baby what would you like to eat for dinner?"
His response, "Whatever you want."
Than I'd say, "I really don't have a taste for anything."
And he'd respond, "Neither do I."

The conversation would go back and forth until eventually I decide to drink a slim rite shake for dinner; sense I was trying to maintain a healthy weight and he'd just starve. I even had to spoon feed him sometimes just to get him to eat; also while talking to him like I would Kenise.

"Come on. You have to eat something. Come on. I know that tummy wants some yummy," I'd say.

As a wife, there's only so much I was able to do for him. I wasn't equipped with the things needed to cheer him up. I understood he's worked hard to get where he was at. He graduated from high school with honors, attended college and also graduated a year before I with a three point eight GPA. But in life, obstacles get's thrown in our path.

Everyday just seem to be much worst than the day before. Kwame just doesn't seem to care. And if he didn't than why should I have? Let me guess…because I was his wife. Well I was trying but it was as if he was purposely letting go of himself. Things had been so hectic that we haven't been able to sleep in the same room; and were married for peat's sake.

After the fight between my father and my husband I told Kwame I couldn't continue on with our marriage unless he got help. That I was prepared to leave because I feared death. This wasn't the first nor the second time that he "mistakenly," as he calls it placed his hands on me. It was starting to become a habit.

I was scared that after last night, if it wasn't for my father coming by things could have gotten a lot worst. He could have seriously hurt me and I just wasn't ready to leave earth yet. Kwame said he understood and would do whatever it takes to keep his family together. *And at this point I believed him.* He sound like my Kwame. Like the man I fell in love with the moment he confessed his love to me.

After about two months of discussing things I took a day off from work to keep things disclosed from my parents. Kenise and I was still with my parents so I didn't have to worry about her. Kwame asked to be taken to the emergency psychiatric department. He said that would be the quickest way for him to see a shrink. And though he wasn't fund of seeing one, he too knew something was wrong. The moment we got to Jackson's Hospital I couldn't help but to flashback our memories from the very first time we stepped foot in there; the moment I collapsed trying to run down the bus. I think Kwame knew what I was thinking of because together we begin to laugh. And it was a laugh at this point that has been needed for quite some time.

"Remember the way your mom looked at me the first time she met me here?" Kwame teased while approaching the front desk. "She could not stand a hair on my body. And remember she called me a big headed little boy," he laughed. "Little did she know the big headed little boy she didn't like would be confessing his love for a…beautiful…woman," he said while kissing my hand.

I smiled but the fact of the matter is we were here to see what was wrong and so I had to keep a serious face. I wanted him to know and feel; *while yes I shared that brief moment and laughed with you, but that still don't excuse you needing help. And if need be, I am still prepared to leave.*

That afternoon Kwame was diagnosed with depression and told that he had an anxiety attack. Because he had gone through so much trauma; loosing his job, not being able to keep up with bills and then I was speaking of leaving with his daughter, he snapped.

And though all of this sound reasonable would this happen again? How could I be sure he wouldn't hurt us again?

The doctor prescribed twenty milligrams of Citalopram to be taken by mouth every morning. He also gave us references for family counseling as well as individual counseling. The doctor reassured me that he didn't see Kwame as the type of man that would harm his family ever.

With Kwame being depressed who knows what he's capable of; he was becoming someone else.

A year had passed and Kwame had become worst. The medicine was no longer helping and he quit going to counseling.

"I don't need that shit!" he would say. "There's nothing wrong with me."

I didn't know what to do. Just a year ago I said how I would leave and he wasn't giving me much of a choice. As much as I wanted to leave, my vows *for better or worst* kept replaying in my head.

Till death do us apart.

What does that mean? That I have to suffer because Kwame took a turn for the worst? One that not even my father saw coming. And would he have done the same for me if the shoe was on the other foot? As much as I wanted to leave I just couldn't; so I held in there and followed my heart. Till the day he died.

"You mean the day you watched your husband lay lifeless while he overdosed on drugs?" Mr. Ohio suggested.

"That's not true! I loved Kwame and it isn't in my heart to watch something as selfish as a life being tourn a part from the man I love."

"But your life was already tourn a part. Kwame wasn't able to pay bills anymore because he wasn't working, am I correct?"

"Yes, but,"

"And after he became depressed you had already repeatedly told this court room, that you were prepared to leave! Is that not correct Mrs. Woods?"

"That's true but,"

"Your honor, I don't see while we're still here. Its clear the defendant had prior knowledge of her husband's abuse and she did nothing to stop him from being murdered."

"Murdered? He killed himself!"

"Maybe, but he couldn't have done it without your help."

"Objection," Mrs. William yelled. "Your honor this is ridiculous. There's more to tell; a chance to approach the witness please?"

"You may," Judge Lanai Brown ordered.

"Mrs. Woods, how did you find out Kwame was on drugs?"

It took a while before I answered. I didn't want to confess to the courtroom that this wonderful man I had been in love with took a turn for the worst. I wasn't prepared to open up about every little dark secret that happened these last few years. But I was in a court room, on trial for the murder of my husband. Because he overdosed on drugs and I knew he was doing them, I was to blame.

"Mrs. Woods," Mrs. Williams continued. "I know it's hard to discuss these things with a bunch of people you don't know. If you don't tell someone about the things you experienced, you'll be doing time for a murder you didn't commit. Do you understand?"

I looked at her with teary eyes and shook my head that I did. And as much as I fought with not wanting to be guilty, in my heart I felt just as guilty as Mr. Ohio wanted me to be. He was right; it's my fought. Shouldn't I be punished? I deserved to be.

"Mrs. Woods we've gone through this before. You have...to... answer...the question." Judge Lanai Brown asked.

"And I plan to as I'm ready to push this behind me and the only way I can do so is to let all of you into the world that once existed for Kwame and I."

Taking a deep breath while closing my eyes I evoked the first time I found out he was on drugs. By any means possible, he would have never told me. We were close but he wasn't stupid enough to shout out, hey honey, I'm on drugs.

To start out...I was devastated and slapped him over and over again. It wasn't because he was doing the drugs; it was because we had a three year old daughter in our house that was very curious.

Because Kwame was depressed, I had to find work. Since Kenise was still a toddler at the time I wanted her to interact with other children her age. Do to the social and emotional skills needed to help our baby grow; I decided it would be best for me to work in a childcare center as well; as a teacher's assistant. Preferably, the center our daughter would be at. With this position I would be able to support our family as well as spend time with our daughter. Kwame talked against it saying he could babysit her while I worked but I knew better. After the incident when she was one, I never left him alone with her again. Not purposely.

On that particular night work had gotten the best of me. My shift was from nine am to six pm but when you're working with children; seventeen to say the least, it's exhausting; so naturally I was tired. Drained to the point that I couldn't keep my eyes open. Mentally I knew I was worn out and so should have been Kenise being that she never slept at school. This was the perfect opportunity to give her an early meal as well as bath. I figured afterwards she would go straight to bed and that would be the end of our day. But…I was wrong.

I remember placing her in her bed and kissing her goodnight. Shortly after I closed her door; just a little, like always than preceded towards our room. Kwame was asleep already or at least that's what he wanted me to believe. Tiptoeing pass him, I placed my pajamas on and laid in bed. The moment I closed my eyes I was dreaming. I'm not sure if you'll believe me when I tell you what happened next but here it goes.

As I was dreaming, visions of happy thoughts emerged. For instance my favorite flower; lilies were flashing continuously and in different colors. Scenic colors of pink, orange, yellow. At this point in my trance I had to be smiling because that's what I did any and every time I say a Lillie. The next flashing images were of sceneries such as the beach with a shining hot sun and water that's so clear it almost looks pure; drinkable. What was once a dream went black. There was nothing to see or hear. I remember turning over onto my side as I thought wow that was weird. But it wasn't as eerie as the approaching dream to come.

Again, I'm dreaming while feeling for Kwame who felt unusually different. His body wasn't as muscular and he appeared softer than normal. Rolling over to my left I looked at the lumps that were placed in bed. I don't know why, but I remember thinking they looked very suspicious. Something was wrong. Slowly I pulled the cover off of what I thought would be my husband but it wasn't Kwame at all. He wasn't there. On his side of the bed laid two pillows to make me believe he was there. My first thoughts were why? Why would he want me to be certain he was in bed if he wasn't? And what did he have to hide that he felt the need to cover it up? I had no way of being prepared for the truth behind our empty bed.

Hearing a commotion caused me to rush and check things out. At the time I didn't think to grab a lamp, stiletto shoe or something that had weight or even could possibly do damage long enough for me to stall while getting my family to safety. As a mother, my first instinct was to check Kenise room first. When I got there her door was closed and I knew it wasn't done so by my hand. I rushed into her room as if to stop someone in the act of harming her but to my surprise she wasn't there. Checking in her closet and under her bed just made me become more furious. Her window was closed and locked just the way I had it before bed. Biting my nails I played the, *If I was three where would I be* game? That's when I heard her cough. It sound as if she couldn't breathe. Taking no time to rush to her aid I couldn't believe what I saw. Kwame was lying in the tub with a belt wrapped around his arm asleep. There was a puncture wound that bled a bit. Worst, Kenise had found the needle he'd used and she too bled in the same arm. She put two and two together and tried to react what her father had just done to himself.

Immediately calling 911, I thought to myself how could he be so stupid! While your child and wife is in the house! Eventually the dream became unbearable causing me to awake in a cold sweat. The perspiration from the nightmare was so bad that I sat in a puddle of fluid. Jumping out of bed I withdrew the blanket not thinking twice of disturbing Kwame while he slept. To my surprise, he wasn't in bed. Two pillows laid in his place, just like the dream. My heart began to think fast as I tried to remember what happened next.

"Ok, ok," I begin to breathe. "I checked Kenise room and she wasn't there. SHE...WAS...IN...THE...BATHROOM. OH MY GOSH..." I yelled. "KENISE, KENISE," I screamed as I ran in that direction.

To my relief, I scared her before she even got the chance to pick up the needle and puncture herself.

"Thank God," I said repeatedly. "What are you doing here?" I said in a frantic.

"Mommy, I had to pee," she responded not knowing why I was so upset. "Why is daddy in the bath tub bleeding mommy?"

I couldn't tell her the truth so I took her in her room and told her a story. It was about a princess who saved a king. She took well to the story and fell asleep. All the while Kwame was still asleep. I was so pissed that I cut the cold water on him. Shockingly it didn't wake him. Becoming even more pissed I slapped him over and over until he awaked. Eventually he did but it wasn't due to the cold shower or me hitting him. I took a moment to catch my breath and sat down on the toilet that was positioned next to the bathtub. The moment I sat down he mysteriously opened his eyes.

"Hey baby what you doing in here?" Kwame asked stoned high.

"What the hell is this Kwame?" I said picking up the needle that sat on the floor by the tub and throwing it at him. "You doing this shit in my house? IN MY FUCKING HOUSE? AROUND OUR DAUGHTER? HOW COULD YOU BE SO DAMN STUPID!"

"What the fuck is that? That ain't mine!"

"You lying son of a bitch! The evidence is left on your arm. It bled after you stuck yourself!"

"It's not what you think!"

"It ain't what I think! It ain't what I think! My fucking husband is on drugs. That's not what I think that's what I see!"

"I can quit. I'll quit," Kwame said standing up.

"Can you Kwame? Can you really?" I asked calmly. "Do you think I'm fucking stupid? That shit is addictive so tell me how you're going to kick your habit? Oh let me guess," I said crossing my arms. "You're going to quit cold turkey?"

"And I can. Just believe in me baby. I need you to believe…in…me," Kwame said trying to woo me.

"You almost killed our fucking daughter, how could you be so irresponsible? Our daughter could have gotten hurt let alone taken away from us. Do you understand that?"

"I'm sorry baby. It won't happen again."

"It better not because if it do,"

Interrupting me, "Please don't say it."

"I'm leaving Kwame."

"Nooo," he wailed like a newborn.

"And I'm taking Kenise with me," I said while walking out of the bathroom

"Karma please… please don't say that. I can't live without you and my baby."

I didn't give a damn about what he said. He was not going to do that shit in front of my daughter. If he didn't care about his self than fine, but don't drag us down with you.

"Did he stop using drugs?" Mrs. Williams asked.

"No…he didn't," I said wiping my nose with my sleeve. "He couldn't."

"Because he was addicted?"

"Yes."

"How often did he use drugs?"

"I can't be certain. Several times a day I guess."

"And did he only use heroine?"

"Heroine and cocaine at first. And when they no longer supplied his depressions he turned to meth."

"Where were you and Kenise when Kwame did these drugs?" Mrs. Williams asked with her back facing me.

"Out of the way," I sniffled.

"What do you mean by out of the way?"

It wasn't long before I found Kwame high again and I knew it wouldn't be. One can't just take a dose of something and think that all of a sudden they would quit. Because I loved him I was willing to deal with it I guess you can say since that's what I did.

After our first incident, to protect our daughter I slept in her room. I needed to know at all times she was safe, especially since Kwame wasn't being careful about where he was choosing to do his drugs. I honestly couldn't believe the man I loved who once was so strong, could easily space out. His own mother wouldn't have believed me if I told her he was using drugs. So I never did. His drug use became **our** secret. One that I'm not proud of but that's what it was.

The second time I caught him he was lying in bed. Passed out cold! And I knew…that he was high. I felt it deep in my soul. This gut feeling of sickness reached over me and I puked all over what used to be my side of the bed. I guess he felt it was safe to do the drugs in our room since Kenise wasn't allowed in there and I no longer slept with him. Who knows, but the whole time I barfed he didn't budge. When I was finish, I wiped my face and attempted to wake him so I could change the bedding. Kwame never budged. Didn't move, didn't twitch, he didn't even as much say one word. Becoming irritated I rolled him over and by chance he fell onto the floor. He just laid there as stiff as a dead man. And for a moment I thought, maybe he was. It wasn't until I saw the needle placed beside his pillow that I knew for sure he was high. Had the evidence that he was still injecting his self even though he said he would quit; promised to quit. I became so upset that I took the needle and began stabbing him over and over again.

I must admit it probably wasn't the smartest thing to do but that's what happened. That's how I reacted.

After so many cuts he woke up right away.

"Woman, what the hell are you doing? Are you crazy? Have you gone mad?" he asked while he blocked his body.

"You mutherfucka! You been using this shit again," I said holding the needle in my hand. "After I told I would leave. You don't care about us," I stabbed. "You…don't…give a damn," I stabbed over and over again.

"Woman STOP!" he yelled while standing. "I'VE HAD ENOUGH! GET YOUR SHIT AND GET OUT! This my house!"

"It's our house! Or did you forget," I said showing him our wedding ring. "So if anyone is to leave it's to be your dumb ass. So you GET THE FUCK OUT! GEEEEET OUUUUUTTTT!"

"I'm not going anywhere. I just paid the bill yesterday."

"Really Kwame," I asked while crossing my arms. "What bill did you pay? I'm just curious. And how did you get there since YOU DON'T HAVE NO FUCKING CAR! IT WAS REPOSSESSED DUMB ASS!"

"What you mean I don't have a car?"

"Oh they came and got it baby. And I happily gave them the key cause I knew you were on that shit. I couldn't prove it but I knew it. And before you thought of giving a car away for a nice fix, I voluntarily gave it up."

"You DID WHAT?" he stood.

That was the very first time Kwame ever put his hands on me. He slapped me so hard that I knew my mother would call to ask what happened. I literally began to see stars.

"Oh, you ain't that strong of a bitch now huh? Talk all that shit and got all that mouth. Guess you never saw it coming huh? Beg me not to hit you again. BEG!"

When I came to my senses it was on. We fought like cats and dogs on a rainy day. He banged my head into the mirror and I crashed his into the tub rail. He pushed my head into the wall and I pushed his into the bottom half of the door causing his nose to break on the knob.

"YOU BITCH! AHHH, YOU BITCH!" he yelled while falling to the floor. "I think you broke my nose."

"As high as you are you felt that?" I asked sarcastically. "Well bitch feel this," I said while kicking him dead in his face. Taking his chin and guiding him to look me into my eyes, "And if you ever…disrespect me out of my name again," I said while grabbing a piece of broken glass from the mirror. "Bitch, I'LL KILL YOU!" I threatened while cutting his face.

"Where was Kenise when the two of you were fighting?" Mrs. Williams asked.

"Believe it or not, through the sounds of our yelling and as much noise as we were making fighting, she was sound asleep. Never heard a thing."

"So the two of you were lucky huh?"

"Yes but that was probably the only incident."

"So you two fought regularly in front of Kenise?"

"Oooh yea. And I'm not proud to say it but it happened."

"Why didn't you just leave?" Mr. Ohio interrupted. Standing up and walking towards me, "You said he was using drugs and that you couldn't get him to stop. You also said he became abusive. Regardless if you fought back, it's still abuse."

"I couldn't," I said not happy about the answer I gave.

"So your husband was that important?"

"Yes he was. I loved him."

"Have you ever heard of the words *tough love?*"

I stared quietly. Of course I heard of those words. At this point in my life I wished I had used them but there isn't anything I can do now. I can't turn back the hands of time. I can't threaten to leave Kwame once more and this time actually do it. I fucked up. I made a mistake by staying with him when I should have left a long time ago.

"Your honor," He said to Judge Lanai Brown to get me to answer the question.

"Mrs. Woods," Judge Lanai Brown said while looking into my eyes.

I could tell by the way she looked at me she sympathized but would have to do whatever the law told her too.

Mr. Ohio continued, "Mrs. Woods I'll ask you again. Have you ever heard of the words,"

Interrupting him, "*Tough love*? Of course; I wasn't born yesterday."

The court room begin to laugh. I think they were getting frustrated with Mr. Ohio as well. He was a mean ass that knew how to get under your skin and was hard. The toughest prosecutor in the city of Covington. I was two point five seconds a way from completely loosing my sanity. If it wasn't for Mrs. Williams who warned me, I don't think I would have made it this far. I might even be in a holding cell for slapping the shit out of him.

"Great, than you can explain to us why you didn't use tough love."

"Your honor this is ridiculous," Mrs. Williams stood up.

"I agree. Mr. Ohio what is the point you're trying to make?" Judge Lanai Brown said.

"The point is, Mrs. Woods seemed to sacrifice a lot for Kwame and I want to know why?" Her daughter, herself, their families. Why didn't she simply leave the way she told him she would if she caught him again?" He said while talking to the jury. "They fought on numerous occasions...in front of their daughter. Why didn't she leave? It was obvious Kwame wasn't going to stop using drugs so why didn't Mrs. Woods move on with her life? That's what I would have done if it was my wife abusing drugs. I would have told myself, *this...is...what's best*."

"Than maybe you've never been in love before," I said defending myself.

"No further questions."

"Mrs. Woods, did you ever at any point in your marriage, after Kwame begin to use drugs leave?" Mrs. Williams asked.

"Yes…I did…but it wasn't for long."

I dealt with Kwame and his drugs for three years at the time. I was sick of it. There was always an excuse here and an excuse there. *Oh Baby I'm going to stop. I promise this is the last time. I love you and my daughter. I want to do right by yall he would say.*

During the mist of his drug using, Kwame and I had an intimate encounter that I wasn't happy about. The reason being is because I had become pregnant. Once I told Kwame the news he was excited. He couldn't believe it. Immediately he wanted to change, except this time I believed him. He went into a drug facility and received treatment throughout the months of my pregnancy. We also had family counseling as well as marital counseling. Due to his years of using drugs, the trust I had for him just wasn't there.

One particular morning I had cramps really bad. I mean they seriously hurt. They started at about four am and never stopped; just a repeated shock being delivered to my body. At six and a half months I knew I couldn't have been in labor, I was way too early. I called the facility that Kwame was at to tell them I was in premature labor. Kwame said he would meet me at the hospital. Before I placed the phone on the hook I began to feel a wetness between my legs. At the time I thought my water broke. The first thought that came after the moisture was Kenise . I needed to call my parents and let them know I'm in labor. Before I got to Kenise room I screamed an agonizing shout. The pain was worst and horrible. She came running out of her bedroom following the cry.

"Mommy what's wrong? What's wrong mommy?"

"Baby, I need you…to…get the phone…for mommy. Can you do that like a big girl?" I breathed between contractions.

"Do you need the phone because you're bleeding down there mommy?"

The moment she said I was bleeding I knew…I was having a miscarriage. I called Kwame back but the nurses said he was gone. They said he didn't even change. And that he received a ride from one of the staff. I didn't know what to think or do. I was too caught up on thinking of loosing our baby. We just found out two months ago we were having a boy. Kwame's first son. He was doing so good. How can I break this news to him? Let alone he's going to be there to see everything. What will happen to us? While I cried thinking of our future Kenise became my hero. She called 911 just like I taught her in case of an emergency.

"Hello…my mommy is bleeding. Down there in her no no spot. She's having me a baby brother. You have to hurry," Kenise said to the 911 operator before hanging up.

Forty eight minutes passed before I finally reached the emergency room just to be told they couldn't save the baby. Looking to my left I saw Kwame who fell to the floor. He had heard the news and believed it was his fought. *If only I had been here quick enough maybe the baby would have made it,* he began to say. *If I'd just taken better care of you.* The nurses and doctors reassured him that it wasn't his fought; things like this happen all of the time. But it didn't help.

That's when things in our marriage became worst.

After the lost of our son we began to pull apart. I blamed him for doing drugs and ruining my chances of having another baby.

"If you hadn't been on that shit, my baby would have made it," I'd yell.

"You have to remember Karma, the moment you became pregnant I stopped. How was I supposed to know you'd get knocked up?"

"What the fuck you mean knocked up? We're married. You mean you didn't expect us to become pregnant again?"

"No I mean exactly what I said! I was happy being high. For once all the pain went away. How I know you didn't do something to harm our son?"

"Why would I do that?"

"Why wouldn't you?"

"Kwame you're full of shit! You may have stopped taking drugs but it's only a matter of time before you start back. Once a crack head, always," I said in regrets as I walked away.

I actually feel bad for saying that now that I think about it. Maybe him getting back on drugs was my fought. I provoked him to do it.

"Mrs. Woods, are you confessing to the murder of your husband?" Mr. Ohio asked.

"Don't answer that Mrs. Woods," Mrs. Williams interfered. "Your honor, can we take a recess so I may talk to my client.

"Recess will be for the equivalent of an hour. All parties are expected back in court by 4:30pm," Judge Lanai Brown spoke followed by a clink of her hammer.

"Mrs. Woods let's go out for lunch. You've been speaking about your life's memories since 9:00 am and must be exhausted. I know it's hard telling the court about a lot of things that has happened but you're doing an excellent job."

"Am I?" I interrupted with a look of guilt.

"Of course. You're a strong woman who has been through a lot with what used to be a good man. Deep in your heart you believed he would change and that's why you hung in there.

After the death of our son, Kwame changed. Even though he fought so hard to overcome it, he just couldn't pull through. Kwame slept for four hours at a time on numerous occasions throughout the day. I had to remind him several times to eat or at least drink something. He didn't smile the same, laugh the same or have that look of joy in his eye anymore so I made him an appointment to see a therapist. The therapist said it was a good idea for him to come. A lot of people commit suicide due to depression. The pain is unbearable and hard to cope with. Beside the point, some people need medicine in order to help them through their depression.

After hearing from Kwame, the therapist decided to put him on seventy five milligrams of Effexor, to be taken one time daily and for a month straight before he would see him again. It took exactly two weeks before I started to notice a change. By then Kwame was a responsible father again; and for once I thought our problems were behind us. He was involved in Kenise schooling practically every other day. The moment the alarm went off he would kiss me and tell me to stay in bed. That is was time for me to rest and allow him to be the man again. At this time he had been clean for exactly one year and so trust was no longer becoming an issue. I believed him and allowed him to pick up where he left off at.

In the midst of his morning routine with Kenise, he would get her dress using the clothes that I had prepared the previous night. Her hair was never an problem because I kept it braided and beaded. And some sort of way, he always managed to have just enough time left to fix her breakfast; which consisted of a bowl of cereal while they sat in front of the television laughing at a cartoon of Tom and Jerry.

It was seven thirty four in the morning to be exact. The sun was slowly rising along the horizon. I was lying on my belly and had rolled over on to my back. Reaching for Kwame, I noticed he wasn't in bed. In fact, his side of the bed was made. Seeing that the bathroom door in our bedroom wasn't vacant and hearing a crackling sound coming from downstairs made me suspicious. I took a baseball bat out of the hallways closet and crept down the stairs. Peeking around the corner I couldn't believe my eyes. Pancakes, waffles, French toast, eggs, bacon, sausage links and patties, hash browns and tater tots; with orange juice, tea and milk to drink. Standing there in what seemed to be a part of my imagination, I didn't know what to do or what to think. Continuing to stand there the cook revealed his self and was…my husband. It was then that I knew we were going to be ok. At least that's what I thought.

Everything was shared as far back as I could remember. There was nothing left to say, no questions left to ask. Both parties did their final speech to present me as guilty or not guilty. It was very convincing and at this point I'm not sure which direction I'd be pushed in. My lawyer held my hand as we awaited the results.

"Has the jury reached a verdict?" Judge Lanai Brown asked.

"Yes we have your honor."

"Let's here it," she straightened herself in her seat.

"We...the jury...find Karma Woods...Not...Guilty."

"Thank you sweet Jesus," my mother announced.

"By the power invested in me Karma will be released immediately to her family as she was found...Not guilty. Court...is adjourned."

My father walked towards me and immediately embraced his arms.

"I'm proud of you baby girl. You did an excellent job sharing your life with a lot of people that are with you and against you. You're a strong young woman...like your mother."

"Awww, you're just saying that," my mother kissed him.

"Mrs. Woods, my job here is done. You're officially free."

"Thank you...thank you so much," I hugged her. "For believing in me."

"Well honey, lets go home," my dad announced.

Opening the doors that led outside felt like a bird being released from its cage. The sun hurt my eyes but after long was readjusted. Camera crews rushed toward us asking tons of questions.

"Mrs. Woods how does it feel to be free?"

"Mrs. Woods do you feel judgment was served?"

"Mrs. Woods, what are you going to do now that you're a widow?

"I just have one question Mrs. Woods. Just one. Did you really do it?"

"We won't be answering any questions. Thanks for your support," my mother motioned. "I'm sorry Karma, if I would have known they'd all been here we'd gone another way."

Speechless I didn't say anything. All I could think about was "I'm free...I'm free."

The ironic thing about it is, on the way down the concrete steps her question kept replaying in my head.

"Did you really do it?"

If only I could have said, "You know what…to be honest…yes…I did."

Preview of
The Moth's Light

Kwame and I have been having problems in our marriage for about two years now. I've used all the strength and patience I could have possibly ever had dealing with him. It was like dealing with a teenage child. Being that I was under a lot of stress that made me completely lonely… and…vulnerable.

One particular night I went to a convenient store to get Kenise some pampers and wipes. I had a quiet thought to take Kenise with me but it was extremely cold outside. Beside the point I would only be gone for fifteen minutes. Thirty minutes tops, if there was a shortage on cashiers. So I left Kenise in the care of her seemingly depressed father. I thought this would be a good time for the two of them to do some catching up. Even Kenise liked the idea. She smiled as I walked out of the door.

On the drive to the store I felt at peace. No man to argue with, no responsibilities of caring for Kenise or household chores; just peace and quiet. It felt so good to be alone for once that I screamed to the top of my lungs. I never realized till now just how much stress I was under. I felt like a single parent on the road to divorce. How could things go so terribly wrong when they have gone so right up until now? Is this what I deserve? Did I do something God didn't like? Hundreds of thoughts crossed my mind but none of which made sense.

By the time I had finished crying and gathering my purse I had already been gone for an hour. Getting out of the car just to get the items Kenise needed seemed like the hardest thing I had to do. My body was weak. So was my soul and heart.

"Are you okay?" someone asked.

"I will never be ok again," I snapped.

"God only put on us what we can carry. He will never make you hold more than that."

"Thank you but I don't want to hear that shit right now," I excused myself.

"I'm sorry if I offended you. I was there at your wedding. You are married to Kwame right?" He asked following me.

Crying even louder, "Yes…yeeeessss." Trying to calm down, "Why? Is he in some sort of trouble?"

"No, no. Not at all. I just remember the two of you having a very nice wedding. Since than, no one has seen much or heard anything from yall. Is everything ok?"

"Of course it is. Why wouldn't it be?"

"Well this is a small city and we heard Kwame lost his job. You don't appear to be happy. You're here…in the parking lot of a grocery store crying. Your hair is a mess and you look as if you're falling a part."

"Do I look that bad?"

"Yes; very," he laughed. "Why don't you come to my place and I'll help clean you up?"

"That sounds very kind of you but I have a husband and kid to take care of," I said walking away again.

"Well here's my card if you shall ever change your mind."

"Thanks but I'm sure I won't need it," I suggested. "Will I?" I questioned once I got inside the store.

Special Thanks!

This novel couldn't have been made possible without the most high giving me the strength to entertain other's thoughts.

I want to thank my wonderful man Randy for entertaining our family so I could focus. For the countless nights he massaged my neck and shoulders as well as rubbed my back while writing. For all of the times he has waited on me hand and foot to make sure I had plenty to eat and drink while concentrating. I am grateful for all he has done.

My best friend Tremeka has spent countless days away from her seven children to edit this novel personally. We've shared many hours of laughter as well as dry red eyes and I appreciate it.

Paul; a friend of a friend for recommending the title of my novel. After reading my book, he mentioned it was very different and needed a name to stand out. The Moth's Flame was the first thought to come to mind and we've agreed to it since. He has also been a tremendous amount of help by editing the novel and providing incredible information on life that I wasn't aware of.

The support of my parents; Michael and Patricia, grandparents; Diane and Virgil, besties; Tamela, Willie, Arlesha and Benita whom always held their faith in me. They always told me that I would publish both my poetry books as well as my stories. I am in debt for their confidence; they were right!

Monday, Wednesday, Thursday and Fridays I productively used 90 minutes of Reginald Stroud Sr. time to work and edit The Moth's Flame while my children attended class. He as well as the brothers and sisters within STROUD'S JINEN-DO SCHOOL OF MARTIAL ARTS gets exceptional thanks for the support and time needed to be mentally alone.

One other particular thanks go out to Metro Bus Services; Routes

21 and 64 for their smooth rides Monday through Saturday. Because of how comfortable and relaxing the drive was I was able to concentrate better on my goals for this book.

To my supporters, I pray that the benefit of reading this novel gives one the strength to move forward if have been faced with this type of trauma. Through GOD, all things are made possible!